IN A
MIRROR
Dimly

A NOVEL
G. ROGER COREY

HARVEST HOUSE PUBLISHERS
Eugene, Oregon 97402

Scripture quotations in this book are taken from the New American Standard Bible NASB, © 1960, 1962, 1963, 1968, 1971, 1972, 1973, 1975, 1977 by the Lockman Foundation. Used by permission.

Cover design by Design Point, Salem, Oregon

Library of Congress Cataloging-in-Publication Data

Corey, Roger, 1951–
  In a mirror dimly / Roger Corey.
    p.   cm.
  ISBN 1-56507-920-5
  I. Title.
  PS3553.O6465I5 1998   98-5763
  813'.54—DC21   CIP

For Claudia

For now we see in a mirror dimly,
but then face to face; now I know in part,
but then I shall know fully just
as I also have been fully known.

1 Corinthians 13:12

Acknowledgment

*I would like to thank Frank C. Leitnaker, M.D., Col. (retired),
for his technical assistance with medical
portions of this book.*

Chapter One

"Bon nuit, Doctor."

"Goodnight, Tran."

Dr. John Brindle leaned against the clinic railing and watched as his assistant walked nimbly across the courtyard in the darkness, the small Asian form disappearing beyond the protective glow of light cast by the open office door. The doctor rubbed his eyes wearily, massaging them with the flat of his palm, trying to rub into them the eight hours of sleep he needed to think clearly. He had not been able to get any rest for the past several nights because of a sudden breakout of cholera among the refugees. He watched Tran disappear along the trail that led to the camp, the hundreds of makeshift shelters that had been thrown up to protect people dumped on the beach by an unsympathetic Indonesian navy. Some of the shelters were no more than branches with palm thatching. Others, built by refugees who had been here longer, were constructed of bits of scavenged wood or discarded corrugated metal. They were fine for now, Brindle thought, but what would happen when the monsoons came? He gazed up through the palm trees to the night sky. There was a heaviness in the air, a pressure more evident than the usual dripping humidity, that meant the West Monsoon was developing out there somewhere above the Asian mainland. Soon it would be strengthened by the wind-flows coming in off the Indian Ocean, and then the rains would begin. The rain would bring mud and more infections and dysentery.

Brindle watched another figure moving slowly through the shadows. Anyway, he thought, the Vietnamese knew more about monsoons than he did. They could probably tell him what day the storm would hit. Such incredibly resilient people. Did anything ever really get to them? Was there any hardship they couldn't overcome—or at least survive? A mosquito buzzed past Brindle's ear and his hand waved it away automatically. He had been at the clinic for six months now, a brief start to a new life, but in some ways it seemed like years.

"Going to the celebration?" came a voice out of the darkness.

He turned to see Hal Aldridge, the camp administrator, coming up the steps. The Indonesians would have nothing to do with running the camp. Typically, the work had fallen to an American from the WRO, the World Refugee Organization.

"I think I'm too tired to appreciate it," he replied.

"Should be fun," Aldridge said. "The Vietnamese don't often have a chance to celebrate."

"Maybe later."

Brindle could hear the scattered beat of drums as the New Year celebration began.

"What year is it?"

"Year of the Dog, I believe," Aldridge answered.

"Figures."

"Pity they don't have any firecrackers," Aldridge added. "Doesn't seem quite complete without them. How can they scare away the evil spirits without firecrackers?"

"The guards could toss in a few hand grenades."

Aldridge frowned.

"Hope it doesn't come to that," he said.

"Of course."

"Michele will be there."

Brindle looked at him.

"I just meant. . ."

"It's okay."

"Well then," Aldridge said, "see you later."

Brindle nodded and watched as the older man, balding, thick through the middle, dressed in a white shirt and khaki slacks, moved off toward the sound of the drums. He wanted to tell Aldridge that he had seen plenty of celebrations in San Francisco's Chinatown. They had always filled him with a sense of momentary excitement followed by sadness, but perhaps that was only how he interpreted things now. Perhaps he viewed every moment of his life now as beginning in excitement and ending in sadness. But it was nothing to dwell upon. Pushing away from the railing, he walked down the clinic steps and across the courtyard to his bungalow.

A ceiling fan powered by the camp generator moved listlessly in his room. Brindle pulled off his shirt and shoes in the dark and dropped onto his metal frame bed. A green mosquito net, balled up and swung off to one side, glowed palely in the moonlight coming in through the slatted windows. He knew he should untie the netting and let it fall around him, but he was too tired. Anyway, he wasn't really going to bed, he told himself, only resting. He still planned to take in some of the New Year's celebration before midnight.

Closing his eyes, he let himself drift. He could hear the distant beat of the drums, the muffled shouts of dancers, the metallic creak of the ceiling fan, a mosquito hovering near the bed, and finally the heavy sound of his own breathing. It was just when he felt his body sagging into the mattress and the darkness was settling over him that the feeling came—an uneasiness slowly developing into dread, a sickness of heart, a feeling that one more thought would cause him to collapse into despair. In the past he had always fought off the feeling by trying to ignore it, by simply going on one minute at a time until it passed; it always did with the coming of sunlight. But now the feeling made him angry.

"I'm too tired for this," he muttered and rolled onto his side. He pushed his face into the pillow and smelled its damp, mildewed scent. Nothing ever really dried in this climate. Everything rotted, including people, he had decided.

He tended to think of himself in terms of the living John Brindle and the existing John Brindle. He was existing now.

How long had it been? Two years. Existing, hollow, no fire, no feelings, no relationship with God, only the accomplishment of working out the day and tolerating the uneasiness at night. He saw no end to it, *once the salt has lost its taste. . .* , but that didn't bother him much. Perhaps the one benefit of being hollow was that nothing bothered him much; it required feelings to be bothered.

After half an hour Brindle realized he wasn't sleeping, but only lying in a state of exhausted anxiety. Without turning on the light he rolled off the bed and walked over to the shelf where a bottle of tequila waited, the last remnant of a trip to the Philippines. It bothered him a little that the tequila—it had been a bottle of whiskey before that—was becoming such a routine, but you either killed the despair with sunshine or alcohol, for there was nothing else. God could not help him now because he had rejected God—rejected all that He stood for on that rain-slick highway two years ago. Perhaps if he were back in California, he could get pills that would do the same job, but on Boromu Island there was only the most basic of medical supplies. He held the bottle to his lips and felt the first burning swig of tequila flow over his tongue. It would only be a matter of minutes now, he thought, and the despair would be gone. He took another swig. That did not mean he would be able to sleep, but being tired without despair was good enough, better than enough. It was a victory that would last until morning when maybe he could doze off a bit before the first patients arrived.

He took another long swig and then replaced the bottle on the shelf. The warming started in his back and shoulders as he waited, standing in the darkness and gazing at himself in the mirror. This was the way it should always be, he thought, to look at oneself in dim light so that the facial contours were softened, the eyes vague, the weakness and pain lost in the shadows. He stared hard at the darkened mirror, trying to find the face he had grown up with, the face that had attended medical school in San Francisco, the face that had married and been a father, the face as it had been before the accident.

There was a knock on his door.

"John?" asked a soft feminine voice through the slats. It was a hesitant voice, filled with subtle hope and a slight twinge of embarrassment. "Are you awake?"

He waited a moment before answering, giving the face in the mirror one final glance, wondering if the absence of light came more from within than without. "Yes," he said.

"They're having the New Year's celebration down in the camp. I thought you might like to go."

"Just a minute."

He lit the lantern and pulled on a shirt. He was still wearing his trousers.

When he opened the door Michele Fallon, Aldridge's assistant, turned from the railing and flashed him a shy but pleasant smile. Her dark blonde hair was brushed back from her face, exposing refined cheekbones and accenting hazel eyes. In the darkness he could not see that her eyes were hazel, but he knew their color. He had studied them, seen signs of pride, insecurity, a need to be loved, a protection against love, hurt, and defiance. Could so much be discovered from one glance into a woman's face? he wondered. But he had seen it, and on another occasion, in another lifetime, he might have been attracted. But that would have been the living John Brindle, not the one who existed now.

"I thought perhaps we could walk down together," she suggested.

Across the darkness and the tepid air, he caught a scent of powder and perfume. It was still fresh, as if she had just applied it as she waited for him at the door. Perhaps she had.

"Fine, Michele," he said. He had no wish to be rude or insensitive. Actually, he rather liked her. He was just concerned that she might start making assumptions about their relationship—that something more intimate might develop.

"These steps are rather difficult to manage in the dark," she said and took his hand. He felt the cool fingers slip gently into his and held them respectfully until they had descended

the five plank steps to the soft earthen path. They were surrounded by darkness for a few moments, the jungle was closing
in on them and blocking out the stars as they left the courtyard. Ahead they could see the dim glow of orange lanterns
and hear the music of the celebration.

"I've never been to a Vietnamese New Year's celebration,"
she said happily, and Brindle realized that she was sincere; that
she was still young enough, or innocent enough, or cared
enough to feel the excitement of new things. He envied that
in her. At another time he would have put his arm around her
right then and kissed her, but now there would be no emotion
behind it, only the physical action, and that would only lead
to trouble later. She was so close to him as the path narrowed
that he could feel her dark blonde hair brush his cheek, and
yet he made no move.

"Oops," she said and took his hand again, this time to
steady herself.

The intensity of what might have been hung for a moment
in the air between them and then dissipated in the heat and
humidity.

"Are you all right?" he asked. It was not the comment of a
prospective lover, but of a doctor. The moment had passed.

Bang. Bang. Bang. A few makeshift firecrackers went off
among the shanties as Brindle and Michele entered the camp.
Music sounded in creaking, scratchy tones from an old cassette
player. People moved about in the darkness. Some had fash-
ioned masks of paper and grass. As Brindle watched, a young
man wearing a dragon mask danced around the clearing. The
doctor felt a sudden envy, a longing to be that uninhibited.

"It's amazing," Michele said.

"In Vietnam, New Year is called Tet," he added.

"As in the Tet Offensive?" Michele asked.

"Yes, it's the Lunar New Year or Spring Festival."

Aldridge came up to them.

"I'm glad you decided to come."

Michele gazed through the palm trees to the full moon. "This is one of those evenings I'll always remember," she said.

Brindle looked at her. "Try Chinatown on a Saturday night."

"Come on, John," she said, taking his hand. "Let's walk around."

They moved through the dancers and past a group of children carrying torches. Some of the shanties were decorated with placards, homemade lanterns, and pieces of paper cut to resemble good-luck symbols like plum blossoms and fish.

"We're supposed to get another group tomorrow," said Aldridge.

"How many?" Brindle asked.

"Fifty. I hope they stop coming before the monsoons hit."

"When will that be?" Michele asked.

"A month or so," Aldridge said.

They passed through the shanties and the celebration and moved out to the beach. There was a slight breeze coming in off the China Sea, and Brindle listened to the rustle of palm fronds above their heads.

"Do you ever feel ridiculous being here, Hal?" he asked.

"What do you mean?"

"Sometimes I feel like—I don't know."

The drums beat behind them.

"You mean like 'here we are, the great Americans, taking care of the Vietnamese after they threw us out ten years ago?'"

"Not quite so arrogant." Brindle said and smiled. "But something like that."

Someone was running down the beach toward them. Brindle could just make out a white shirt and dark trousers moving rapidly over the pale sand.

"Who's that?" he asked.

Three Indonesian soldiers appeared behind the runner.

"I don't know," Aldridge said. Then he shouted, "Watch out!"

One of the soldiers had raised his rifle and was firing. The bullets struck the sand at the man's feet. Another soldier fired, and the runner took two falling strides and then pitched forward on the sand.

Michele let out a cry.

"Stay back!" Aldridge warned.

The soldiers ran up to the runner and turned him over. One shined a flashlight in his face.

"I should see if he needs medical attention," Brindle suggested.

"No," Aldridge said, taking his arm, "wait a moment."

The first soldier searched the man's pockets and came up with a small plastic sack. He began talking rapidly. The other two soldiers nodded. After a moment the first soldier stood up. He shouted something to Aldridge in Indonesian and then laughed. The soldiers left the runner lying in the sand and began to walk back up the beach.

"What did he say?" Michele asked.

"He said here's another refugee for us," Aldridge explained, his voice sounding tired.

Brindle knelt beside the body.

"Take my flashlight," Aldridge offered.

The dead man's eyes were fixed black opaques in the light of the beam. His face was twisted into a grimace of fear and pain. His white shirt was stained front and back.

Brindle checked his pulse.

"He's gone," he said finally, leaning back on his heels and gazing up the beach to the disappearing backs of the soldiers.

"Why did they shoot him?" Michele asked.

"Drugs, probably," Aldridge commented. "The first soldier took something off him."

"If we leave him here, the crabs will get him," Brindle said.

"I'll have some workers bring him up to the clinic," Aldridge replied. "We can have him buried in the morning."

Up the beach they could still hear the sounds of the New Year's celebration.

"I didn't expect this when I came here," Michele said.

"Think of it as a no-man's-land," Aldridge commented. "The refugees here are lost between the world they left behind and the world they hope to reach."

"It's horrible."

Brindle gazed out at the dark waters. "It's not so hard, really," he said. "You just accept the new rules and learn to live by them."

"What rules?"

Brindle turned back to the beach. "Nothing. Let's go."

"I'll get the workers," Aldridge said.

"Do you need me to stay?" Michele asked, gazing at the body.

"No," Brindle replied, "I'll walk you back."

They took the path through the palm trees to the clinic and the bungalows.

Brindle felt Michele press close to him again.

"John?" she asked thoughtfully.

"Yes?"

He knew there was something she wanted to say, something she had thought of before the shooting on the beach, but death, even the death of a stranger—and that is death in its purest form—had a way of making light of fantasies, of making emotional problems seem trivial. So she did not speak again but only walked quietly beside him. Her unspoken words hovered like her faint perfume in the humid air just beyond them. At her door Michelle gazed searchingly at him for a long moment, her eyes moving back and forth from his, as if she hoped to find the answer to her unspoken question there. But eyes that only exist, without life, do not give away secrets or answers, and so she turned and offered him the flicker of a smile. He smiled too.

"Goodnight, John."

"Goodnight," he said, feeling her eyes on him as he went down the steps and crossed the compound to his bungalow. The smile he had given her in return had not shown the discomfort he felt at having someone trying to complicate his life. His life was complicated enough. Somewhere or sometime after the accident, he had decided that emotions were unnecessary, even dangerous. If he did not feel anything and just kept his mind on the job, then time passed and he felt okay. Emotions were no longer a part of his life. All of that was buried with two graves in a Marin County cemetery. The wall had been built and he had no interest in tearing it down. Anyway, he told himself bitterly, by now there was probably nothing behind that wall—only dust, something lost.

In his room, Brindle could hear the sounds of the celebration drifting up through the palm trees. He dropped onto his bed and closed his eyes. After a few minutes however, he got up again and walked across the room to the shelf and his bottle of tequila.

"Here's to the rules," he said to a face gazing vaguely back at him in the mirror.

Then he lifted the bottle to his lips and drank.

Chapter Two

At first he did not hear the knocking because he assumed, in his half-boozed state of exhaustion, that the sound was coming from somewhere else, perhaps the camp. But then he heard the familiar sound of Tran's voice, calling with more respect and consideration than Brindle felt he deserved.

"Doctor?"

He managed a perfunctory, "Yeah?" and then coughed.

"The refugees are arriving, Doctor."

"All right," he said and gazed at his watch. It was just past seven. "Wait for me at the dock."

"I will prepare the kit."

"Fine."

Brindle swung his legs over the cot and felt the rough floorboards under his bare toes. He put his fingers over his face as if to block out the sunlight streaming in through the slatted windows, and when he removed them, the light hit his face and he breathed heavily. Another day.

The arriving refugees were usually suffering from exposure, dehydration, malnutrition, and occasionally knife cuts or wounds when they disembarked on Boromu Island. Brindle had handled one case where two sisters had fought over a mango, and one had stabbed the other in the face. Brindle had been pleased with the job he had done on the girl's cheek, making the stitches small so that the scar running from just under her left eye to her jaw would not be severe. The same resilience that brought these people to the haven of the island carried them through the pains of refugee life. If there were

17

any deaths on board the little boats as they drifted in the China Sea, the deceased were put over the side, so Brindle rarely saw anyone in critical condition. When he arrived at the wooden dock, he saw that Tran had already brought down the stretchers and medical kit.

"I think this group not so bad, Doctor," the young man remarked as they waited for the launch to dock. "Maybe they get lucky. Indonesians pick them up quickly."

"I hope so," he said.

An Indonesian soldier jumped onto the dock and tied the launch. Another put down a walkway, and the refugees began to come off in groups of twos and threes. They had ceased months ago to be separate individuals in the eyes of the camp workers. Now each boat load that arrived appeared to be the same group as before, with the same white shirts and black trousers, plastic sandals, gaunt faces, and frightened, suspicious eyes. The older men tried to put forth the last remains of their broken courage, the mothers clung tightly to children, and the young men and women gazed around in the desperate hope that they had finally arrived someplace where there was a future.

As the refugees came down the dock, Tran herded those who needed medical attention over to the stretcher area.

Brindle checked the pulse and eyes of one refugee.

"Set this one up for malnutrition, Tran," he said.

"Yes, Doctor."

He noticed a young woman being helped down the dock by an older woman and a young man. They were probably family, Brindle thought. The young woman and young man resembled each other.

Tran started to direct them toward the stretcher area, but the young man pushed him away.

"We're here to help you!" Tran told the young man in Vietnamese. "This is the doctor."

But the young man only scowled at him as he replied.

"He say no need for doctor," Tran translated.

"Ask him what's wrong with the girl," Brindle said.

Tran repeated the question in Vietnamese.

The young man snapped back an answer.

Tran shrugged.

"He say nothing wrong, Doctor."

"Very well," Brindle said. There was far too much work to bother treating patients who did not want his help.

A boy staggered down the dock and collapsed. A man and woman knelt beside him, chattering fearfully.

Brindle hurried over to the boy and saw that he was not breathing. He began to quickly apply mouth-to-mouth resuscitation while Tran explained to the man and woman that Brindle was a doctor.

The woman set up a fearful wailing.

The boy gave a cough and began to breath again.

Brindle leaned back and wiped his mouth.

"Ask her if the child has a history of seizures."

"She say no, Doctor."

"Then it's probably heat exhaustion or dehydration. I've seen that happen before." Brindle stood up. "Get him on a stretcher and tell that woman to shut up. The boy will be okay."

Tran explained and the woman fell into a trembling silence.

As he worked on his patients that morning, Brindle thought of the young woman being helped up the dock by the older woman and the belligerent young man. For some reason, he could not get the image of her out of his thoughts. Usually he did not even notice the appearance of the refugee women; they were just patients, medical problems to be treated. But there had been something about this young woman which had lingered. As he gave oral rehydration therapy to the boy who had collapsed on the dock (he had found that just a teaspoonful of water every minute could be absorbed by the stomach immediately and worked better than trying to get down a lot of fluid at one time), Brindle tried to carefully examine the picture he had retained of her. How had she been any different from all the others?

"Doctor?" Tran asked.

"Yes?"

"Miss Fallon. She here for inoculation list."

"All right," he said, noting the boy's temperature on a chart. It was still high.

⮂

Is it possible that there could ever be a rebirth of the human heart? Brindle thought to himself that evening as he sat in a wicker chair outside the clinic. He gazed up at the tropical night sky. It had been a good day. He had performed an appendectomy in the afternoon. Normally a case like that would have been sent to Jakarta, but the patient's abdominal pain suggested that the appendix had ruptured. So he had operated with Tran standing in as assistant. Tran had done a fine job, and Brindle was proud of him. Then the workers had come for the body of the runner who had been shot on the beach.

"How about a game?" Aldridge asked, coming along the path from the administration office with a chess board in his hands.

"Sure," Brindle said. "I can play for a while."

Aldridge sat across from him and began to set out the chess pieces. He kept the pieces in an old first-aid box.

"Did you get them all registered?" Brindle asked.

"Of course. But you never know if they're telling the truth. They're all so suspicious."

"Would it make any difference if they lied?"

The administrator frowned and made his first move. "I suppose not. It's just that we like to have the paperwork done accurately."

"And is there a place on the form that asks about drug dealing and communist sympathies?"

Aldridge chuckled. "I wish there were."

Brindle moved his pawn to block Aldridge.

"They're starting over anyway, Hal," he said. "Maybe it's better if they have new identities."

"I suppose so."

"For example, my name isn't really Brindle. It's actually Schweitzer. This is Africa, isn't it?"

"You're drunk," Aldridge said disappointedly. "John, you'd better lay off the alcohol. It makes people rot in this climate."

"I'd like to lay myself off."

Aldridge moved out his knight.

"And what would we do without you?"

Brindle shook his head. "We don't have any importance here, Hal. These people are survivors. Without us they might lose a few, but the rest would keep going."

"I know you don't believe that," Aldridge said. "I saw you giving mouth-to-mouth to that kid this morning."

Brindle slid his queen's bishop across the board.

"Sometimes I forget myself."

There was movement in the shadows. Several figures were hurrying up the path from the camp.

"Company?" Aldridge asked.

Brindle shook his head.

"Tran?" he called.

Tran came out from the clinic as the figures came into the light. Brindle could see two men carrying a woman between them. He recognized the first as the rude young man from the dock that morning. He did not recognize the other. He assumed they were carrying the same young woman.

Tran spoke to them rapidly in Vietnamese, and they responded breathlessly.

"The brother say this girl very sick now, Doctor," Tran said. "She have infected arm. Much sweating. Temperature."

Brindle thought about the twelve hours they had wasted with their pride and lack of trust. Well, he thought, if she died, it was their own fault.

"Bring her into the clinic."

The two men carried the woman into the clinic and placed her on a table.

"You'll have to crank up the generator, Tran," Brindle commented. "I'm going to need lots of light for this."

"Yes, Doctor."

"Anything I can do?" Aldridge asked.

"Stick around for a few minutes, Hal. I don't trust these two."

"Do you want me to call security?"

"Probably a good idea."

"Fine. I'll be right back."

But Brindle did not hear the administrator turn and hurry down the clinic steps, because he had pulled back the sleeve of the young woman's white cotton blouse and caught a glimpse of her forearm.

"Oh no!" he exclaimed.

A three-inch slash, partially healed over but discolored and oozing pus, ran along the inside of the young woman's forearm. The skin around the wound was swollen and infected. Red streaks—inflamation of the lymph channels—ran up the arm from the wound. It smelled, and as Brindle daubed the area with disinfectant, he glanced up angrily at the brother.

"This is terrible," he said to Tran. "Tell them they should have brought her to me this morning."

"I think he know that now, Doctor," Tran said.

The brother asked something.

"He want to know if you have medicine—fix her up quick."

"She'll be lucky if she doesn't die," Brindle snapped. "How did she get this wound?"

When Tran asked the question, the brother looked away guiltily.

"Well?"

Tran asked again and the brother muttered something in reply.

Tran nodded and shook his head disgustedly.

"Family hide gold necklace in girl's arm. Make cut, put necklace inside, cut open again when gold needed."

"What barbarians," Brindle said.

"Many refugees do this, I think, Doctor," Tran explained.

Aldridge appeared at the door with two Indonesian soldiers.

"How's it going, John?" he asked.

"I can't believe these people," Brindle said. "They've stuck something in her arm and now it's infected. If she's gone septic, there's nothing I can do for her."

"Where do you want the guards?"

"Oh, just outside the door. And keep these two out of here."

Tran explained to the brother, and he and the other man went outside.

Brindle pulled the medical light close to the woman's arm and examined the wound carefully.

"Prep for surgery?" Tran asked.

"Yes," Brindle said. "If it were just infected, I'd let it soak overnight, but we've got to remove whatever is in there now."

"Take arm off, Doctor?"

"I hope not."

Brindle jabbed a needle into the vial of penicillin and drew out one million units.

"Hold her arm, Tran."

Brindle cleaned the injection area with a cotton swab and gave her the shot. She winced as the needle went in. She began to sit up, her eyes opening with a kind of wild, feverish panic, but Brindle grabbed her firmly by the shoulder and pressed her down again.

"Maybe I get restraining belts," Tran suggested.

"Okay. I don't want her thrashing around while I'm giving her the anesthetic."

While Tran was getting the belts, Brindle went out to the terrace to speak with Aldridge, but the camp administrator had gone and taken his chess game with him. It was just as well, Brindle thought, glancing at his watch. It was after ten and he did not know how long the procedure would take. The brother and his friend sat quietly on the clinic steps. They looked at Brindle expectantly as he stood in the doorway. Tran came from the operating room.

"Tran," Brindle said, rubbing his eyes. "Will you explain to this guy that I'll have to keep his sister in the clinic for at least a week."

Tran spoke to the men.

"He say she called Kim Thi."

The brother said something else.

"Kim Thi Van Quang. This her brother—Hoang."

"Okay," Brindle said. "Explain to him about her arm, and then tell him to go back to camp. He can return in the morning."

Tran and the brother spoke together.

"He understand you very good doctor, but he no leave," Tran translated. "Besides, he sleep here on steps or in camp on ground—all same."

"As long as he knows that I don't want him in the clinic," Brindle said sternly. "Tell him if he comes in here without asking me first, I'll have him arrested."

Hoang nodded his head.

"He understand," Tran said.

The young woman was sleeping fitfully now and tensed as Tran began to put on the restraining belts. When she was immobilized, Brindle lifted her arm and gave her a brachial plexus anesthetic block. It was a difficult injection, and he hoped he had gotten it right the first time. As he waited for the anesthetic to take effect, Brindle gazed at his patient. She was an attractive young woman, despite the paleness of her skin and the black, perspiration-soaked hair that clung to her face. What had there been about her, he wondered, that had caused him to think about her all day, to find himself remembering how it was that she had come along the dock between her brother and mother.

"Blood pressure okay, Doctor," Tran said.

"That's good," Brindle replied. Perhaps she had not developed septicemia after all. An early sign of it was a drop in blood pressure and fast pulse. He had already checked her pulse and found it steady. She was feverish, but that could simply be from the localized infection, and not from tetanus or gangrene. Or it could be from exposure or dehydration. There were so many variables.

It was time to begin.

Brindle opened the wound with a scalpel. Probing with his hemostat, he found a speck of something metallic in the subcutaneous layer. A pocket of fluid had formed around the object. Pulling gently, he removed a long strand of finely woven gold, a necklace. Brindle shook his head in disgust as he placed it in a sterile tray. He probed the wound again but found nothing else. He spent some time cleaning the infected tissue and removing a sample for a culture test. Brindle was proud of the little refrigerator he had rigged with a light bulb and thermostat set at 97 degrees to serve as an incubator for testing cultures. It was one of many medical improvisations he had developed since his arrival. He expected to find little clumps of staphylococcus bacteria in the smear he had just taken from the young woman's arm. If that were true, then the penicillin he had given her would prove effective as an antibiotic. Effective if Kim Thi had not, as had so many other Vietnamese, purchased diluted penicillin over the counter and used it improperly so that the bacteria in her system had become immune. Brindle had discovered early on that this was often the case with the refugees. He would know by the following morning.

"Suture?" Tran asked.

"No," Brindle said. "The best thing we can do is to leave it open to irrigate. Put some pillows under her arm for now.

We'll rig up a suspended support later. We need to keep the arm elevated."

"Yes, Doctor," Tran said.

"If the infection doesn't spread, she has a chance," Brindle offered. "We'll keep her on the antibiotic—one million units four times a day."

He made a notation on her chart.

"So now we wait," Tran said.

"As always," Brindle sighed.

"What I tell brother?"

"That he can get his gold necklace back in the morning."

"Very dangerous time for these refugees," Tran explained. "Never know what come next. Sometime might need gold."

Brindle pulled off his gloves. "I know," he said thoughtfully. "But when it doesn't work . . ."

"Sometime you no believe thing work, but it come out okay anyway."

"What is that?" Brindle asked. "Vietnamese fortune cookie philosophy?"

Tran smiled. "Hope, Doctor. Always hope something good happen when in bad place."

"Like here?"

Tran looked around the surgery. "This place not so bad."

"I suppose it isn't," Brindle said.

Chapter Three

The following morning Brindle returned to the clinic sober, with a calmness of mind and heart now. Hoang Van Quang was still sitting on the steps. The young man looked haggard as he leaned against the railing, and Brindle wondered for the first time if he was really such a barbarian after all. Hoang apparently cared for his sister, or at least felt a responsibility toward her. Had it been his idea to put the gold in her arm, or had it been the mother's? She would no doubt be around the clinic later in the morning, and then Brindle might learn the answer to that question. In any event, the young man was here now and had spent the night outside the clinic, not breaking the rules by trying to enter, and Brindle respected that.

Hoang said something in Vietnamese which sounded like a question as Brindle passed, and the doctor motioned for him to wait.

Kim Thi Van Quang was sleeping peacefully and Brindle observed that the gauze pad beneath her arm was spotted with drainage. Her color was better, and putting a hand to her head, he did not feel the fever of the night before. The red streaks running up her arm from the wound were still there, however, and he did not like that. It would be a shame to have to amputate the arm after she had improved so much.

Tran was off duty, and the Vietnamese assistant who had replaced him spoke almost no English. So Brindle walked out to the steps and motioned for Hoang to come inside. The young man came into the clinic hesitantly and followed

Brindle over to his sister's bed. Without talking, Brindle showed him the arm and had Hoang touch his sister's cheek. The young refugee's look of apprehension lightened immediately when his fingers registered that Kim Thi's skin was cool. He said something in Vietnamese and nodded his head in thanks.

Brindle tapped his watch.

"Twelve o'clock," he said, pointing to the twelve on his watch. "You come back at twelve o'clock. Okay?"

Hoang nodded and left.

Brindle made his rounds. The boy who had collapsed on the dock was showing signs of rehydration. There was saliva in his mouth and his eyes were no longer dry. Brindle decided that dehydration was indeed the cause of his breathing failure. He explained to his appendectomy patient that it would be another week before the stitches could be removed. The other patients who had been brought to the clinic from the recent arrivals were doing fine. Most of them simply needed a little rest and food.

Brindle finished his rounds in an hour and then returned to Miss Van Quang's bedside. He changed the drainage pad beneath her arm and gave her another injection of penicillin. Then he hesitated for a moment and watched her as she slept, gazing at the soft round cheekbones and the thick dark hair.

"Coffee, Doctor?"

Brindle turned to see Tran holding out a mug.

"Thanks," he said and then looked at the young woman. "She's doing much better. I told her brother to come back at noon. We should be able to tell him something by then."

"Yes," Tran said and smiled. "Much better now."

There was no celebration in the camp that evening as Brindle crossed the courtyard to the dining mess, just the muffled chirp of cicadas in the palm trees and the rustle of wind off the sea. Dinner was served at eight, and Aldridge preferred that all camp administrators attend. He considered it an opportunity to hear from each member of the team regarding the events of the day. Usually present were Aldridge, seated at the head of the table, Michele on his right, then Brindle, and seated across from them Captain Salinem. Salinem was in charge of the Indonesian soldiers who helped with security in the camp. Next to the captain sat any guest who might have come over from Java, Sumatra, the Philippines, or a visiting WRO official.

"I was just telling the captain that I may have to attend a meeting in Jakarta," Aldridge said as Brindle seated himself at the table. "You know Soeharto would love to close us down. He doesn't care about the refugees."

"Is there any reason why he should?" Captain Salinem asked.

Brindle saw the pain on Aldridge's face but didn't say anything. Brindle did not like Captain Salinem. There was something sleazy about the man, the way he slicked the few strands of black hair across his balding head, the dark suspicious eyes with a tinge of yellow at the corners, the tightness of the skin across his cheekbones which gave him the impression of being an opium smoker. For all Brindle knew, perhaps he was, which would make the captain doubly dangerous as an Indonesian official (they hated the Vietnamese) and a possible opium dealer. Brindle had discovered shortly after his arrival on Boromu Island that most of the Indonesian soldiers were corrupt, so he assumed Captain Salinem was corrupt as well. The danger lay in not knowing how corrupt. Seeing the soldiers every day in wrinkled and unbuttoned uniforms which hung loosely on them, with their dark hair growing wildly, Brindle often wondered if they were culturally a step above, or below the Vietnamese. But it did not matter. The weapons they carried, the food supplies they brought each month, and the fact that they were able to come and go from the island defined the soldiers' status.

"The problem is that we're caught in the middle," Aldridge said. "It isn't the refugees who make the trouble. It's the communists, the black marketeers, and the opium smugglers. Unfortunately, Soeharto lumps the Vietnamese refugees in with the others as just another problem for his government."

"The smugglers have used some of your refugees before," Salinem commented. "And I believe there are some communist dissidents planted among them also."

"I know," Aldridge said. "They try to escape all that mess and just end up bringing it with them."

"Your heart is too large, Mr. Aldridge," Salinem suggested. "You Americans let so many people into your country and look what you have—economic weakness, increased crime, international debt. We in Indonesia intend to learn from the mistakes of others."

"Perhaps if we weren't the only ones who ever helped, we wouldn't have so many problems," Aldridge replied.

Brindle picked up his water glass. He was not in the mood to enter into a hopeless political discussion.

"Here's to dictators and despots everywhere," he said, raising his glass. "May they live long and multiply unto themselves."

Captain Salinem gazed at him. "Surely you do not include Indonesia in this toast, Dr. Brindle."

"Of course not, Captain," Brindle said. "Hands across the water and all that. We can't do enough for each other, can we?"

"John," Aldridge cautioned.

Salinem shook his head slowly. "Your sense of humor has always baffled me, Dr. Brindle."

"Baffled?" Brindle said, laughing. "Not confused or frustrated, Captain Salinem? Only baffled. I'll have to try harder."

"That's enough, John," Aldridge said.

"I think John is trying to say that there has always been corruption in the world, and there always will be. It's out of our hands," Michele suggested.

"Did I?" Brindle asked.

"Now you are bringing things into the spiritual realm," Salinem suggested. "This is very different, you being Christians, and we Muslims."

"Christians, Muslims, Hindus, Buddhists. What difference does it make?" Brindle asked.

"Do you really believe there is no difference?" Salinem asked. "That is very interesting, Dr. Brindle."

Aldridge laughed nervously. "John likes to stir things up sometimes, Captain." He shot an accusatory glance at Brindle.

"Are you familiar with the wayang drama?" Salinem asked.

"Yes," Brindle answered.

"I'm not," Michele said. "What is it?"

"It's a form of Indonesian drama where puppets or human performers portray gods or heroes," Brindle explained. "A variation on this is the shadow theater using leather puppets."

"Very good, Doctor," Salinem said. "Full marks."

"So which character do you identify yourself with?" Brindle asked.

"Oh," Salinem laughed. "I am much too modest to identify myself with any of the wayang gods, Doctor. Although I do prefer Bima, the warrior-hero."

"As did Sukarno."

"Right, again. But our current president identifies himself with Semar, the clumsy, comically obese, but immensely powerful clown god character."

Salinem ran a hand across his thinning hair. "And personally," he said, a sarcastic smile on his face, "I believe Semar would be an excellent choice to represent the United States."

"The immensely powerful clown god," Aldridge said. "I suppose so."

"I would like to see some of this drama," Michele said. "I love puppets."

"Then I must take you," Salinem said. "Or perhaps we might be able to put on a drama here at the camp."

"Is that possible?"

"Yes. I imagine so."

"Then let's do," Michele said.

Captain Salinem nodded his head courteously.

Aldridge asked, "How is that young woman with the infected arm, John?"

"She's doing better."

"It's the strangest thing," Aldridge said, picking up a butter knife. "They sliced open her arm and stuck a gold necklace inside—under the skin." He motioned with the knife across the skin of his left arm. "Can you believe that?"

Salinem's eyes glinted briefly. "Really."

"And she's an attractive girl too," Aldridge said. "What a shame to disfigure her like that."

"She'll be all right," Brindle said. "We all have scars."

"Yes," Aldridge laughed. "We do, don't we, John?"

⤝⤞

After dinner Brindle excused himself and stepped outside. He was just heading back across the courtyard to the clinic when someone called his name. He turned to see Michele coming down the steps.

Are you heading back to the bungalows?" she asked.

"Yes."

"May I walk with you?"

"Of course."

Michele folded her arms and gazed up at the dark sky.

"I'll be going to the Philippines in two weeks."

"I hadn't heard," Brindle said.

"Yes. I need to check on the relocation programs. I was supposed to go last month, but I've been putting it off."

"I'm running low on Scotch."

"I certainly wouldn't be going for that," she said.

"Then make it tequila."

Michele looked at him. "Would you like to go? We could have fun exploring Manila together."

His hesitation was enough to provide her with an answer, but he went through with the formality anyway.

"I've got too much work here," he protested.

"There will always be work, John. You could use a break from this place."

"I'll think about it."

"The offer is good right up to the time my plane takes off on the fifteenth. Even after. . ."

"Thanks," he said.

When Brindle returned to his room, he splashed water on his face to cool off and then picked up a book. He was reviewing Warren and Mahmoud's book *Tropical Medicine* in preparation for what he expected to happen when the monsoons came. There was more humidity and pressure in the air again tonight. He could imagine the storm clouds continuing to gather above China, like some malevolent force which affected not only the body but also the soul. He had found that a small quantity of alcohol not only fought off the depression, but also soothed his nerves to a point where he could study the medical journal calmly, without mental distraction. So he poured himself a drink. This was actually one of his more preferred times of the day—just after dinner when the night had settled in and the whine of mosquitoes had diminished. It was not late enough yet to worry about sleep, and he had no pressing obligations, except if there were a medical emergency. So he sat quietly and read chapters on intestinal parasites, typhus, and trachoma.

He had always enjoyed this time of the evening at home in California. By this time his daughter would have brushed her teeth, been read a story, said her prayers, and finally fallen asleep. Then he and Sarah would have spent some time together as a man and woman—not as parents. He smiled, thinking of his daughter sleeping so peacefully. Sometimes he used to sit in Carrie's room for a time after she had fallen asleep and listen to her breathing, the dim nightlight casting shadows on her blonde hair against the pillow. He had felt at peace on those evenings, happy, safe in a strange way that perhaps even he could not define. He remembered Carrie's prayers: "Now I lay me down to sleep, I pray the Lord my soul to keep, if I should die before I wake. . ."

If I should die . . .

Brindle threw his medical book against the wall.

When will you ever learn? he snapped at himself in the mirror. *When?*

Taking a swig from the tequila bottle, he dropped onto the edge of his bed.

In the morning he had felt so peaceful, calm, wanting to be sober and even feeling a kind of amnesty with life. Hadn't he even felt a certain amount of tenderness toward Miss Van Quang?

So what had happened?

"It's the darkness," he muttered to himself. "The lack of sunlight."

But he knew that was not true. The truth lay in what he had given up and what that had done to him. When you rejected God, he had decided, it left a void in the spirit which had to be filled by something, and if it was not from heaven, then something else slipped in at night, in the darkness, and took root. Brindle was beginning to feel as if that metamorphosis was happening to him now, and he rubbed his heart. It was as if he were a vacant room from which one occupant had been forcefully evicted and another had entered without permission. Did it always have to be that way? he wondered. Couldn't a person just decide not to be filled—to just go on living one day at a time without spiritual thoughts or feelings? Did God have to make it a choice of one way or the other? What was wrong with neutrality?

There was a knock on his door.

"Doctor?"

Brindle did not answer.

"Miss Van Quang awake, Doctor. She want leave clinic."

Brindle tilted his head back, breathed deeply, and then exhaled slowly. How loudly had he shouted earlier? he wondered. This was something he would have to control. He could not have everyone thinking he had gone off the edge. At least now, for another evening, work would occupy his thoughts and he would not have to deal with the darkness.

"I'm coming, Tran," he called.

Kim Thi Van Quang was indeed awake and gazed at him timidly as Brindle walked up to her bedside. She had dark eyes that resembled her brother's—distinct, and yet the same as every Vietnamese refugee who had ever come into the clinic. If he saw only the eyes, would he know her? he wondered as he took her temperature. He checked the drainage pad beneath her arm and saw that it was clean. The red streaks were beginning to fade also.

"Well, Miss Quang," he said. "It looks like we got you just in time."

She smiled and said something, but he could not understand. He assumed she had spoken in Vietnamese.

Clearing her throat, the young woman tried again.

"I very sorry cause you trouble, Doctor," she said. "My brother here?"

Brindle was surprised. Very few of his patients knew any English, and this young woman spoke very well. She had a soft pleasant voice.

"Yes," he replied. "Your brother was here all day. He is at the camp now."

"And mother?"

"She was here this afternoon."

Kim Thi nodded weakly and closed her eyes. After a moment she opened them again.

"I . . ." she coughed.

"Don't talk now," Brindle said. "Just try to rest. I'll have your brother and mother here for you in the morning. Okay?"

She nodded.

Brindle turned to Tran. "Let's keep her on the penicillin. We can remove the arm support tomorrow morning if she's doing okay."

"Yes, Doctor."

Chapter Four

Vo Nguyen could see the beach and the lights from the refugee camp as he paddled around Surabi Point. He planned to put in just north of the camp in a deserted cove and hide his skiff under palm branches. From there he would slip into the camp unnoticed. It was a moonless night and he had worn black pajamas. Moving his paddle smoothly, without noise, he guided the skiff toward shore. When he felt the skiff bottom brush against sand, he slipped out and crouched motionless in the water, carefully gazing up and down the beach. Finally assured that no one was watching, he grabbed a rope attached to the prow of the skiff and began to drag it across the rocky sand to the trees. With a machete he hacked enough palm branches to camouflage the skiff. Taking another branch, he brushed the sand from the water's edge up to the trees to remove any footprints or marks from the skiff. Then he moved stealthily along the tree line to the camp. In his pack he carried a small radio receiver and transmitter.

Within thirty minutes Vo Nguyen had reached the outer edge of the shanties and stepped casually in among the refugees. He passed men squatting together and talking quietly, women working over cookfires, and children sleeping on mats outside the shanties. *These were the deserters*, Vo Nguyen told himself, *the weaklings who did not have the moral courage to follow the party rules*. They had forfeited their right to the new society. But they would not get off so easily for having abandoned Vietnam. It was his job to see that they paid for their betrayal and that the Indonesians would no longer want to

37

help them. A dead soldier here, a fire there, a feeling of distrust, it would not be a difficult assignment. He would begin soon, but first he wanted to work quietly—spread a little dissent, make a few comrades among those who had developed second thoughts about leaving Vietnam. Certainly there would be men who were not satisfied with the life desertion had brought them—living in shanties on the edge of this jungle island. Nguyen would find those men and begin to organize. *Tomorrow*, he told himself, as he stepped into the darkness around the side of a shanty. Tomorrow he would begin. Now there was still time enough to get some sleep and let his pants dry before morning. It had been a long trip from the fishing trawler.

John Brindle gazed at the sleeping form of Kim Thi Van Quang. She had been moved from the post-surgery room into the main ward where two dozen beds lined the walls. It was still early in the morning and she had not awakened. Brindle had not slept much during the night himself. There was the usual depression, but mostly he had been thinking of her. Yesterday evening as he had spoken to her, he had suddenly realized what had attracted him to her that day on the dock: her fragility. To be in a fragile state physically was nothing new for the refugees, most of the patients he saw were in that condition. With Kim Thi, however, he had perceived a fragility that did not correspond with physical health but which went much deeper—into that area where one spirit touches another. In response, he had felt a sudden opening of his heart toward her. What surprised him, as he thought about it during the night, was that this release of emotion was so instantaneous, so natural. He could not have predicted or believed that it would have happened. Yet, quite naturally, he had begun to experience a trickle of happiness. As he stood beside Kim Thi this morning, he enjoyed the feeling within limitations. After all, he had

learned the painful lesson that life was cruel. When he had
given his love before, to a wife and infant daughter, life had
seen his vulnerability and had taken them away. The living
John Brindle had loved openly and without reservation. The
existing John Brindle could only remember what love felt like
and try to imitate its unbarred expression—as if going through
the physical motions represented the same emotional impulse.

"I feel better now, Doctor," someone said and Brindle
looked up to see that Kim Thi's eyes were open.

"Are you hungry?" he asked.

"Maybe a little."

"Good. I'll have some food brought in to you."

The young woman lifted her head and gazed at her arm. "I
was frightened. I thought I would lose arm."

"It's okay," he said. "You will have a scar, but that's all."

She smiled and he noticed how the pink of her cheeks
contrasted with the buttery tan of her skin. It was as if her
cheeks had been faintly dusted pink, but he knew this was her
natural complexion. He was pleased to see color in her face.
She was improving.

"Your brother is waiting outside," Brindle said. "Would you
like to see him?"

Kim Thi nodded, her eyes brightening.

Hoang came into the ward, and Brindle moved on to his
next patient. As he examined a chart, he glanced over to Kim
Thi's bed and saw that she had taken her brother's hand and
that they were talking quietly.

What would he be saying to her now? Brindle wondered.
That he was sorry? That cutting her arm had been a bad idea
in the first place? Or was that beyond them now? Were they
already discussing plans for the future?

Brindle felt irritated somehow that he had begun to feel an
emotional attachment to this woman that he knew so little—
basically nothing—about. He remembered the advice Aldridge
had given him when he had arrived at the camp.

"Don't get involved," Aldridge had warned him. "Every one of these refugees has a story to tell that would break your heart. You can't help them or yourself if you're reacting emotionally."

"I'm a long way from getting involved with anyone," Brindle had said, and he meant it. But he felt differently now. And this was a specific case, he told himself, not just an impractical need to care for all the refugees.

What am I doing? he asked himself disgustedly and walked into the dispensary. When he returned, Hoang had gone and Kim Thi was eating her breakfast.

"Everything all right?" Brindle asked, feeling stupid at the shallowness of his question.

"Yes," she said. "Hoang has built a shelter for us."

"I'm glad he found the materials."

"Hoang very re. . ." she searched for the word in English.

"Resourceful?" Brindle guessed.

"Yes. Resourceful."

"That's a big word. Where did you learn to speak English?"

Kim Thi smiled, remembering. "I had American girlfriend. We spent all time together." A look of sadness came into her eyes. "Before Americans go home. Long time ago."

"Yes," Brindle said. "Ten years."

"Many things change in Vietnam. Cannot speak English now."

"I'm sure."

"So I keep little book. Read English in room."

"It must have been difficult."

"Yes," she said, frowning. "Always problems."

"Someday you'll have to tell me how you got that necklace in your arm."

He realized immediately that he had overstepped his boundary when the smile vanished from her face and she looked away.

"I'm sorry," he said. "I was only trying to make conversation. You don't have to tell me anything."

Kim Thi continued to look away, her eyes moving back and forth nervously.

Was she trying to make up her mind about something? Brindle wondered. He turned to leave.

"Doctor?"

Brindle stopped.

"Maybe someday," she said quietly. "No good time now."

"I understand," he said.

Hoang was talking with Tran when Brindle left the ward.

"He want to know how sister doing," Tran said, as Brindle walked up to them.

"Much better. Her temperature is down and the wound is draining."

"So, no lose arm?"

"No lose arm."

"When she leave clinic?"

"In three or four days, depending on how quickly she recovers."

Tran translated.

Hoang nodded.

"Hoang say good," said Tran.

"Tell him I heard that he built a shanty," Brindle said. "Where is it?"

Tran asked.

"He say on north side of camp. Near beach."

"I would like to see it sometime," Brindle said. Was he already planning that far ahead, he wondered. Had it actually become such a reality to him that he was thinking of visiting the family?

"Hoang say you help sister. You come anytime. Always welcome."

"Thanks," Brindle said.

∽✕∾

The South China Sea was gray blue that afternoon when Brindle walked down to the beach. He usually took a walk along the beach in the late afternoon to clear his mind and to set things in perspective. Far off on the horizon a bank of very white cumulus clouds hovered above the water. Brindle sat on a fallen palm tree and gazed at the water. Sometimes now he had the impression that he, or whatever part of himself he had always considered as being the real he, had been lost or misplaced somehow, and that his body or physical actions had continued on through time on simple momentum. For example, he thought to himself, what on earth had ever brought him to a refugee camp in Indonesia? Had it been a conscious decision on his part—the part that he had always thought of as being himself? Or had this sudden interest in Kim Thi sparked enough life into the previously living John Brindle so that he could peek through the despair and hollowness to see life as he had once known it? In any event, he was beginning to look around himself now and to ask questions. He picked up a small seashell and turned it over in his hands.

"It's really nice out here today."

He turned and saw Michele walking barefoot toward him across the sand. She was carrying her sandals.

"You were looking so pensive," she said, looking at him from behind her sunglasses. "Thinking about something important?"

"Nothing much." He shrugged.

Michele sat beside him on the fallen tree and dug her toes into the sand. She had polished her toenails bright red. Brindle noticed that her feet looked young. He could imagine her wearing braces, or talking for hours on the phone with a girlfriend about boys, or trying new shades of lipstick to see which ones made her look the most seductive. Although any hint of her desire to have a relationship with him caused Brindle to feel uneasy, he had actually given Michele Fallon a lot of thought. She was twenty-six years old and from San Diego, so they were both Californians. She had attended nursing school, but had dropped out when her engagement to a pediatric intern had fallen through. Then she had worked on a relocation project for illegal immigrants—mostly Mexicans. From there she had moved on to the refugee organization and Boromu Island.

Brindle handed her the seashell. "Here's one for your collection," he said.

"Thanks," she said, laughing. "I didn't know I had a collection."

"So now you can start."

The fundamental difference between them, Brindle had decided, was that Michele was open, willing to commit her feelings, take the chance of being hurt. He, on the other hand, had trained himself to become elusive. He did not mind the questions of others as much as the answers. It was the answers which hurt and stirred up the feelings of despair. So he avoided the questions. Michele took them head on. He respected that quality in her. He also knew that she still believed—in fact had a devout faith—but he was careful never to bring up that subject with her. There was no point in starting down a path which could only lead to pain.

"May I ask a personal question?" she asked him now.

He tried to see her eyes behind the dark glasses.

"What?"

"Well," she said, laughing, "I know this sounds completely crazy, but I had a dream last night that you had fallen in love with someone."

"Nice dream. Anyone in particular?"

"Someone here on the island."

"So what do you want to know?"

She looked down at the seashell in her hands.

"Is it true?"

Her voice was hesitant.

So, Brindle thought, there were answers she was afraid of too. Perhaps they were not so far apart as he had first imagined.

"Not that I'm aware of," he said.

"I just thought," she said, then hesitated. "That new girl with the infected arm is very pretty. . ."

"I only look at her wound."

Michele let the seashell slip through her fingers and drop to the sand.

"I guess I need to get away from here more than I realized," she sighed.

"Would you like to go for a walk?" Brindle asked. He was being sincere now. He would like to have her company. For a moment he felt like telling her everything. It seemed completely right to do so, but something held him back.

"All right," she said, brushing the sand off her legs. "Maybe for a few minutes."

They walked along the beach in the direction of Surabi Point. Two refugee boys were fishing in the surf with a handmade net.

"Do they ever catch anything?" Michele asked.

"Sometimes," Brindle said, "though I think it's more to keep them busy than anything else."

"And to stay out of trouble."

He nodded.

Michele walked into the water up to her ankles.

"I've been reading about wayang drama," she said. "Hal has a book."

"Is it interesting?"

"I've decided that you are Karna, the undefeated warrior," she commented. "Sired by the sun. Born out of the ear of his mother, Kunti." Michele laughed.

"Undefeated?" Brindle said questioningly. "I can't even claim that on my good days."

"Do you have good days, John?"

Brindle gazed out to sea. Far in the distance he could see an old fishing trawler.

"Once in a while," he said, shrugging. "Not very often."

"Is there anything I could do to help?"

He thought about this for a moment. Was there anything anyone could do to help? he wondered. Turn back time, possibly. Stop the argument. Keep the car from skidding. Have his side of the car swerve into the approaching truck. Change the mind of God.

"Walking helps," he said. "Just like this—having someone to talk with."

"Are you sure you can't get away for a few days and go to Manila?"

"That would complicate things, wouldn't it?"

She looked at the water as they walked.

"Maybe," she said. "Maybe it would help."

"I need to get back," he said.

"All right, Mister Doctor," Michele said. "See you at dinner?"

"Yes."

She turned and walked back along the beach. As he moved out of the hot sun into the shade of the palms, Brindle glanced back and saw her talking to the boys with the fishing net. They were showing Michele how to throw the net into the water. Brindle smiled and headed up the path.

Aldridge was waiting for him when he returned to the clinic. The camp administrator looked tired.

"Have you been taking your cloriquine?" Brindle asked. "We can't afford to have you come down with malaria."

"Yes, yes," Aldridge answered. "It's just something intestinal that I picked up. Bad fish, probably."

"If it isn't better tomorrow, let me know."

"Right," Aldridge said. "Now, I've got this report from Captain Salinem."

He held out a folder.

"What report?"

"About the runner on the beach. The one who was shot."

Brindle opened the folder and glanced at the single sheet of paper inside.

"They claim he was an opium dealer," Aldridge said, wiping his face with a handkerchief.

"Was he one of ours?"

"I'm afraid so."

"He must have been cutting in on their trade."

"Let's not get negative, John," Aldridge said. "And please, don't ever let Captain Salinem hear you talking like that."

"It's okay, Hal," Brindle said, smirking. "We're pals."

"We're getting the refugees out. That's the important thing."

"I'm just glad I'm not one of them, if they have to depend on Salinem and his gang."

"Well, anyway," Aldridge said, "that's the report. I thought you might like a copy."

"I'll have Tran file it with the others."

"Oh, and I almost forgot," Aldridge added, picking through a handful of mail. "A letter came for you."

Brindle took the envelope and slipped it into the pocket of his medical coat. He looked embarrassed.

"Thanks," he said without enthusiasm.

༈

It seemed curious to Brindle that he had no desire to spend a few days in Manila with Michele. Could the heart really make decisions that quickly, he wondered. Could a few days spent with a patient really alter his feelings that much? The practical thing would be to go with her, spend a few days away from the clinic, maybe share the lingering impression of a relationship, but then what? He would invariably return to the camp and then have to spend his time distancing himself from her. On the other hand, he felt compelled to be near this new refugee woman. He felt good when he was beside her, that his life was opening up again. So, what was the difference? If he could be attracted to Kim Thi, then why not Michele Fallon?

He knew Aldridge was curious about the letter he had received—there had only been two in the past six months— but Brindle had tried not to show the anguish such letters caused him. Seated behind his desk now with the door closed (meaning that there would be no ventilation and that within a few minutes he would be soaked with perspiration), he withdrew the letter from his pocket and gazed at his name scrawled in the familiar penmanship. Could the sender of this letter possibly know how much it pained him to see the address written in the return corner? The California postmark meant only one thing—that it was from his past, from a life he no longer wished to remember in any way. His first impulse was to pitch the letter into the trash without opening it, but a feeling of responsibility, of curiosity even, prevented this. Had life really gone on without him back there? It seemed to him now that everything he had ever known, people he had cared about, places he had visited, should have crumbled into that dark void which had become his memory. The idea that life in California continued on as before—with people traveling to work each morning across the Golden Gate bridge, going out to dinner, hiring babysitters, taking school photos, going to church—seemed incomprehensible to him. It had ceased to exist in the reality of his life, and therefore it truly did not exist. This letter, then, was like a time capsule sent from the past.

Brindle opened the envelope with an increasing feeling of despair.

> *Dearest John:*
>
> The WRO has given us this address in hopes that we may be able to reach you. We have tried to find Boromu Island on our world map, but the scale is not large enough. Have you really gone so far away from us, that we are not able to find you even on a map?
>
> John, we understand why you wanted to leave your practice and start a new life, but we hope this does not mean you have abandoned your family or

faith. We have been praying for you. They say that
intercessory. . .

The letter continued on for three pages about how much
they were praying for him in Napa Valley, of nephews growing
up, jobs changing, and of a new pastor at his former church. It
ended with an imploring request to hear from him:

> *Please write to us. Even a postcard would help*
> *so much. We are so concerned about you. Know that*
> *we love you.*
>
> > *May God bless you,*
> > *Carolyn*

May God bless him, Brindle thought bitterly. What was
the chance of that happening? And what was there left to
bless, anyway? Slipping the letter back into the envelope, he
tossed it onto his desk. He knew that he would never respond
to his sister's letter, but he was not ready to throw it away yet.
As he had with her first letter, he would keep this one around
for a few weeks until the message it contained had become a
part of the past. Then he would discard it subtly so that not
even he could be sure of when it was truly lost. That would
lessen the guilt.

Glancing at his watch, Brindle saw that it was nearly time
for dinner. Opening the door to his little office, he felt the hot
air of the island strike against his sweating face.

Chapter Five

"How far is it?" Brindle asked as he climbed into the truck beside Tran and an Indonesian driver. Ahead of them in a jeep were Captain Salinem and two soldiers.

"Thirty minutes, maybe less," Tran replied. "We just follow the Captain."

Brindle glanced behind him to where four Vietnamese workers sat in the truck bed.

"Did you load the stretchers?"

Tran nodded.

"And the body bags?"

"All okay, Doctor."

They had been informed earlier in the morning that an Indonesian patrol had picked up the trail of six refugees who had strayed from camp. Although there were no fences around the camp, there were well-defined boundaries, and refugees were not allowed beyond those areas. The patrol had opened fire and three refugees had been killed. Two had been captured, and one had escaped.

Brindle watched Salinem's jeep bounce and sway over the dirt track. Boromu Island was covered with thick tropical growth in the coastal areas, but inland the ground jutted upwards in volcanic hills. To reach the site where the refugees had been shot, they were required to take a road which led to the west and then turned north. Despite the gruesomeness of the occasion, Brindle found himself pleased to be out of the camp and headed into the highlands. The air whipping through his open window felt cool and smelled of hyacinth.

"Much good land here," Tran said as he looked at the passing jungle. "Remind me of Chu Lai."

"Is that where you're from?" Brindle asked. It surprised him that he had never before asked Tran this question.

"Yes, Doctor. Good land. Much farming."

"Do you ever miss it?"

"Chu Lai?"

"Yes."

"Most time miss Chu Lai, Doctor. But not miss communists."

The heavy vegetation was beginning to thin out now, and they turned north. As the ground began to rise, Brindle looked back across the treetops to the sea, which sparkled in the morning light. They had gone about three kilometers when Salinem's jeep came to a halt. Brindle's driver pulled the truck to a stop just behind the jeep, and everyone climbed out. The road went straight on for another hundred meters and then disappeared around a bend. On the right side of the road the ground dropped away into trees and thick undergrowth.

"We assume, Doctor, that the refugees were planning to connect with the road here and then follow it across the island," Captain Salinem explained.

Brindle was aware that this was the only possible route of escape from Boromu. Once on the western side of the island, the refugees might find a way to cross the Strait of Malacca to Sumatra.

"So where are they?"

"Just down there," Salinem said, pointing into the trees.

Tran came up with the Vietnamese workers who carried the stretchers and body bags.

"If you don't mind, Doctor," Salinem said, "I will remain here. I have seen far too many bodies, and I've just polished my boots."

Brindle shook his head and followed the soldiers down the slope.

Two of the bodies lay close together in a position of unexpected death. Surely they had not anticipated an ambush when they had come so far from the camp and so close to the road. As Brindle had expected, they were both young men—for the old do not seek a future in distant lands. Standing over them and gazing at the blood-brown stains on their chests, he felt the helplessness of human life, that irrevocable cessation of blood pumping through the veins, of laughter and memories and pain. The young men's quest for freedom had led them from Vietnam to this damp, overgrown slope with its rotted leaves and clinging vines. If they were not moved soon, they would quickly be drawn into the slope and its vegetation.

The third man lay a few meters away, sprawled in a position of escape, his back ripped with darkening wounds in the shoulder and spine.

Brindle shook his head sadly. "Why couldn't they have trusted us to get them out?"

"Always sometimes bad people, Doctor," Tran explained as he put down one of the stretchers. "Not listen. Want freedom quick."

"It was a stupid thing to do."

"They free now," Tran said with dry humor. "Plenty free."

"Let's get them back to camp."

Brindle and Tran rolled out three bags as the workers lifted the bodies. They carried them one at a time up the slope to the truck.

Salinem was talking quietly with one of his men when Brindle reached the road. Brindle felt suddenly, without any logical reason, that there was something sinister about Salinem and this ambush of escaped refugees. How had the patrol managed to spot them down there in the trees? Where were the two who had been captured? Had one really escaped?

"I can see that it bothers you, Doctor," Salinem said from his jeep. "Death is always unfortunate. But we must maintain discipline. We cannot have these Vietnamese running all over the island."

Brindle looked at the bodies in the back of the truck.

"What happened to the two you captured, Captain?" he asked.

Captain Salinem said something to his driver, who started the jeep.

"They were taken back to the camp, of course," he answered.

"I would like their names."

"Yes, Doctor. Now may we return to camp. It is getting hot."

Brindle looked back at the truck. The workers had covered the bodies with a canvas tarp. Tran leaned out the window. "All ready."

"Then let's go," Brindle said.

∾

Paperwork. It seemed as if there were no end to the forms and regulations that had to be filled out on the refugees who arrived at the camp. The WRO required that each refugee be documented, with an additional form requesting refugee status and relocation. Also, Brindle had to do a general physical on each refugee selected for transportation to the Philippines. Aldridge and Michele had been authorized to select 150 the day before. That meant they were moved from the regular camp to a special holding area. From there they would be taken on a launch out to the WRO-chartered ship for transportation to Manila and another camp. It was all one long process of geographical movement toward a free life in the West, or whatever a green card in the United States implied.

Brindle put down his pen and rubbed his eyes. Then, of course, there was the paperwork on the dead. He had filled out four death certificates since Monday and hoped there would not be any more. As he pushed away from his desk, he decided to walk over to the holding area. There, for a moment at least, he would be able to get away from the thought of captivity and

death and enjoy the excitement of those who had been
selected to depart.

He passed the Indonesian guard at the entrance to the
holding area and looked at the families huddled in the courtyard. They sat together with their meager belongings, expectant glances, and the implied hope of a smile, and he thought
that *here* were truly the resilient ones, for they had beaten the
odds. Tomorrow they would board the ship for the Philippines.
Whatever hopes they had when they had pushed off from Nha
Trang or Vung Tau or Ben Tre were now coming true. He could
not have known that they were more safe now than he realized, that there was a reality to life in the camp which had
nothing to do with him or Aldridge or the WRO. There were
pressures and dangers of which he was unaware. Because the
camp had been set up for the benefit of the refugees, he
assumed that their plight had ended when they stepped onto
the shabby wooden dock and scrawled their names on the
admittance forms. They knew, though, that it was not until
they had stepped from camp life into this area of departure
that they were actually safe. In their spirits they were already
moving eastward in anticipation of freedom, though their bodies remained on Boromu for the moment.

A young women who vaguely resembled Kim Thi smiled
at Brindle as he passed, causing him to think. All he had to do
was sign the health form, speak to Aldridge, and she and her
family could leave with this group in the morning. The idea
appealed to him to help Kim Thi in this way, but at the same
moment he became depressed at the thought of losing her.

The young woman bowed slightly and smiled, showing bad
teeth.

"Good luck," Brindle said. He turned away.

Kim Thi was sitting up in her bed and sipping a bowl of
broth when he entered the main ward. She held the bowl del-
icately in her right hand. Her left arm, the wound bandaged
now, lay on a pillow for support.

"You're looking much better," he said, gazing at her.

His expression must have been obvious, for her eyes only briefly touched on his and then she looked away demurely.

"Yes," she said. "Arm no hurt."

He had always been aware of that Oriental vagueness, of his Western inability to understand the inner workings of the Vietnamese mind, but now this inability frustrated him. He wanted to reach out to her, to let her know in some polite, respectful way of his growing attachment to her. But how could he? Where would he begin? Each encounter with Kim Thi left Brindle feeling more and more as if he were reaching out to something which did not exist or was so illusive that he was incapable of grasping it. And this was what caused the frustration—this realization that he was somehow not good enough or lacked the qualities to establish a connection between himself and this young Vietnamese woman. Looking at her now, he realized that it was true; she saw him as nothing more than a doctor.

"Be okay soon," she said.

Brindle looked at her chart.

"Hoang say he get money. Help go Philippines."

Brindle put down the chart. "You don't have to pay. The WRO takes care of everything. All free."

For the first time, she leveled her eyes on his inquisitively. He saw the darkness of them, the softness around the edges, the delicate upturned corners, and it occurred to him that she did not believe what he was saying. He was aware that Hoang had been visiting her several times every day. But what had he been telling her? That they had to pay to get to the Philippines?

"It's true," he repeated. "Everything is free. You don't have to pay."

"All same," she said. "Hoang make money. Have money for Philippines."

"How?" Brindle asked. "How can he make money? By selling your necklace?"

Something about his questions must have sparked a memory of danger, for she stopped talking immediately and withdrew into herself.

"Listen, Kim Thi," Brindle explained. "I'm not the police. I'm a doctor. My job is to take care of you. Okay?"

"Okay."

"If I happen to ask you a question that you don't like, simply tell me to shut up. You don't have to be afraid."

She nodded.

But as he left the ward, Brindle wondered if he had told Kim Thi the truth. If he discovered that her brother was involved in something illegal or dangerous, would he really remain silent? Or would he feel compelled to do something about it? He did not know and hoped the situation would never arise. He had already made a decision about her leaving early, and that was to pass on doing anything out of the ordinary. It was not exactly being selfish, he told himself. After all, she was not scheduled to leave tomorrow. He would simply let things play out as they were destined. What harm could it do?

The air pressed low and heavy against the sea the following morning as Brindle watched the transport group loading on the dock. Because of the haze, he could not see more than a hundred meters out from the beach, and everything had been filtered into shades of blue—waves, sky, Surabi Point, cargo ship. It was like walking in a dream, and as he stood there and watched the refugees stepping onto the swaying launch, he felt that they came out of nothing and moved silently into nothing. And here, he thought, was the truth more graphic than any reality he could ever imagine. He looked up the path through the nearby palms. Soldiers were posted every few meters from the holding area to the dock to prevent stowaways from slipping into the transport group. This was always a touchy time for the administration, because there was such a great potential for trouble, and it always made Aldridge nervous.

As Brindle leaned against the railing, he saw again for a moment the girl who resembled Kim Thi, and he suddenly felt

that he had made a terrible mistake. If he was attracted to Kim
Thi for her innate purity, and by this he did not imply sexual or
even mental but rather purity in a spiritual sense, then wasn't
it his obligation to protect her from the cruelties of this harsh
life, more so than he had with his own family? Now it was too
late, and anything he might try would be too obvious. Aldridge
had worked hard to establish the idea among the refugees that
there was no favoritism played here by the staff. When their
time came, the refugees would be sent on to the next camp
without jewelry or bribes or special duties performed by the
women. It was all numbers and paperwork.

There was a muffled cry. It drifted through the haze like
something without form, without certainty, but with an unmis-
takable undercurrent of surprise. Had it been a seagull, Brindle
wondered. He gazed up at the hazy sky above his head but could
see nothing, and the sound did not come again. Then he glanced
at the faces of the passing refugees to see if they had heard it also,
but their expressions were focused, concentrated on the necessity
to put one foot in front of the other until they had reached the
launch. It was a fear born of the realization that at any moment
something might happen to stop their journey.

A woman with a baby passed him, and the child let out a
little squeal of hunger. So it was the baby, Brindle thought. He
began to wonder about the powdered milk they had distributed
to the refugees. Some of the mothers had watered the powdered
milk down to the point where it had practically no nutritional
value. They had done this to stretch the powder. Brindle had
gone through the camp with Tran and explained to the mothers that there would be more powdered milk available every
month, and that they should follow the instructions fully. Yet
there were still women who watered down the powder, and
their babies suffered for it. Brindle gazed at the child and pon-
dered how much all children looked alike when they cry. We
pretend to be different from each other, he thought with some
bitterness, but when we cry, we are all children from the same
womb, with Eve as our mother.

The woman with the baby moved out onto the dock.

There was a commotion behind him, voices talking excitedly, a shout. Brindle turned to see a soldier coming quickly toward him.

"Doctor," the soldier commanded. "Come."

The haze gave one an odd sensation that only in the exact place where you stood did life really have substance. Brindle could see quite clearly the green and black striped uniform of the soldier in front of him, the webbed belt, the black boots, but beyond that there was only the filtered blue of obscure forms. On his left moved the steady line of transport refugees toward the dock. As they hurried up the path, Brindle could hear the voices more clearly. There was the voice of Aldridge, sounding strained and tired, and Captain Salinem, sounding angry. Then the guard stopped and Brindle saw Aldridge standing beside a form on the ground. It was another soldier, one of the guards. He was dead. Brindle examined the body and found blood below the man's left shoulder blade. Pulling up the soldier's fatigue shirt, he saw a puncture wound about an inch wide.

"Looks like someone got him from behind with a knife," he said. "Between the fourth and fifth ribs. Straight into the heart."

"We must take them all off the ship," Captain Salinem said. "We must check each one. There will be an investigation."

"None of the transport refugees would have done this," Aldridge argued. "What reason would they have to kill a guard now? They're leaving."

"All the same," the Captain snapped. "One of my men has been killed."

Captain Salinem shouted an order to his men, who began to butt the refugees with their rifles.

"Wait," Aldridge shouted. "These people haven't done anything."

"Of course not," said Captain Salinem. "That is why you are no longer in Vietnam."

Aldridge looked to Brindle for help.

"Let's just put a hold on everything until the haze clears," Brindle suggested. "Right now, we can't see a thing."

"Yes," Aldridge agreed. "We'll keep these people in the holding area and wait until the sky clears."

"Very well," said Captain Salinem.

Two soldiers began to pick up the body, but the captain stopped them.

"Leave him," he ordered. "Nothing changes until the haze clears."

It did not take long. By eight-thirty the tropical sun had burned off the haze, and when Brindle looked at the sky, he could see a thin wafting of cirrus clouds high up in the atmosphere.

It was apparent that the refugees who were just coming from the holding area could not have reached the scene by the time the soldier was killed, so they were simply detained. Also, the ones who had already been taken out to the ship could not be considered, as Brindle had heard the soldier's cry only moments before the woman with the baby had passed him. That meant anyone who had reached the dock before her was eliminated as a suspect.

"So if one of the refugees did it, and I don't believe they did, then it had to be one of these," Aldridge said, motioning to the line of men and women squatting on the ground near the dock.

Brindle had immediately sent for Tran, who was moving casually along the line, passing out a chocolate bar here and there, and asking a few questions.

"What do you think?" Brindle asked.

"They very worried," Tran said. "They know soldier killed. Maybe cause trouble for them, no leave camp."

"Do they know who did it?"

"They live with communists for ten years," Tran explained. "Know when to keep mouth shut."

"So they didn't tell you anything?"

Tran shook his head.

"Maybe they don't know," Brindle suggested.

"Most, I say yes," Tran responded. "But someone know. Too many people passing. But ones who see too afraid. Not say anything."

"Do you think one of them killed the guard?" Aldridge asked him.

"No," Tran said. "Only cause trouble for them. No reason."

"That's what I think too," Aldridge said. "We have no proof that it was a refugee. It could have been anyone."

"We'll never convince Salinem of that," Brindle said.

"I know," Aldridge said, rubbing a hand wearily across his chin. "I'm afraid we're going to have to hold these . . ." he looked around him. "How many are there?"

"Thirty-five," Tran said.

"Okay. We're going to have to hold these thirty-five back and select another thirty-five to replace them."

"They no like that," Tran said.

"It has to be done," Aldridge said. "I'll have Michele get to work on their papers right away. I want to get this ship out of here as soon as possible."

Aldridge sent one of his workers to notify Michele and then conferred with Captain Salinem.

"What's the matter?" Brindle asked.

Aldridge shook his head. "He still wants to search the ship."

"And look for what?" Brindle asked. "Some guy standing there with a knife and blood on his hands?"

"Yes," Aldridge said. "And we have to do it."

While Michele was busily coming up with names for the thirty-five replacements, Aldridge and Brindle escorted Captain Salinem and four soldiers out to the ship. As he stood in the launch, Brindle felt relieved that he had not gotten Kim Thi into this mess.

"What's the delay?" asked the captain when they had climbed aboard.

"An unfortunate situation," Captain Salinem replied. "One of my men has been killed—apparently by a refugee. . ."

"We don't know that," Aldridge interrupted.

"In any event," said Captain Salinem, "we would like to search the refugees who have already come on board."

The ship's captain shrugged. "It's your charter," he said. "Have at it, if you like."

The cargo hold had been rigged with rows of shelf-like bunks three high to accommodate the refugees. As Brindle walked through the quarters, the refugees gazed at him fearfully, suspiciously. He could imagine what they were thinking. Was this some sort of trick? Were they being sent back to Vietnam? Or was it something worse? Each shelf had a bit of worn curtain hanging from a cord for privacy, as if there could be any privacy on a ship when you were surrounded within touching distance of 150 people. Brindle noticed the rows of plastic sandals beneath the shelves, the plastic bowls, bits of orange peel, and burnt matches. On the black metal frame of each shelf a number was painted in white: 17A, 17B, 17C, and so on along the rows. He immediately thought of animals crated for shipment, though this was a ship of the living, the potentially free.

Captain Salinem's men searched the ship for two hours before he seemed to be satisfied. They had, of course, found nothing to link any of the refugees with the killing.

By the time they had finally left the cargo area, Brindle's shirt clung to his back with perspiration. The sun seemed to be just overhead as they stepped down the ladder to the launch.

"Those people are going to bake if we don't get the ship moving soon," Aldridge said.

"Have you chosen the replacements?" Captain Salinem asked.

Aldridge nodded. "Michele should have them done by now."

Chapter Six

The remaining refugees were not loaded onto the ship until almost noon, so those who had boarded at daybreak were beginning to suffer from dehydration and heat exhaustion. Brindle had extra containers of water taken out to the ship on the launch. It was the least he could do, he felt, for people who had been punished for no cause. Afterwards, Aldridge called a meeting in the mess hall so that they could sort out the death of the soldier and its ramifications. Everyone realized it was a terrible incident, but no one had any idea what to do about it.

"My man did not just fall with a knife in his back," Captain Salinem argued with reason. "Someone on this island killed him."

"We all agree," Aldridge said. "But we have no proof that it was one of the Vietnamese. The only reason that I can imagine for one of the refugees to kill the guard would be to slip into the transport group. But you checked the ship yourself and found no extra passengers."

Captain Salinem nodded.

"So we can assume that was not a motive."

"Unless the perpetrator killed my man and was then frightened off somehow before he could join the line," Captain Salinem said.

Aldridge shook his head slowly. "Don't you see, Captain, that doesn't make any sense? If you wanted to slip into the boarding line, you would have to do it without any disturbance. To kill a guard would bring about an investigation and a possible search of the ship."

"So what are you implying, Mr. Aldridge?"

"What do we know about this guard?" Aldridge asked. "Is there any reason why someone would want to kill him?"

"You mean another Indonesian?" Captain Salinem was barely able to mask his hostility.

"I'm not accusing anyone," Aldridge said. "I'm just suggesting that we examine all the possibilities."

"Very well," Captain Salinem snapped. "I will have this man investigated. And in the meantime, I expect you to begin questioning the thirty-five refugees you have detained. It would be better for them to give you the information. When I begin my interrogation, I will not be so compassionate."

He pushed back his chair angrily and stalked out.

Aldridge rested his head on his hand. "Can you believe this?" he asked.

"The poor guard," Michele said.

"I've thought of two points we might consider," Brindle offered. "First, whoever killed the guard knew what he was doing. The man was stabbed very skillfully. Second, we've never had a guard killed on the island that I know of..."

Aldridge shook his head. "No."

"So now," Brindle continued, "we have a guard killed only days after three refugees are shot trying to get away from camp."

"You think there might be some kind of connection?" Michele asked.

"Who knows," Brindle said, shrugging. "But it could be a revenge killing."

"I don't think so," Aldridge said. "Why kill a guard when the transport group is loading? The guards are on patrol around the clock. Why not just stab one in the darkness? Why punish the transport refugees?"

"Jealousy, perhaps," Michele suggested. "Perhaps whoever killed the guard wanted to be on the ship but wasn't chosen. So they tried to spoil it for those who were selected."

"That's the first honest possibility I've heard," Aldridge said.

"Then there's no problem," Brindle said sarcastically. "Out of the nearly one thousand refugees we have left, we just find one who regrets that he wasn't chosen to get off the island."

Aldridge sipped his coffee. "You're not making this easy, John."

"There's another possibility," Michele suggested. "I just got a report from our camp in Malaysia. They said they've been having trouble with Vietnamese infiltrators, communists sent to stir up trouble in the camps."

"You mean infiltrators who have arrived with the boat people?"

"They didn't give any details. Only that communists have been stirring up trouble."

"Well," Aldridge mused, "it seems remote, but who knows? Will you send them a telegram and ask for more information?"

Michele nodded and made a note on her pad.

"If that is the case," Brindle added, "then we can assume that it will happen again."

"Yes," Aldridge replied, "and what can we do about it?"

"Nothing, really," Brindle said. "If we had some informers among the refugees, we might be able to come up with something. But that isn't our style."

"Definitely not," Aldridge continued.

"So Captain Salinem may be right. Our best bet may be the thirty-five who have been detained."

"Okay," Aldridge said, "I'll start questioning them."

"You'll have to promise them that they won't be put back into the general camp," Michele suggested.

"I know," Aldridge said. "We may have to construct a new area just for them. And of course, none of them will leave this island until we find the killer. We may even have to send them back to Vietnam."

"That should be some incentive," Brindle commented.

He left the meeting and walked down to the dock. It was peaceful now, with the late afternoon sun glinting off the water. Brindle leaned against the dock railing and watched a gull floating on the wind at the water's edge. He was relieved that he had not made special provisions to get Kim Thi and her family onto the ship. What a mess of investigations and paperwork they were in for now. He looked back up the path to where the soldier had been killed. It seemed inconceivable that someone had died there only hours before. As a doctor, Brindle had been around death for years, and yet the sound of that muffled cry in the haze kept replaying in his mind like a stab of pain. Was it that his patients had always known what to expect, that there was some framework to their suffering? Or was it the absurd quickness of it? He began to experience that hollowness of feeling which usually came upon him only at night. It was rare for him to have this feeling in the daytime. He knew the best thing to do was to keep busy, so he walked over to the clinic. When he entered the ward, he saw Kim Thi talking to her mother. The old woman turned when she heard Brindle coming and gave him a kind smile. She said something to Brindle.

"My mother thank you for making arm all better," Kim Thi explained.

"She is welcome," Brindle replied. "But please don't let it happen again."

When Kim Thi told her mother this, the old woman shook her head emphatically. "No, no," Kim Thi translated. "We go Philippines soon. No problem."

"Good," Brindle said.

The old woman said something and bowed several times.

"She go now," Kim Thi translated.

Brindle smiled and watched as she left, her plastic sandals brushing softly against the floorboards.

"She is very nice," Brindle said.

"Much courage, my mother," Kim Thi said. "She get us out of Ho Chi Minh City. On boat at Nha Trang."

"I can imagine," Brindle said.

"She say we all go free or die," Kim Thi explained. "Many danger."

"So you went free."

Kim Thi nodded.

Brindle examined her bandage and then followed the soft golden curve of her arm up to her face. His eyes must have betrayed his thoughts, for she looked away quickly.

"Arm okay now," she offered.

"I was just wondering . . . " Brindle paused. He felt as if he were crossing a line which would somehow expose him to emotional danger. He felt nervous, despite his desire to know this young woman. "Have you ever been married?"

Kim Thi leaned her head back on the pillow. "No," she replied. "One time block chairman like me. Want for his girl. But he have wife in Hanoi. My mother no let him."

Kim Thi touched the gauze bandage on her arm. "You have wife, Doctor?" she asked.

Brindle shook his head.

"No wife? No woman?"

"No."

She gazed across the ward thoughtfully.

What was she thinking, Brindle wondered.

"I wanted to ask," he continued, "when you are released from here, may I come and visit you sometime?"

Kim Thi looked at him now, and Brindle could see that for the first time he was not a doctor to her.

"You like me?" she asked with some surprise.

Brindle blushed. "Yes."

She patted his hand, and he felt the gentleness of her fingers.

"I ask mother. Must be careful. All things new now."

"Of course," he said.

When he left the clinic Brindle felt like a new man, or rather like the old Brindle as he had been in college or medical school. Walking across the compound to his room, he felt a surge of new energy entering into him, an excitement about life he had not felt for years. His room was hot and smelled of mildew when he entered, but he did not notice. Going over to the shelf he picked up his bottle of tequila, unscrewed the cap, and lifted the bottle to his lips. Then he hesitated, lowered the bottle, and gazed at the label. It was the picture of a matador and a bull in red and black. He gazed at it for some moments and then walked over to the sink and turned the bottle upside down.

You're becoming a cliché, John, he muttered to himself in the mirror as the tequila flowed from the bottle. *Screwed-up doctor meets young woman who turns his life around. What chance is there of that really happening?* He lifted the bottle and saw that it was nearly three-quarters gone. Replacing the cap, he set the bottle on the edge of the sink and stretched out on his bunk.

He was beginning to think that the promise of happiness which hovered out there beyond his reach was worse than the depression he had lived with for two years. Or was it that he had lived with the feeling of emotional hollowness for so long that it had become the only reality he could accept? Then there was the other thought, feeling, which even he could not acknowledge, the thought which he kept hidden away even from himself. Motives.

The crumbling of Brindle's faith had begun two years before on a rain-slick highway in northern California and ended a few hours later in an hospital emergency room as he waited to have the contusion over his left eye examined. He could not have foretold that evening as he dressed for the party that he would be rejecting God within a few hours, or that he had ever considered any feelings of bitterness toward the Almighty. But after the accident came an overpowering moment when he realized that his faith was gone, had vanished as if he had been trying to hold smoke in his hands. He did not stop believing in the existence of God, but he could no longer accept a God who seemed to play with his life as if he were Job, constantly testing to see if he would remain faithful.

The Lord had populated the Earth for His glory. Glory be to God in the highest! Praise the Lord! Brindle had never questioned the Scriptures before, but now he saw God's purpose in creating human life as the supreme expression of egotism.

And he was no longer playing that game.

Rising from the bed, he walked over to the window and gazed out to the fading sunlight. The trunk of a palm tree cast a long shadow in the hot dust of the compound. He saw someone coming up the path from the camp and realized that it was Hoang on his way to the clinic.

"There is still a chance," Brindle muttered to himself, thinking of Kim Thi. "Still a chance."

Aldridge had questioned twenty-five refugees by the time Brindle returned to the mess hall that evening. Soldiers were bringing them in one at a time and then waiting outside so the men and women would not be frightened. Aldridge had a basic command of Vietnamese, but Tran had volunteered to help translate if necessary. As Brindle was entering the mess, the woman with the baby was leaving. She glanced at Brindle but showed no sign of recognition. He dropped into a chair beside Aldridge.

"Any luck?" he asked.

"Nothing," Aldridge snapped. "None of them has seen anything."

He looked tired and Brindle wondered about the dysentery.

A young man in a tattered white shirt came in and sat in the chair across from them. He had long hair that grew down over his ears and the back of his collar. He gazed at his hands nervously.

"Name?" Aldridge asked in Vietnamese.

"Duong," the young man said.

"All right, Duong," Aldridge said kindly, and Brindle was reminded again just how much the administrator cared for these people. "Perhaps you have already heard, but there was an incident during the loading this morning. A soldier was killed."

The young man nodded. He had heard about it.

"Did you see anything?" Aldridge asked.

Duong shook his head.

"This is an extremely serious situation," Aldridge continued, gazing intently at the young man. "None of you in the holding area will be released from camp until the person who did this is found. Do you understand what that means?"

Duong continued to gaze at his hands. His cheek muscles twitched.

"You may even be sent back to Vietnam."

The young man looked from Aldridge to Brindle imploringly. He muttered something quickly in Vietnamese.

"What did he say?" Aldridge asked Tran. "I didn't quite get it."

"He say he no want go back. Very dangerous."

"I'm sure," Aldridge said, "but tell him that's exactly what might happen if he doesn't help us."

Tran explained.

The young man nodded.

Aldridge waited for a moment and then asked again.

"Did you see or hear anything?"

Duong shook his head hesitantly.

"All right," Aldridge said. He turned to Tran. "Please tell him that I hope he likes this place. He's going to be here for a long time. Or back in Vietnam."

Tran spoke to the young man in a harsh voice.

Duong nodded and got up from the chair. They watched him walk toward the door. As his hand reached the knob, he hesitated. Finally he turned toward them again and spoke a single word. It came from his mouth so quietly that Brindle was not sure if the young man had actually spoken or if he had just seen his lips move.

"What did he say?" Aldridge asked Tran.

"He say Nguyen," Tran said.

"That's a name."

"Yes."

Aldridge got up from the table and took the young man by the shoulder.

"Listen, Duong," he said. "Whatever information you give us goes no farther than this room. No one will know. Do you understand?"

Aldridge looked at Tran, who repeated the words.

Duong nodded, but at the same time his teeth found his lower lip and chewed on it nervously.

Aldridge directed the young man back to the chair and then sat on the edge of the table. "I don't want to make any mistakes, Tran," he said. "So will you please translate everything?"

Tran nodded.

"Okay," Aldridge began. "He said the guy's name was Nguyen, right?"

Tran nodded.

Aldridge cleared his throat. "We must have two hundred refugees in the camp with that last name. Does he have a first name?"

Tran asked and then said, "Vo. Vo Nguyen."

Aldridge looked at Michele.

"I'll check to see if he has a file," she said and left the room.

"Now," Aldridge said, "what can Duong tell us about this man?"

Tran spoke to Duong for a moment.

"He say this man talk all time about communists," Tran translated. "Say people who leave Vietnam weak."

"That doesn't sound like a refugee," Aldridge said. "Maybe we do have an infiltrator in camp."

Brindle asked, "Does he know if this guy was picked up on one of the boats? Was he brought here by the Indonesians?"

Duong lifted his shoulders. He did not know.

"But he saw this Nguyen stab the soldier?" Aldridge asked.

Tran shook his head. "Not stab. But as soldier fall, this man see Vo Nguyen running into bushes."

"Can he describe him?"

"He say Vo look like people from Central Highlands. Thin, with small black mustache."

Aldridge shook his head.

"Is he sure the man is Vietnamese?" Brindle asked.

"Yes."

Michele returned with a folder. "We have no record of a Vo Nguyen listed as a refugee."

"Then he isn't one of ours," Aldridge sighed.

"Apparently not."

"So we find the guy and arrest him. That should put an end to it. Captain Salinem will be pleased."

"Lord, help us," Michele added.

"Yes," Brindle scoffed, "that's just what we need."

Chapter Seven

The first, imperceptible drops began sometime in the night, beading lightly on the thick leaves and vegetation around the camp, trickling down the palms and falling into the darkness of the compound. It was the beginning of a change which Brindle had felt weeks before, and it would now grow with increasing intensity until there was no cessation at all but constant, unrelenting rain. The monsoons had arrived from the Asian mainland.

Brindle was first aware of the heavy beating sound on his roof as if in a dream. Finally, from somewhere far away in his sleep, he awakened, opened his eyes, and listened. He thought about weeks of low, gray storm clouds, of running between the buildings, of mud in the camp, and the mildew which the dampness brought. Everything which contained any organic substance at all would turn green and rot, and he would have to prepare the clinic for a dramatic increase in infections and dysentery. Glancing at his watch, he saw that it was five o'clock. In the early morning darkness, with the rain pounding oppressively on the roof, he felt despair come to him again like a dog waiting at his bedside, like a shadow that crept upon him at the moment of consciousness. Brindle knew he would not be able to go back to sleep, so he rolled from under the mosquito netting and walked to the window.

When he looked outside, to his surprise, he saw a line of soldiers moving up the path from the beach. Their helmeted forms were just visible in the darkness. They moved quietly in single file, each figure shrouded in a poncho, their faces down against the rain. When he had counted about twenty, he heard a familiar voice.

"Captain Salinem," Brindle whispered.

The line of men moved off to the doctor's left on a path that led into the jungle.

Brindle pulled on his trousers and headed for Aldridge's bungalow, not taking the direct route but moving quickly from his covered terrace to that of the clinic, then to the administrative office, and finally to Aldridge's door.

When Brindle knocked, however, there was no reply.

"Hal?" he called, but his voice was lost in the heavy downpour.

Brindle glanced across the compound to the mess and saw a light glowing dimly behind the shutters. He glanced at the roof and saw a heavy curtain of water splashing down from the thatching. There was nothing to do but make a dash for it. Stepping out into the cold rain, he took a stride and felt his shirt and trousers suddenly clinging to his body.

"Well, John," Aldridge said pleasantly as the doctor entered the mess and stood dripping rain on the floor. "It looks like the monsoons are finally here."

"You sound like you're pleased about it," Brindle said, pulling his soaking collar away from his neck.

"No, no," Aldridge said. "But after several years, you get used to it. Here, have some coffee."

"Thanks."

Brindle took a handful of paper napkins from the mess table and began to wipe his face

"I suppose you saw the soldiers?"

"Yes. What's up?"

"We're going to try and flush out Nguyen this morning. Cream?"

"No, thanks."

Those soldiers have just landed from Sumatra. Captain Salinem is going to position them around the perimeter of the camp—in case our man tries to slip away when we begin the search."

"How will you know when you've got him? That wasn't much of a description Duong gave us."

"Ah," Aldridge smiled. "We have a little trick up our sleeve."

"If you corner this guy, it could get nasty," Brindle said. "Have you thought about that?"

Aldridge nodded. "I've tried to imagine it from every angle, John," he said seriously. "And this is the best bet. We've got to catch him."

"Anything I can do?"

The administrator shook his head thoughtfully. "Not really. You might be ready, though, if someone gets hurt."

Brindle nodded and sipped his coffee. It was bitter, so he added more sugar.

"So when does it begin?"

Aldridge glanced at his watch. "Not till seven. Of course, it will be more difficult now with the rain."

"I bet Salinem can't wait."

"He has lost a man," Aldridge said. "You can't blame him."

"No." Brindle knew about revenge. He had come to realize that it was an emotion as true as love, more so even, because it was focused; it left no doubt as to the motives of the one involved. The complications arose when the object of your revenge was yourself.

"Well," Brindle said, running the paper napkin over his hair, "I'll get over to the clinic. We're going to have more infections and cases of cholera now with the rains."

Aldridge nodded. "I'll send for you if we need you."

"Thanks for the coffee. Did you make it yourself?"

"Did you like it?" Aldridge asked. "I'm not much good at this sort of thing."

"Terrible," Brindle said, smiling.

The doctor kept an eye on his watch as he worked at the clinic that morning, and at seven o'clock he walked back out to the compound. When he stepped outside, the air which struck his face and arms felt impregnated with dampness. It seemed as though every plant and tree surrounding the compound had taken on the quality of water, so that the whole environment seemed to ooze moisture. Off to his right, a squad of men stood in front of the administration office. They were dressed in the usual army fatigues, but on this occasion Brindle noticed that their faces were streaked with camouflage paint. He wondered about that. They seemed to be waiting for something, so Brindle sat in one of the terrace chairs. The canvas of the chair felt damp, but not enough to wet his clothes. Anyway, he thought, he had better get used to it. The dampness was going to be a part of his life for at least four months.

After a few minutes another soldier came out of the office and joined the squad. The men seemed to be ready now and began to form up. Captain Salinem came from the office and shouted a few orders, and they began to move down the trail to the camp.

What orders had Salinem given the squad? Brindle wondered. To shoot if they got a chance? Not to hesitate? Or had they been told to take Nguyen alive at any cost? And how were they going to spot Nguyen anyway? Brindle watched the soldiers moving off. The last one, the one who had come from the office, fell in at the end of the squad. He tugged awkwardly at his carbine as he walked, and Brindle suddenly realized the purpose of the face paint. The doctor cursed angrily under his breath.

"Poor Duong," he muttered.

Brindle watched the squad moving down the slope to the camp. He wondered what their odds were of catching Vo Nguyen. Surely someone who had been trained to stir up trouble knew how to escape detection?

"Do you think they catch him?" Tran asked.

"If they do, he won't leave Boromu alive," Brindle said. He made a slicing motion across his jugular with a finger.

"I kill him myself, no problem," Tran offered.

"We'll wait and see," Brindle said. "How is Miss Van Quang?"

"She much better, Doctor," Tran said. "Eat breakfast okay. Sit up okay. Leave clinic soon."

"I'll check on her," Brindle said.

"I get sling for arm?"

"Yes, and. . ."

Tran hesitated at the door.

"Don't mention to her about being discharged."

Brindle said this in almost a whisper, and Tran looked at him questioningly.

"I know, but that was a nasty infection. It could return if we take her off the antibiotic too soon."

"She come back every day. Outpatient. Get shots," Tran suggested.

"We'll see tomorrow," Brindle said. "Now get the sling."

He had never before used his medical position to suit his personal interests, and Brindle felt guilty. If it were anyone other than Kim Thi, he realized, he would have discharged them that morning. On the other hand, he told himself, it had been a terrible infection and could use an additional day or two of observation. She was not going anywhere, after all. Wasn't it better to keep her at the clinic than to have her out there in the camp and exposed to all kinds of diseases? And now the rain and mud?

Kim Thi was sitting on the edge of her bed when Brindle went into the ward. She was leaning back on her right hand with her legs crossed, a smooth golden thigh showing beneath her hospital gown. She smiled at him pleasantly.

"Much better now," Kim Thi explained as Brindle removed the gauze bandage and examined the wound. The lymph channels were no longer infected, and the new tissue looked pink and healthy. Brindle had closed the slash with butterfly tape after it had stopped draining. "No more hurt."

"That's what we want," he said, smiling.

"Maybe go?" she hinted. "Help family. Mother work all time."

Brindle looked at the dark eyes.

"You'll be leaving us soon enough," he said. "I just want to keep you here a day or two more for observation. That was a nasty infection."

"Two more days?" she said imploringly.

"Tran is bringing a sling for your arm," he continued. "We'll see how you feel when you stand up."

"I stand up already," she said. "No fall down."

"Good."

"So, I go?"

"Tomorrow morning."

The words had come from his mouth before he could stop them, and now he knew there was no way he could hold her. Tomorrow morning. He had only been able to postpone her departure by a day. It was not long enough.

"I tell Hoang," she said.

An angry and frustrated Captain Salinem returned to the administration compound that evening with his squad of soldiers. They had spent all day searching for Vo Nguyen but with no success. The refugees had watched them entering the camp with curiosity and some alarm while squatting around their morning cook fires. No refugees were allowed to get through the perimeter under any circumstances. Once the perimeter had been sealed off, the soldiers began a systematic search of the camp. Duong had remained at the back of the group as they moved through the camp, dressed in the same fatigues, hat, and face paint as the others. They had searched every shanty, but had not found Vo Nguyen.

"It's obvious, the guy is too professional to be caught like this," Brindle said afterwards at a meeting called by Aldridge.

"We've got to catch him," Aldridge said. "Otherwise, he might ruin everything."

"Why don't we let the refugees do it for us?" Michele asked. "We could post notices saying that no more people will leave the camp until Vo Nguyen is found."

"We could try that," Aldridge said.

"Dead or alive?" Brindle muttered.

"Does it matter?" Aldridge asked.

"I have informed the authorities in Jakarta," Captain Salinem said. "I am awaiting their instructions on a course of action."

"Hopefully, we'll have found the guy by then," Aldridge said. "And when we do, he's all yours."

"It would be better for him not to be caught," Salinem said.

"And in the meantime, we keep Duong safe," Brindle advised.

"Right," Aldridge said.

ᘓᕲ

If there was one good thing about the rain, Brindle decided, it was that the steady downpour seemed to drain away his thoughts, to nullify the pain. The constant patter was like a tranquilizer, a distraction which kept his thoughts away from himself. Yet he could not help feeling a sense of loss that Kim Thi would be discharged in the morning. He had not had enough time to go beyond his position as a doctor and establish himself as a man in her eyes. She had gazed at him that once as if he were a man only, but that was more out of surprise than affection. It was inevitable that she must go, but he could not help feeling a sickness, as if something were pulling or tearing at his insides. For this reason he sat now with the tequila bottle in his lap, the cap still in place, without having drunk, but wanting to, and knowing that he probably would before the evening was over. He thought about going to the

clinic and sitting by Kim Thi's bedside while she slept, but
realized that was ridiculous. It was just past nine, not too late
for him to pay a visit to someone else in the camp. Running a
hand through his hair, he stepped out of his bungalow and
stood listening to the light patter on the terrace overhang.

Michele's light was on as he had expected, and he heard
the screech of a chair against rough floorboards when he
knocked.

"John," she said, opening the door.

He saw that she had been writing a letter at the wooden
table beside her bed. The electric bulb shone like a small yellow spotlight on a pad of lined paper, a pen, an envelope, and
a roll of stamps.

"I was just catching up on some correspondence," she said,
but he could tell that it was more than that. He imagined that
she had been pouring out her heart to a friend ten thousand
miles away because she had no friends here, no one with whom
she could really share her thoughts. He felt somewhat responsible for this.

Michele looked at him.

"I, uh. . ." he fumbled for words. He had not given a second of thought as to why he should be knocking on her door
or what he would say.

"Would you like to come in?" she asked.

He moved into the room which was almost identical to his
own, except that here there was life—a vase of flowers on the
washstand, a blue-and-white checked cloth on the table, a set
of books on the shelf. He glanced at the books on the shelf and
saw a half-dozen romance novels, a New American Standard
Bible, a Rand McNally Pocket Atlas, and a book of crossword
puzzles. Brindle picked up the Bible. Its cover was worn, and as
he flipped through the pages he saw that some of the passages
were underlined. A verse in John caught his attention:

*"This sickness is not unto death, but for the glory of God, that
the Son of God may be glorified by it."*

Brindle closed the Bible and returned it to the shelf. "You're a Baptist, if I recall."

"Yes, and you?"

He shrugged. "I used to be an Evangelical—or whatever they're calling them these days. But I don't think about God much anymore."

"You don't believe?"

"Yes, I still believe, but I made a pact with the Almighty a few years ago. I leave Him alone, and He leaves me alone. Or at least that's the way I see my side of the bargain."

Michele opened her footlocker and removed a carton of tea from a cardboard box.

"All I have left are a few bags of English breakfast tea," she said, gazing at the label.

"That's all right," Brindle said and cringed at a sudden memory of a morning in San Rafael with Sarah.

"Is something wrong?"

He forced a smile. "No."

Michele lit a can of Sterno on the table and set a small kettle of water on it. The flame burned blue. "It takes a few minutes for the water to heat," she said apologetically.

"I like your place here," he said. "It's nice."

"You're always welcome, John. You know that."

She folded her legs up under her on the chair. She had removed the red polish from her toenails. Brindle caught a glimpse of something moving on the wall above the door.

"That's Sylvester," Michele said, smiling.

Brindle looked up to see a lizard clinging to the rough walls.

"He lives up in the rafters. We've had some very long talks. He's a good listener."

"It's tough keeping them out of the clinic," Brindle said. "They get on everything."

"Not Sylvester," Michele said, as the lizard moved behind a picture frame on the wall. "He's a very polite little guy. In the afternoons he sits out in the sun and does push-ups. Likes to keep in shape."

Brindle laughed.

"Well. . ." Michele said amusedly, "that's something."

Brindle got up and walked over to the picture. It was the photograph of a family: two parents and three teenage children, all gazing at the camera with enough cheerful energy to make it seem genuine. A younger Michele stood smiling on the right. The edges of the photograph were beginning to yellow.

"You have a brother," Brindle commented, looking at a young man with trimmed blond hair standing behind the father.

Michele took the kettle off the burner and put in two tea bags. "Ricky died almost ten years ago in a motorcycle accident. He was always the wild one in the family."

"I'm sorry," Brindle offered, moving his gaze to a teenage girl with plump cheeks.

"That's my sister, Gail. We're very close."

Brindle thought of the half-written letter on the table. He glanced at his watch.

Michele noticed this and sat up.

"Would you like to listen to some music?"

"Nothing classical, I hope," he said. "I'm not quite up for anything heavy this evening."

"No, no," she said. "I got a couple of jazz albums the last time I was in Manila." She put a tape into her cassette player. "I think you'll like this."

Brindle leaned back in his chair and listened to a saxophone playing a melody that seemed to float through the room.

"It must be very lonely," Michele said, gazing thoughtfully at the brewing tea. "Not having God in your life."

Brindle shook his head. "It's a lot less painful. I got tired of being tested. Finally I just said, God, go test somebody else. I'm not playing anymore."

"Do you know why God tests us?"

"Of course," Brindle said with exasperation. "I've been through this a hundred times. But what is the point of having our faith strengthened or judged? When is the faith we have enough? I used to have plenty. A child loves unreservedly without being tested."

"You sound so bitter."

"I am bitter," Brindle replied. "I should have my name changed to 'Bitter.' Dr. John Bitter."

"I don't know if I could go on without my faith," Michele said seriously.

"You would," Brindle said. "Most people do."

"I certainly wouldn't be here."

"Why not?"

She pulled her Bible from the shelf again and handed it to Brindle. "Look up Isaiah 43."

Brindle frowned and opened the Bible.

"The whole chapter?" he asked.

"Verses 18 and 19," Michele said.

Brindle read:

> *Do not call to mind the former things,*
> *Or ponder things of the past.*
> *Behold, I will do something new,*
> *Now it will spring forth;*
> *Will you not be aware of it?*
> *I will even make a roadway in the wilderness,*
> *Rivers in the desert.*

When he finished reading, he looked up at her.

"I was afraid of coming here," Michele explained. "Boromu Island was so far away, and I had only been out of the States once on a trip to England. Then one Sunday a friend showed me these verses and I knew they were for me."

"I can remember feeling that way," Brindle said. "We used to sit up nights interpreting each other's spiritual dreams."

"But not anymore?"

"No. I've passed the cup to someone else."

"Who?"

"Maybe to you. I don't know."

"It won't work, John. If you didn't believe that would be one thing—but you do, which means you have to accept everything that goes with it."

Brindle shook his head. "Just because I know there is an element of evil in the camp doesn't mean I have to take part in it. I don't. And I don't take part in the good either—at least not where God is concerned. I'm neutral."

"Is that possible?" Michele asked.

"Yes," Brindle said. "Now can we change the subject?"

"Can I tell you one more thing?" Michele asked.

"What?"

"You won't leave?"

"I don't know."

She poured two cups of tea. "I turned to God when I was fifteen. I can still remember the day. I was on my way home from school, and suddenly I just went into a church."

Brindle studied her. "Yes?"

"I needed an answer to a question."

"You wanted to know if there was life on other planets?" Brindle suggested.

Michele pursed her lips and gave him a sassy look. "I wanted to know, John, why so many people seemed to lead such miserable lives."

Brindle nodded thoughtfully. He had wondered the same question himself. "That was around the time of your brother's accident, wasn't it?"

Michele shrugged and wiped a hand across her eyes. "And as I got closer to God, I felt like I was beginning to understand. Not why Ricky died, but why life could be so miserable."

The despair which Brindle had wanted to escape was creeping up on him again. He could feel its cold emptiness settling into his stomach and reaching up toward his heart. He would have to leave soon. This conversation was too close. It was not why he had come.

"I realized," she continued, "that so many people are miserable because they don't include God in their lives. They wait out their time on earth completely blind to the possibilities."

"And you're saying I'm like that?" Brindle asked.

"I don't know, John. I only know that without. . ."

Brindle sat up. "I need to go."

"I'm sorry," Michele said. "I do it every time. I promise not to say anything more about religion."

"No," Brindle said. "It was nice being here. I just need to go."

Michele smiled, wanting to believe him.

"Will you come back again?"

His hand was on the door. "Yes."

"John?" She put her hand on his. "I suppose it's because I'm leaving in a few days, but I'm beginning to see things in a better perspective. I know you only want to be friends. I realize it probably couldn't be any other way."

Brindle touched a hand affectionately to her shoulder.

"I just wanted you to know that," she said.

He saw her eyes begin to tear.

"It wouldn't be any good, Michele," he said. "I'm completely messed up."

"You can talk to me, you know," she urged. "Anytime. About anything."

Brindle glanced at the half-written letter on the table, the substitute for friendship.

"Thanks, Michele."

Stepping out to the darkness of the terrace he heard the rain once again. The moisture settled on his skin and clothes, and he turned back to the door. Inside he could hear the screech of her chair as Michele returned to her letter and the music of the saxophone. The notes sounded lonely now, or was it that he had lost the glow of the conversation and the warmth of the room? Working his way around the terraces, he came to the clinic. The night-duty nurse, an Indonesian, looked up from her magazine and smiled politely.

"Yes, Doctor?"

"Nothing," he said, thinking quickly. "I was just looking for my pen. I think I left it on the ward."

"You need pen?" she asked, reaching into her uniform pocket.

"No," he said. "I just wondered. . ." It was useless. He turned back toward the door. "I'll look for it in the morning."

The nurse had already dismissed his visit as unimportant and went back to reading her magazine.

"Kim Thi," he sighed. He began to count the hours until morning.

Chapter Eight

Brindle did not know exactly what he expected, but Kim Thi's discharge the following morning was remarkably uneventful. Hoang arrived after breakfast with some clean clothes. She changed behind the dividing curtain, signed a form, and within minutes was walking down the clinic steps and heading toward the camp. Kim Thi smiled appreciatively at Brindle as she passed him on the terrace, and he felt the instinctive urge to touch her but refrained when he saw a nurse approaching. It would not have been proper anyway, he told himself. If he were going to pursue her now, after she had left the clinic and his proximity, then he would have to follow the Vietnamese rules of courting as correctly as possible—whatever they might be. He would have to speak to Tran.

Kim Thi and her brother moved down the path congruously, with a freedom of movement which Brindle somehow took as a rejection of himself. Near the administration office he saw Aldridge tacking up a notice. "I've tacked up twenty of these things already," Aldridge said when Brindle walked over to him. "The soldiers are putting up another fifty."

"I hope it works, Hal," Brindle said.

"We drew a crowd with the first ones we put up. The refugees are reading them."

"What does it say exactly?"

Aldridge stood back and examined his work.

"That a communist infiltrator named Vo Nguyen is wanted for the killing of a guard, and that no more refugees

85

will be sent on to the Philippines until he has been captured," Aldridge explained.

"That should do it."

"We'll see how long it takes," Aldridge said.

As he made his rounds that afternoon, Brindle felt an emptiness which he discerned from his usual feeling of hollowness because of the pain that came with it. How could the feeling that he was empty inside be painful? he wondered. Where had the pain come from? He could only surmise that the feeling came from an area of his heart where something had been removed. Kim Thi, or at least his feelings about her, had filled that space, and now that she was gone he felt the loss as living tissue might when it has been incised. He wondered also how long he should wait until he visited her. Surely it would be an intrusion if he appeared at her hut that very evening. She would be busy adjusting to her new life in the camp. So would tomorrow be too soon? Or should he wait longer? There was some reassurance in the fact that Kim Thi had an appointment at the clinic as an outpatient on Friday. But the Vietnamese often did not show up for their outpatient appointments. Once they had been discharged from the clinic, many of the refugees believed they could take care of themselves. They only returned when their wounds became infected again or the symptoms of their illness reappeared. Thinking of this, Brindle recalled the way Kim Thi and her brother had walked down the slope to the camp. Was there any reassurance, he thought to himself, that he would ever see her again?

Brindle examined one of the new cholera patients who had been brought in the night before. The teenage boy was running a high temperature; his thin wrist hung limply in Brindle's hand as he felt for a pulse. The rain was going to mess up everything, Brindle thought with despair, including the search for Vo Nguyen. He worried about Kim Thi out there in the dampness and decided that he would visit her the following afternoon. Perhaps he could take her a little something. At the moment he did not know what. He would have to think about it. For some awkward reason he felt the need for an excuse.

As he crossed the courtyard that evening to the dining hall, he saw Michele coming out of her office. When she saw him, she smiled sheepishly. "Still angry with me?" she called.

"About what?"

The rain had stopped momentarily and the setting sun peeked from behind a line of palm trees on the beach. Michele closed her office door and walked toward him. "You know," she said, "I was preachy and self-righteous last night, and you didn't deserve that." She ran a hand through her dark blonde hair. "You've always been honest with me."

Brindle wondered if that were true. Had he always been honest with Michele? Or with himself?

"Anyway," she continued, "sometimes I just try to cram religion down people's throats and it never works. So I'm sorry."

"It's all right. Really."

"The next time, I promise, all we'll talk about is jazz."

"Do we have to?"

"Unless you want to talk about Nguyen. Do you think they'll ever catch him?"

Brindle shrugged. "It could take weeks. He might even be off the island by now."

"It's amazing how one person can botch things up so completely," Michele muttered. "The question is, how long do we wait?"

"Until he is found or we're sure that he is no longer here," Brindle said. "We made a stand when we put up the notices, and now we have to stick with it for the sake of discipline."

"That's what I mean," Michele added. "We may never know."

"We have to know," he replied tersely.

Brindle had noticed a change in Michele. She was more pensive, thoughtful, reserved around him now. It was an expected change, but he had enjoyed being with her more previously, if enjoyment was the appropriate term. The change in her implied some effort on his part, which he had never given. Still, he took this new attitude as another rejection of himself—the second in one day. He did not mind that Michele was beginning to distance herself from him; he merely noticed her reaction as one might follow the outcome of a medical test. If he had minded, it would have implied that he actually derived some type of pleasure by her interest in him, which he did not. It was because he had no feelings to share that he could look dispassionately on the situation and notice her change in behavior. But was that true anymore? Did he really have no feelings? If so, then where did the sense of pain come from at Kim Thi's departure?

At dinner, Aldridge held up his glass of iced tea and looked at Michele. "Our lovely lady will be leaving us tomorrow for several weeks," he said. "And we will miss her."

"Three weeks," Michele added. "I'll be back on the seventh."

"However many it is," Aldridge continued, "it will be too long."

Brindle lifted his glass while watching Michele. She seemed uncomfortable this evening. She was a sensitive young woman. He wondered if she felt awkward about leaving now with the Nguyen mess still hanging over the camp.

"I have concocted a little surprise for you on your return, Miss Fallon," Captain Salinem spoke up.

"The wayang drama?" Michele asked.

"I have located a *dalang* in Sumatra. He has been kind enough to volunteer his services for a special performance on the Saturday after your return."

"I understand they're usually pretty expensive, Captain," Aldridge said.

Salinem flashed that ingratiating smile which caused Brindle not to trust him.

"This dalang has been most reasonable," the captain said. "I should not worry about that."

"Well, then," Michele broke in, "I'll have to buy a new dress in Manila. I can't go to a wayang performance in jeans."

"Wayang dramas are usually for weddings aren't they?" Aldridge asked, slipping a fork into his rice.

Salinem glanced at Brindle.

"Would you like to answer this question, Doctor?" he asked.

Brindle shook his head. One glance into Salinem's eyes told him the question was rhetorical. Salinem obviously did not want to share his little surprise with anyone. Realizing this, Brindle was suddenly concerned about Michele's welfare. What were the implications of Salinem's effort to put on this drama for her? he wondered. What did the captain expect in return?

"Yes, you are right, Mr. Aldridge," Salinem continued. "The wayang drama is used at wedding ceremonies. But it is also performed at certain rites of passage such as circumcisions, the birth of a child, and at funerals."

"Well, let's hope it's not for the last," Michele said.

"No, let's hope not," Captain Salinem repeated.

Brindle could not sleep that night. The sense of loss which had come upon him earlier still gnawed away, causing his heart to pound and the perspiration to dampen his shirt. A new patient was now occupying Kim Thi's bed in the ward, and this sense of literal change seemed to bother him more than any abstract feeling. Perhaps it was because the absence brought back so many memories: a pink-and blue-comforter, a baby doll nestled on the pillow, a nightlight which played "Jesus Loves Me". Brindle sat silently in his chair with a hand to his mouth, his eyes gazing blankly into the darkness.

Someone knocked.

He considered not answering for a moment, but what would that leave him?

"Yes?"

"John?"

Michele opened the door. She looked tired. Her hair was damp from the rain.

Brindle did not smile. He searched down within himself to find an attitude of pleasure but found nothing.

"I just wanted to tell you that I'll get the tequila for you while I'm in Manila," she said.

"You don't have to."

She held up a hand. "I don't like to see you drink so much, John, I admit. But I haven't been through what you've been through."

"It's no excuse," he said. "There aren't any excuses."

"And it's not the answer, either. My father had a drinking problem, and it wasn't the answer," she said.

Brindle gazed at her from his chair. He saw the damp hair, the innocent cheeks, the inexperienced eyes. Didn't she understand? he thought. Couldn't she see the difference between him and a living man?

"I could have helped you," she said.

"Michele," he said, standing up.

She came toward him, and he felt her arms slip around his waist. He found her mouth and tasted the coolness of her lips, the longing for something beyond her reach, the unspoken promises.

"Goodbye, John," she said suddenly, pulling away from him.

"Michele."

She lingered in the doorway. Outside there was nothing but darkness and the rain. "Yes?"

"Be careful of Captain Salinem."

Michele gazed at him thoughtfully. "You mean the drama?"

"Yes."

"It's only a performance, John. They have them all the time in Indonesia."

"I know, but . . . "

She gave a soft laugh. "You're worried about me?"

"In Asia things have meanings, and hidden meanings, and shadow meanings," Brindle explained. "Just like in the wayang drama. The performance is actually very symbolic of their culture."

"And my dream was true, wasn't it?"

Brindle gazed awkwardly at the lantern on his table.

"I've seen the way you look at her, John. You can't hide that expression in your eyes. It's obvious."

He shrugged his shoulders. "I don't know."

"It's true," Michele said. "And I don't know whether to be happy or sad."

"Believe me," he began. He hesitated.

"I have to go," Michele said. "I'm leaving first thing in the morning."

Brindle stood there without moving, the feel of her kiss still upon his lips, wondering why he did not want her to leave.

"I have to be at the clinic," he said. "Or I would see you off."

"I know," she said. "I'll be back on the seventh."

Then she was gone and he suddenly felt that there was no wall or defense between himself and his destiny now, that Michele with her firm grip on reality and faith had taken all that with her. He felt as if he were adrift, just as the refugees were adrift when they pushed off from Vietnam into the South China Sea. He wondered if this was the way Kim Thi had felt when she had made the silent, heart-pounding run down the dock and then huddled and waited as the fishing boat moved slowly, ever so slowly out to the sheltering darkness of the open water.

∾∾

The next morning as he made his rounds, Brindle followed the steps of Michele's departure in his mind. She would be waiting at the helicopter clearing with Aldridge now, he thought as he gave an injection. Later, while filling a prescription, he could hear the helicopter approaching from the south. Then at seven-thirty he could hear it lift off and knew with the diminishing whine of the motor that she was gone, that she had rid herself of Boromu Island, at least for a while. She would be going places where people were alive again, he thought, where there was movement and a sense of future— not this implacable stagnancy, tropical rot, and heat, this sense of coming from nowhere and going nowhere. She was away now and, for all her good intentions, perhaps she should stay in the Philippines.

But Brindle had other things to think about. He had promised himself that he would visit Kim Thi in the afternoon, and this began to occupy his thoughts. Would she be glad to see him? he wondered. What should he take? Walking into the dispensary, he spied a roll of gauze and some tape. Of course, he thought. She would have to change her bandage regularly to keep it from becoming infected. The gauze was not only a probable excuse, it was a medical necessity. He slipped the gauze, a roll of tape, and a tube of antiseptic cream into his pocket.

The rain had stopped by ten o'clock, and as Brindle stepped out of the clinic he noticed that there was some intangible element in the air, as if the rot had been washed away from the camp and therefore depression had receded with it. Or perhaps it was simply his excitement at the prospect of seeing Kim Thi again. This caused him to stop and think for a moment. Was he really excited? Had that feeling which had been dormant in his heart for two years actually returned— the ability to not only care about but to actually look forward to some event in the future? Brindle did not know. Still, lingering on the step in front of the clinic, he felt as if there was something new, something invigorating about the day.

"Do you smell that?" he asked Tran.

"What, Doctor?"

"I don't know," Brindle said. "Something different in the air. It reminds me . . ." He was lost in thought for a moment.

"Miss Fallon leave, Doctor," Tran said. "Philippines."

"Yes, I know. She flies out of Jakarta this afternoon."

"She very nice lady, Miss Fallon," Tran said. "All time smile."

"She'll be back."

"No good in camp all time men, men, men. We need good women like Miss Fallon."

"I know what you mean," Brindle said. He started to ask Tran about Vietnamese courtship but hesitated. He was not sure how far he wanted to go with this or how much he wanted others to know about his interest in Kim Thi.

"No good all men."

"Tran?" Brindle began. "How do men find a wife in Vietnam?"

Tran scratched the back of his neck. "Most time make arrangement with family, Doctor. No date like in America."

"Who do Vietnamese girls like to marry?"

"Vietnamese men," Tran said. "If no can marry Vietnamese man, then marry Chinese man. Chinese smart people. Many ancestors of Vietnamese come from China long time ago. Maybe next, Filipino man."

Tran gazed at the palm trees thoughtfully.

"What about American men?" Brindle asked.

Tran shook his head. "For most Vietnamese, no good. Americans too different. Culture too different."

"But they want to live in the States."

"Want escape communists," Tran said. "You see snake in jungle come toward you, you think snake come to bite you. But no, snake run from tiger. Look same, but not."

"I see," Brindle said, his heart sinking. "So Americans are way down on the list?"

"Maybe nine or ten," Tran said encouragingly. "Always all time better than communists."

"How does an American man get to know a Vietnamese woman?"

"Stand on street corner, have money in pocket," Tran said, laughing.

Brindle smiled. "No, a good one."

"Meet family. Let parents see you have good heart. Show respect. Very important—respect."

"Okay."

"So you go see Miss Van Quang today?"

"Miss . . . ?" Brindle played dumb.

"Girl with bad arm," Tran explained. "You visit today in camp?"

Brindle realized that the pretense of impartiality he had shown for Kim Thi had been only for himself. Everyone else on the staff seemed to know of his interest in her. But how could they know? He had never said a word to anyone. Had his actions actually been that different?

"You fine man, Doctor," Tran continued. "Miss Van Quang fine woman too. But she refugee and you doctor. I think no can work."

"Even if I follow the rules?" Brindle asked. "Show respect?"

Tran looked to the south, in the direction Michele's helicopter had taken. "Too bad Miss Fallon go Philippines," he said, not meeting Brindle's eyes. "She okay woman."

Brindle muttered and walked down the steps. "I'll be back in a while. Check the IV on that kid with the cholera."

"Yes, Doctor."

The air was now so permeated with moisture that the ground gave way in soft, padding squishes as Brindle walked down the slope. Above his head the clouds were low and gray, almost seeming to touch the tops of the palms, and he knew that it would begin to rain again soon. But in the time of monsoons precipitation took on a different perspective. Light drizzle and soft patter were not even considered rain but only a precursor to the real rain, which fell in hard blowing sheets and banged against the roofs and footpaths of the camp.

Although he realized he might get wet, Brindle did not believe he would be caught in a downpour. That would come later in the afternoon.

Entering the camp he felt nervous. In the past he had moved among these people as a doctor, with a specific task to perform. Now, as he walked through what had essentially become a large Vietnamese village, he realized that he had left his medical identity at the clinic. He was a visitor here, a stranger among people he only knew as patients. When he reached the northeastern section of the camp near the beach, he began to look for Kim Thi. Hoang had built a hut in this area, she had told him. Outside one hut a group of children were playing. They were dressed in ragged shirts and shorts, and their bare brown legs were mud-spattered. When the children saw Brindle, they got up and began to follow him, rattling away happily in Vietnamese.

Brindle realized the comical absurdity of his situation. As he went from one hut to another looking for Kim Thi, the group of children followed him and drew attention to his every move. He could not have been more conspicuous, and with each additional face that gazed at him from the shelters of palm thatching, his courage diminished by a degree. He was just about to turn back when he saw her. Kim Thi was kneeling beside a cook fire and stirring something in a large black pot. Rice, Brindle assumed. He hesitated for a moment and watched her. She stirred with her right hand; her left arm, bandaged, was held carefully at her side. She looked different somehow out here in the camp, Brindle noticed. She was more than ever one of them now—a Vietnamese and a refugee— and this caused Brindle to doubt. Had he only been attracted to her vulnerability as a patient? he wondered. Now that she was a whole, well person, would he still feel that attraction to Kim Thi? Or would she now be like the others and blend into that ever-present stream of refugees which flowed around him in a coexistent yet separate reality?

"Doctor," she said sweetly, gazing up at him. Her voice was pleasant, but it did not hold the warmth which Brindle had desired. Madame Van Quang sat quietly on a stool in the doorway of the hut. Clothes were strung on a line from the hut to a nearby palm tree. Brindle found it beyond optimism to believe that anything would dry in this climate. Nothing ever seemed to dry during the monsoons.

"I brought you some things," he blurted awkwardly, reaching into his pocket and pulling out the gauze, tape, and cream. He seemed to need positive proof that he had come for a justifiable reason, that he was not just acting on foolish compulsion. Clutching the objects in his hand, he held them out to her. When her fingertips brushed against his, he smiled.

"That's antibiotic cream," he explained as Kim Thi examined the tube. "Perhaps you won't need it, but . . ."

"Thank you, Doctor," she said.

Brindle wished she were not so polite. Her carefully affected manners seemed to put a distance between them. He wished the mother was not there either.

"I wanted to see how you were doing," he continued with embarrassment. He was relieved that Madame Van Quang did not speak English, though the mother of any young woman would have known what was happening here—even if no words were spoken.

"Work hard all day," Kim Thi said.

Madame Van Quang said something to Kim Thi. The young woman nodded and began to unwind the bandage.

"Mother want you see arm all better," Kim Thi explained.

A lightness came over Brindle when he took her arm in his hands. The skin was smooth, delicate. Indeed, the wound showed very good red granulation tissue and was well oxygenated. Brindle held her arm for as long as he thought proper and then disengaged himself professionally and smiled at Madame Van Quang.

The children behind him giggled knowingly.

Kim Thi shouted something at them and they skittered away.

"Where is Hoang?" Brindle asked, searching for conversation.

"Gone for walk," Kim Thi explained. "With friends."

"Is there anything you need?" he asked, feeling that this could eventually be a mistake. He did not want them to think of him only as a source for special supplies. The WRO supplied the refugees with all the basics. However, he still felt the need to have a specific reason for his visits. What could an extra packet of tea or sugar from time to time hurt?

"A good knife," Kim Thi replied, holding up what appeared to be a large, dull butter knife. "This knife no good." Then she smiled. "And some chocolate?"

Brindle returned the smile, hoping that she understood.

"I'll see what I can find."

Madame Van Quang spoke again in that nasally whine which seemed to be so typical of older Asian women.

"I sorry," Kim Thi said. "You want tea, Doctor?"

"John."

"John," she repeated.

Brindle began to relax.

"I say wrong?" Kim Thi asked.

"No," he said. "You said it beautifully."

"Tea, John?" she asked again.

"Yes."

Kim Thi went in the hut and came out with three tin cups. From a kettle beside the fire, she poured out the tea and handed a cup to Brindle. The cup was almost too hot to handle, and he held it around the edges. Sitting on a stone near Kim Thi, he sighed contentedly and took a sip. The tea was weak but tasted good. It smelled of rice paddies and hooches and water buffalo.

"Thank you," he said.

"How do you say. . . ?" Kim Thi began thoughtfully, and Brindle watched as the soft brown eyes searched inwardly for the correct term in English. "Tea time?"

"Yes," he said, "tea time."

He was here with her now, just being himself, and he felt accepted. He could hear the soft lilt of her voice and knew that whatever happened, he would take this memory with him—the low, rain-swollen clouds, a rustle of wind in the palms, the wisp of smoke from the cook fire, Kim Thi in her black trousers and lavender shirt, and the hot cup of tea in his hand. Something broke within him, and he felt like crying, in fact had to fight hard to keep the tears from flowing. Kim Thi and her mother would not understand this emotion coming from him, so he kept it down. But something had broken, and he felt the deadness within him, the void, filling up with warmth. His own tears perhaps—or just the tea? he wondered. Whatever, it was okay.

"More tea?" Kim Thi asked, touching his arm.

"Please," he said, holding out his cup.

Chapter Nine

"I don't know what to do," Aldridge said two days later at a hastily called staff meeting. "We still haven't found Nguyen and now Soeharto is rethinking the whole idea of the refugee camps. He might actually shut us down."

"That's a bit of an overkill, don't you think, Hal?" Brindle asked. "A dramatic change in Indonesia's foreign policy because of one soldier's death?"

"They're looking for an excuse, John," Aldridge explained. "I'm telling you."

"I sympathize with you, gentlemen," Salinem said. "I myself have grown quite fond of some of these refugees. I am not without compassion, you know. But I will not tolerate the murder of one of my men without retribution. You must understand that."

"Yes, yes, Captain," Aldridge said, his frustration adding an edge to his voice. "We all want to see Nguyen brought to justice. But do we make two thousand refugees suffer because of the actions of one man?"

Salinem shook his head. "History has shown, Mr. Aldridge, that great political events are often set into motion by the actions of one man. Take Lee Harvey Oswald, for example. There is a case in which one man changed the whole destiny of a nation. From Genghis Khan to Ho Chi Minh, there have been similar examples."

"You never cease to amaze me, Captain," Aldridge replied, while raising his eyebrows at Brindle.

"We always seem to be either baffled or amazed," Brindle said sarcastically.

After the meeting, Brindle waited for Aldridge outside his office.

"Something troubling you, John?" the administrator asked.

"I wondered if you would mind coming over to the clinic," Brindle replied.

"What for?"

"A quick checkup. I promise it won't take more than five minutes."

Aldridge glanced at his watch. "Well, all right."

They crossed the courtyard in the darkness. There were no stars or moon out because of the low storm clouds which had swept in from the sea, so Brindle carried a flashlight. The beam bounced weakly across the sand as they walked. Above their heads a wind that smelled of salt and rain bent the tops of the palm trees. They could not see the tops of the palms, but they could hear them rustling and felt the movement all around them, as if they were surrounded by a powerful and audible force which spoke a language they did not understand.

"If we could just get this Nguyen business over with," Aldridge sighed as they turned up the path to the clinic. "At least Soeharto wouldn't have that to use as an excuse."

"Do you really think that would solve anything?" Brindle asked.

"Maybe not, John. But we have to think short term. Every day, each week here counts for these people. We're almost ready to get another group out to the Philippines. All we need to do is find Nguyen."

In the clinic Aldridge sat on a table and removed his shirt. He had been perspiring heavily. With his stethoscope, Brindle checked the administrator's heartbeat and then took his pulse. All normal. Finally he took his blood pressure.

"Have you experienced any shortness of breath lately?" he asked as he pumped up the wrap.

Aldridge shook his head.

"Chest pain?"

"In the chest?" Aldridge said, smiling. "No, not there."

Brindle noted the blood pressure reading. It was 140 over 90, a normal reading for a man of his age and weight—designating mild hypertension.

"Headaches?"

"A few."

"Where?"

Aldridge reached his fingers behind his head and traced a line from the base of his skull around and over his ears to his forehead.

"Just along there," he said. "They're bad when I get them."

"Any temperature or chills?"

"Not that I'm aware of in this heat and rain."

"And you've been taking your cloriquine?"

Aldridge nodded.

"Have you missed any?"

"Maybe a few here and there."

"Okay," Brindle said. "I'm going to take a blood sample." He got out a syringe and attached a needle. "Make a fist."

Aldridge bunched up his hand, and Brindle tapped for a vein.

"Do you take the usual two tablets every Sunday?"

"Yes."

"Okay," Brindle said. "I'm going to switch you over to quinine sulfate. You may have been infected with Falciparum malaria. If so, that strain is resistant to the cloriquine."

Brindle made a note. "We'll start you on 600 milligrams, three times a day for seven days."

"Is that all?"

"Yes, for the moment."

Aldridge pulled on his shirt.

"One more thing. . ." Brindle said.

The camp administrator looked at him.

"How about finishing that chess game?"

Aldridge grinned knowingly. "If you think you're ready."

"I can't let you go on thinking you were going to win."

"I'll get the board," Aldridge said.

While Aldridge was gone, Brindle went into the makeshift lab he had constructed and prepared a Giemsa stain for his microscope. Aldridge's color had worried him lately. He believed the administrator had been taking too much of the camp stress on himself, as it was always the obligation of those who cared the most to work the hardest. But what else could he do? Of all the people on the Boromu staff, Aldridge's motives seemed to be the purest. Brindle had noticed a navy anchor tattoo on Aldridge's upper right arm and wondered if the administrator's time in the service had anything to do with his desire to help the Vietnamese. Was there some incident in Aldridge's past which had caused him to serve month after month on this remote island? Or was it simply that Aldridge had run his course, had done those things in life which you talk about later, and now was content to make his contribution to the refugees?

Brindle twisted the focusing knob on his microscope and the slide came into view. He gave another slight turn and there it was, a textbook example of Falciparum malaria with its crescent-shaped gametes. Well, Brindle thought bitterly, he couldn't keep anyone from getting malaria on this island. They probably all had it by now. The main thing was to keep it contained in the liver. It only became serious when the parasite traveled up the spinal column to the brain. And there was no point in cleansing the malaria from Aldridge's system now if he were going to stay on the island. He would only be reinfected the moment he walked outside. The best thing was to keep him on the quinine sulfate.

"When are you up for your next leave, Hal?" Brindle asked as he sat across from the administrator on the terrace. Aldridge had already set up the chess board.

"September."

"You can't make it before that?"

"Not really, John. You know how busy it gets around here after the monsoons."

"If we're still here after the monsoons," Brindle said.

Aldridge did not appreciate that kind of talk.

"We'll be here," he said, holding out his hands.

Brindle tapped the administrator's left hand.

"Black," Aldridge said, opening his hand and displaying the black queen on his palm. "I open."

Brindle leaned back in his canvas chair and sighed. "I could use some coffee."

"Even mine?"

"Well . . ."

"That's okay, John. I think I can round some up."

He called to one of his assistants who was passing in the courtyard. The man turned and headed toward the mess.

Brindle moved his queen's pawn to check Aldridge's advance. Aldridge was a sound but uncreative player. He moved his pieces with elementary precision.

"You're from Illinois, aren't you, Hal?" Brindle asked.

"Chicago," Aldridge answered, while studying the board.

"Do you ever miss it?"

Aldridge moved his rook to queen's bishop three. Then he glanced up and looked around him at the darkness of the jungle beyond, the yellow lights of the camp, the bright doorway of the clinic.

"Not much," he said. "Sometimes I miss that feeling of walking down Michigan Avenue. You know, that big city feeling you get with the traffic and people on the sidewalks and all the stores. I can never quite imagine it. Every time I go back, it's bigger and faster and brighter than I remembered."

Brindle nodded. "I know what you mean. San Francisco is that way for me."

"But no, I don't really miss it. My life is here. Time slows down here."

Brindle took Aldridge's pawn. "What do you mean?"

Aldridge ran a hand through his thinning gray hair. He laughed, somewhat embarrassed. "It's like, you know . . . the standard of living is higher in Chicago, but the quality of life is better here. Do you know what I'm saying?"

Brindle nodded, though it had been a long time since he had thought of life in terms of quality.

"You're an optimist, Hal. That's what you are. A bloody optimist."

Aldridge grinned. "I certainly don't often feel that way. Especially when it comes to this camp."

"I wanted to ask you about that . . ." Brindle began but was interrupted by a commotion in the darkness beyond the perimeter of light. He peered in the direction of the commotion until there emerged a group of people moving rapidly toward them. A guard ran up to the clinic railing and spoke hastily to Aldridge in Indonesian. Brindle saw that two men in the center of the group were carrying a bamboo pole on their shoulders. His heart sank a little when they came closer and he could see that a body hung from the pole. It swayed from side to side as the men hurried up the slope.

Aldridge pushed away quickly from his chair. "They say it's Nguyen."

"It's about time . . ." Brindle said.

He followed Aldridge down the steps to the crowd.

The two carriers dropped their load at Aldridge's feet with no more concern than if it had been a heavy sack of rice. The other refugees formed a circle around them and shouted excitedly.

"You'd better have a look at this," Aldridge said after glancing at the figure.

Brindle knelt and examined the body. As he did so, the crowd stepped in closer.

"Stand back," he shouted. A soldier forced the group to part so that Brindle could at least partially see in the light from the clinic. When the yellow light fell upon the dead form, he saw that it was a male. The face had been slashed several times with a knife or machete. The back of the head was bloody.

"Bring him into the clinic," Brindle said. "It's too dark out here."

"If this really is Nguyen . . ." Aldridge said. "I'll get Duong and inform Captain Salinem."

Aldridge hurried off.

The refugees carried the body into the clinic and placed it on a table in the treatment room. Brindle flicked on an examination light and adjusted it over the face. With a pair of scissors, he clipped the ropes which bound the man's hands and feet. Pulling on a pair of surgical gloves, he moved the head tentatively from side to side. Two deep gashes ran from the man's left temple to the right side of his jaw. The blows must have been powerfully swung when the man was lying flat on his back. There were no marks on the upper torso. When Brindle examined the back of the head, he found that the injury was traumatic enough to have caused death. Then why the slashes across the face? Brindle wondered. A thought occurred to him, and he glanced into the outer room to see if Aldridge was coming. The administrator and Duong had not yet arrived, so Brindle began to quickly search through the dead man's pockets. In the right trouser pocket he found a worn photograph of a young woman. Brindle held it under the light. It had been taken in a photo booth. He turned it over and saw a telephone number with a San Francisco prefix scrawled in ink on the back. In another pocket he found a folded piece of paper. It appeared to be a letter written in Vietnamese. He could not read Vietnamese, but scanning down the single sheet which had been folded and refolded numerous times, as if the reader had dwelt upon each word, he noticed an address. The ink was faded, but he could readily make out a street name and number for an address in the Sunset District of San Francisco. Again San Francisco, Brindle thought. Why would a communist infiltrator. . . ?

But at that moment he heard footsteps in the outer room and quickly slipped the photograph and letter into his pocket.

Aldridge hurried into the examination room followed by Duong. The young refugee looked pale and frightened as his eyes flicked briefly over the body, the face grotesquely disfigured with the two deep slashes and blood. Brindle could appreciate the young man's discomfort, for not only were the wounds gruesome, but Duong could probably envision himself lying there under slightly different circumstances.

Brindle gave the young man time to study the face.

"Is that Nguyen?" Aldridge asked, finally.

Duong looked at the face more closely, his jaw muscles twitching.

"Let me turn his head this way," Brindle suggested. "Perhaps that will help."

A guard appeared at the door.

"What is it?" Aldridge asked.

"A message for you, Sir."

Aldridge glanced at Duong and then at Brindle. "I'll just be a moment," he said, following the soldier outside.

Brindle leaned toward Duong.

"Is this Nguyen?" he whispered.

Duong looked confused.

"Nguyen?" Brindle asked again, pointing to the dead man.

Duong shrugged and shook his head.

"Yes," Brindle coached him. "Vo Nguyen."

Duong gazed at the doctor questioningly.

Brindle glanced toward the outer room and then moved his head up and down exaggeratedly in a motion of affirmation. "Yes. Nguyen."

A sign of understanding began to reflect in Duong's eyes. If this really were Nguyen, then all his troubles would be over. "Nguyen," he proclaimed hesitantly and tapped the dead man's shoulder.

"Yes," Brindle said emphatically. "Nguyen."

"Vo Nguyen," Duong repeated.

Brindle nodded and smiled.

"Vo . . . Nguyen," Duong said again.

"Now, just don't blow it," Brindle muttered as Aldridge came back into the room. Tran was with him.

"Well?" Aldridge asked.

"The poor kid's frightened to death," Brindle said. "I don't think he knows which end is up."

Aldridge frowned. "Has he identified the dead man yet?"

Brindle shrugged.

Aldridge let out a groan of exasperation. "Tran, will you ask Duong if this is the guy he was telling us about?"

"Yes, Sir."

When Tran translated the question, Duong glanced quickly at Brindle and then nodded his head.

"He say, yes," Tran interpreted.

"Please ask him one more time," Aldridge said. "I want this to be perfectly clear. Is this the body of Vo Nguyen? The man he saw behind the guard in the fog?"

Tran translated.

Duong nodded again, but looked nervous.

This isn't going to work, Brindle thought bitterly. He's going to blow it.

"The kid isn't used to blood," Brindle offered. "I think he's going to faint if we don't get him out of here."

Aldridge nodded. "Okay." He watched as Duong left the room.

Brindle put a towel over the mutilated face.

"Well," Aldridge said, wiping his forehead with a handkerchief. "We have the body and a positive ID."

"That should make Captain Salinem happy," Brindle said. "And the Indonesian government."

"John . . ?" Aldridge began and then hesitated.

"What?"

Aldridge wiped his face again.

"Are you all right, Hal?" Brindle asked.

"It's awfully hot in here," Aldridge said.

"Let's go outside."

When they stepped into the tropical night air, Aldridge breathed deeply and wiped his face with a handkerchief. It was better for him out here, Brindle thought. Death was not something most people could gaze at under the glare of an examination light. It gave one the feeling of being up against a force which was exasperatingly beyond reach and yet just there, beyond a line which could be far too easily crossed.

"How about that coffee?" he asked sympathetically.

"It's cold by now," Aldridge said. "Anyway, here comes the captain."

Salinem was crossing the compound with several of his men. Brindle could see that the officer was quickly buttoning his tunic.

"Must have caught him at an inconvenient time," he muttered to Aldridge.

"Quiet," the administrator warned.

"Where is he?" Salinem asked as he entered the clinic.

"In here," Brindle replied, motioning to the treatment room.

"Dead?"

"Yes."

"How unfortunate."

Salinem lifted the edge of the towel from the dead man's face. Brindle watched the shock register in the officer's eyes.

"What happened to his face?"

"There must have been a struggle," Aldridge answered. "You know, the refugees hated this guy."

"Nevertheless," Salinem said and let the towel drop. "I'm not sure I could identify that man if he were my brother."

"The face has distorted somewhat, Captain," Brindle said. "That type of trauma will cause swelling."

Salinem regarded the two Americans seriously. "Of course I am pleased that we have apprehended the murderer—even though he is dead. But I have my questions about this affair."

"What do you mean?" Aldridge asked.

"Do you not think it is curious, Mr. Aldridge?" Salinem questioned. "That the face has been so badly damaged?"

"Yes," Aldridge replied. "But we have a positive ID."

"The young man?"

"Yes."

"Where is he?"

"I sent him back to the detention area," Brindle said.

"Perhaps I will question him later," Salinem decided. He looked at the figure on the table. "In the meantime, keep the body here. I will send my men for him in the morning."

"For burial?" Brindle asked.

"That is not your concern."

Chapter Ten

Brindle took a sip from his bottle. It was getting easier, he told himself, this play-acting like a human being. Hadn't he just done a wonderful and self-sacrificing deed, urging Duong to lie about the dead man's identity? Hadn't it been just wonderful how he had saved all those refugees from possible deportation, the camp from possibly being shut down, and Aldridge from all that stress? There was only one small swig of alcohol in the bottle, and Brindle tipped it up to let the liquid drain into his mouth. Then he held the empty bottle up to the lantern light and turned it in his hands. It shone in distorted yellow sparkles. He noticed the faint blond hairs and the well clipped fingernails on his hands as he turned the bottle. The hands of a physician, he told himself. The hands of a self-sacrificer. Then why did he feel like he had traded away his last remaining bit of self-respect?

I can't do this, he muttered. *Anymore.* He threw the bottle across the room, and it broke against his sink. *Have to clean that up, so many things to clean up.* But he did not make any movement toward the sink. Instead he crawled onto his bed and put his hands over his face.

I'm sorry, Carrie, he said, burying his face in the mildewed pillow. *I'm sorry.*

The rain came and went and came again that night as he lay on his mattress, his eyes gazing sleeplessly into the shadows of a void he was beginning to perceive as something real, tangible. It was sometime in the early morning hours that a stillness came over the island, as if something malevolent and noiselessly harsh had moved on. It was not a quiet stillness but rather an absence of sound, and it seemed to ring in his ears more loudly than any actual noise. Dressing, and knowing that it was not wise for him to be seen in such a condition of exhaustion, he nevertheless stepped outside and began to cross the compound toward the food distribution shelter. He knew without being told because he had learned everything there was to know about Kim Thi Van Quang as a refugee, that she would be waiting in line there for her weekly supply ration. The army knife he had given her had been a success (it had been his own), and he had even scrounged a few bars of chocolate, which had caused Kim Thi's face to beam with delight. Now he wanted to know if there was anything else she wanted.

But Brindle had not reached the administration office and the path which led to the shelter before he heard someone yelling his name.

"John!"

He turned and saw Aldridge waving at him from the clinic terrace. Brindle stood for a moment in confusion. His total concentration, his every muscle, had been focused on reaching the distribution shelter and meeting Kim Thi. Now he had to reorganize what had seemed to be an important desire.

"John!" Aldridge called again.

With a sigh, Brindle turned and headed toward the clinic.

"Didn't Tran wake you?" Aldridge asked as Brindle walked up the steps.

"Yes," Brindle said. "Though I was already awake."

"Looks like you've been up all night. What happened?"

"Nothing."

Brindle saw a soldier coming from the camp with a stack of soggy posters under one arm. So they were taking them down already, he thought. From the moment he had stepped from his room, he had sensed a different emotional atmosphere in the camp, as if tension could be physically transmitted through the air. The refugees had lived for days with the ominous threat of being returned to Vietnam. Now that the infiltrator had been caught, the camp was returning to normal.

"Can't you at least comb your hair?" Aldridge asked. "I know we're on an island in the middle of nowhere, but we're still professionals."

"Sorry," Brindle said. He pulled a short black comb from his hip pocket and ran it through his hair. There was nothing he could do about the stubble of beard on his chin, and he scratched it thoughtfully.

"So what can I do for you?" he asked.

"It's just one thing after another," Aldridge said angrily. "Come on, I want to show you something."

They walked down the terrace of the clinic and around to the medical storage shed. Brindle had constructed the shed with a double roof made of corrugated metal which had an air space in between to keep the medical supplies as cool as possible. The wooden door was secured with a padlock.

"One of your aides was in here earlier this morning," Aldridge explained as Brindle opened the lock. "She found some visitors."

"Rats?" Brindle asked.

"No."

Brindle swung the door open and examined the contents inside. To the right were several large metal drums which contained surgical supplies, gauze, tape, bandages, gloves, and cotton. Against the wall were shelves of malarial pills and aspirin in boxes which had been sealed in plastic. Among the boxes on the left were his containers of antibiotics.

Brindle saw that Aldridge was looking disgustedly in that direction, so he picked up one of the antibiotic containers. As he did so, several large black ants scurried out from under the container. Brindle opened the lid and saw that the rubber caps of every antibiotic vial had been eaten away.

"Don't tell me," he muttered.

"Yes," Aldridge said, "they're all like that."

Brindle examined the bottom of the container. The ants had eaten through the heavy cardboard exterior.

"So, are we out of antibiotic?" Aldridge asked.

"No," Brindle sighed, dropping the vial back into the container. "We still have a small amount in the dispensary. But we'll need to contact Michele and have her bring a new shipment."

"Okay," Aldridge said. "I just wanted to make sure we weren't out completely. You'll need to do an inventory and tell me exactly how much to order."

"I'll have it for you by lunchtime," Brindle promised. He closed the shed door and attached the padlock.

"Did Salinem's boys come for the body?" he asked.

Aldridge nodded. "Early this morning."

"So what happens now?"

"We'll keep the refugees we've detained in the holding area where they are," Aldridge replied. "They'll go out with the next group in a week or so."

"And Duong?"

"He'll go with them."

Brindle gazed up at the sky. The atmosphere was so saturated with water that the air around them was a heavy gray blue. Despite of this, he could see a shaft of sunlight breaking through the clouds far beyond Surabi Point. It hung there like a lost promise.

"It's just one more thing, Hal," Brindle said. "That's all."

Aldridge gazed at him seriously. "Listen, John. Last night you gave me a checkup. Now it's my turn. Are you all right?"

Brindle thought about a response to this question. What could he say? That he had cut himself off from the vine, that he was now like a branch that had been dried up and gathered to be thrown into the fire? Is that what Hal wanted to hear? He scratched the side of his face. "Most of the time, yeah, Hal, I'm all right. But sometimes . . ."

"Like last night?"

"Yes."

"And the drinking?"

"You would be surprised how much I've cut back. I even poured some down the sink."

"But not all?"

"No," Brindle smiled. "That would be too much to ask, wouldn't it? Anyway, I'm all out now until Michele gets back."

"She's bringing you some?"

"Is that against the rules?"

"No," Aldridge said. "We don't have rules like that for the staff. But all the same, I'm concerned."

"I know."

"Of course, if you were ever intoxicated while on duty, that would be another thing."

"Don't worry," Brindle said. "Last night was a minor setback. I'm working on becoming a new man."

"Really?"

"Definitely," Brindle said. "You should buy tickets. It should be quite a show."

"I'll have to."

ᔓᖇ

Kim Thi was sitting with a group of other women when Brindle approached her hut that afternoon. He had completed the inventory which Aldridge had requested and had spent an additional hour and a half trying to rid the storage area of ants. Then he had taken a semi-cold shower—there was never any hot water—and had shaved and cleaned himself up before entering the camp. It bothered him as he approached her hut that she never tried to visit him. The impetus of their relationship was all on him. Kim Thi never made any effort to see him or even communicate with him, except when he arrived each time uninvited and unannounced to visit her. Yet she always seemed pleased to see him. Did she really not care about him, or was this an Asian custom of reticence? he wondered.

This afternoon, however, Kim Thi looked embarrassed when she glanced up and saw Brindle standing on the path. Immediately he was sorry he had come. *Wasn't she entitled to any privacy?* he asked himself bitterly. Did he have the right to just drop in on her at any time unexpectedly? She could visit him at the clinic any day, yet she had chosen not to come. Why? What caused her now to gaze at him with a look of almost shame in her dark eyes?

When the other women saw Brindle standing there, they scattered away like orchid blossoms blown in the wind.

"I'm sorry," he said. "I shouldn't have come."

Kim Thi offered a weak smile. "No, no," she said. "Okay."

Instinctively she held out her arm. There was no longer any need for her to wear a bandage. Brindle noticed that the new skin was a smooth pink and beginning to thicken into scar tissue. He had stopped worrying about her some time before when he had seen the red granulation tissue beginning to form. The wound to him now was a case history, a means to an end.

Madame Van Quang stepped from her hut at that moment and stopped cold when she saw him. She rattled off something in Vietnamese to Kim Thi, who shook her head quickly in response and then gazed back at Brindle to see if he understood.

He did not understand, but he could perceive that something was wrong. What could he do about it, though, if they chose not to tell him? He began to think of the problems a refugee family might have on Boromu Island. The only thing he could imagine was that Kim Thi's brother had gotten into trouble.

"Where is Hoang?" he asked.

"Fish," Kim Thi replied, pointing in the direction of the beach. "He go fish."

Brindle believed she was telling the truth, though with each reply came the furtive glance, the flash of embarrassment. He decided not to press the issue. If he remained calm and acted as if he were unaware of any difference in their behavior, perhaps they would tell him in time. Possibly something serious had happened, or perhaps it was simply that Kim Thi had not combed her hair. Looking at her now, he saw that her long black hair hung loosely on both sides of her face. Usually she wore it tied up and secured in the back with a hairpin. Was that it? he wondered. Was there something in the Vietnamese culture about a woman not being seen by a gentleman caller without her hair being put up? How could he tell? Brindle knew he had another question to ask Tran.

Anyway, he decided as she handed him the dutiful cup of hot tea, he would continue with the purpose for his visit.

"I wanted to ask," he began, holding out the tea as Kim Thi sprinkled in some sugar, "if you would like to attend a performance with me."

"Performance?" she asked.

"Yes. It's a wayang drama. I don't suppose you've ever heard of that."

"Wayang drama. No."

Brindle thought for a moment. "It's a kind of play with puppets."

She looked at him, and he could tell that she did not understand.

"Here," he said, picking up a stick. He began to draw a puppet in the dirt. Then he made motions with his hands as if he were moving the puppet.

Kim Thi smiled. "I know this," she said. "Puppets?"

"Yes," Brindle said. "Do you want to come?"

She nodded. "Yes. . . John."

"Good," he said. "Now I need to know one more thing."

She looked at him expectantly, openly, and he wondered how someone could appear so open and yet remain so aloof. It was as if deep inside Kim Thi there was a small sheltered place—like a young bird in a nest—that she was able to keep sealed off from everything else which transpired in her life. She could look at him with complete openness because she was open, except for that one small place. But it was that one small place which would forever keep her at a distance from him. He was beginning to understand that much already. Could he ever find his way there? he wondered. Would she ever show him the way, or let him try to understand? Would it mean anything to him if he did?

"What is your favorite color?" he asked, realizing that he had been gazing at her for an embarrassingly long time without speaking.

"You mean like pink, red, blue?" she asked, pressing the hair against her cheek.

"Yes."

Kim Thi thought for a moment and this gave Brindle the opportunity to study her soft upturned eyes and the curve of her lips. He had spent several afternoons with her now, and yet he sometimes felt as far away from her as if she were still in Nha Trang.

"Blue," she said finally. "Favorite color blue."

"Okay," he said, smiling. "Blue it is."

"Not big blue," she added, motioning with her hands. "Just little blue."

"I understand."

"Why you ask?"

"I wanted to get you a little something," he said.

"For me?" she asked.

Brindle nodded, and for the first time since his arrival, he felt that he had transcended whatever had been bothering her. At the same moment, Kim Thi turned so that he got a full view of her left cheekbone beneath the dark hair, and his jaw tightened.

"What happened?" he asked, anger swelling in him and replacing any trace of intimidation.

Kim Thi immediately realized her mistake and let the hair fall back over her cheekbone.

"Fall down," she said, turning her eyes away from him.

Brindle reached out and touched her cheek. At first she resisted and then she assented as he moved her face toward him. The contusion was just across the cheekbone and resembled the bruises he had seen on battered women in San Francisco.

"You've been hit," he said, disregarding her answer.

"All okay, John," she said and covered her face. "No problem."

"Who hit you?"

"Fall down," she said. "Dark outside . . ."

"Was it Hoang?"

She shook her head.

Brindle gazed angrily at Madame Van Quang. "I bet it was this old biddy," he muttered.

Kim Thi shook her head again. "No Hoang. No mother. Fall down."

Brindle felt that Kim Thi wanted him to know what had happened but was too ashamed to say. Why would that be? he wondered.

Then the possible answer became clear.

Brindle felt a sinking feeling coming over him. He had wanted to protect her, to shield her, to help her because he had begun to care. And what had happened? He began to feel sick.

"Do you want to come up to the clinic?" he asked.

She shook her head.

When had it happened? he wondered. While he was feeling sorry for himself and getting drunk? *Fine, you pathetic wretch*, he told himself. *You've let someone else down.*

He got up to leave.

"You come back tomorrow. Okay, John?" Kim Thi asked.

Brindle stopped. This was the first time she had ever actually invited him to visit her. He looked at the dusted pink cheeks, the golden brown skin, the eyes which had seen more than he would probably ever see and yet still retained a trace of innocence.

"Yes," he said. "I'll come back tomorrow. And if you need anything . . ."

She nodded.

Brindle bowed slightly to Madame Van Quang, who shook her head regretfully, and then he hurried down the path to the beach.

❦

Hoang was fishing in the surf near the dock. Brindle walked along the beach for several hundred meters before he found him. The young man did not see him at first, so Brindle stood on the sand and watched him throwing the net. He felt that if he just watched Hoang, he would somehow be able to tell if he were telling the truth. What was that? he asked himself, a polygraph test through body language? Did you carry yourself differently when you were bearing a lie? he wondered. Did the lack of truth weigh you down, warp your shoulders, tilt your head? Brindle saw only a young man with shaggy black hair. Somehow, though, he felt there was an element of truth about Hoang. Well, he told himself, he would have to find out. Brindle walked to the water's edge and called. Hoang turned with the net in his hands and gazed back at the beach. Brindle waved and Hoang nodded. Gathering the net on his shoulder, Hoang began to wade toward the shore.

At that moment Brindle suddenly realized the absurdity of his situation. He had angrily come down to the beach to question Hoang about Kim Thi. But how could he discuss something as sensitive as rape with a young man who spoke no English? Nor did Brindle speak Vietnamese.

"This isn't going to work," he muttered as he stood there and watched Hoang wade toward shore.

When Hoang came out of the water, his shorts dripping and his t-shirt wet up to the armpits, Brindle noticed with detached surprise that a net bag hung from a strap over his shoulder. In the bag were two fish.

Hoang approached the doctor tentatively. His face held a semblance of greeting, and yet his eyes looked wary, questioning.

Brindle was reminded of the first time he had seen Hoang as he disembarked with his sister and mother at the dock. The young man's eyes had been hard then too, holding up an angry courage against indefensible odds and events totally out of his control.

"Hi," Brindle said, feeling stupid.

Hoang nodded and put down his net.

"I want to talk to you," Brindle explained.

Kim Thi's brother looked at him and Brindle noticed the family resemblance in the facial structure and nose.

He pointed in the direction of the clinic.

"Will you come with me?" he asked, motioning with his hands and pointing again in the direction of the clinic.

Hoang held out the fish bag to Brindle.

"No, no," Brindle said, "you come with me."

Hoang shook his head.

Did he really not understand, Brindle thought. Or did the young man sense some kind of entrapment?

"Fine," Brindle said, "you wait here. I'll get Tran and be right back." He made a stop motion by holding his palm out flat.

Hoang nodded and sat down on the sand. Reaching into his pocket, he pulled out the Swiss Army knife Brindle had given Kim Thi and began to scale the fish. Brindle was somewhat surprised and hurt when he saw the knife. He had given it to Kim Thi. She had never said the knife was only for her; she had simply said they needed a knife. Oh well, Brindle thought, you couldn't clean a fish with a butter knife. He began to walk fast up the beach toward the clinic.

When he returned with Tran a few minutes later, Hoang had finished cleaning the fish and was sitting with his arms around his knees and gazing out to sea.

"Okay," Brindle said as they knelt beside Hoang. "I've seen Kim Thi's face and I want to know what happened."

Tran translated.

As Hoang listened, he gazed at the pack of gum in Brindle's shirt pocket.

"Ask him if he would like a piece," Brindle said, taking out the pack.

Hoang nodded.

Brindle opened the package and gave Hoang a piece. He also offered one to Tran, who declined.

Hoang chewed the gum and breathed deeply. Finally he said something in Vietnamese.

"He say all time trouble," Tran interpreted. "Anywhere go, all time trouble."

"What kind of trouble?" Brindle asked.

Tran and Hoang spoke together for a minute.

"This time he say no big trouble if he not care about sister," Tran explained.

"What about his sister?" Brindle asked.

Hoang spoke quietly while looking up and down the beach.

"Someone in camp want Kim Thi for his woman," Tran continued to interpret. "Make trouble for family if Kim Thi not say yes. Maybe never leave island. Or maybe go back Vietnam."

"A refugee?"

Hoang shook his head.

"You mean someone on the staff?"

Hoang and Tran spoke again for a moment while Brindle sat back on the sand. The sand was hot, and he was beginning to feel sweat trickle down his back and arms from being out in the open. Someone on the staff? he thought to himself. That was impossible. It was strictly against Aldridge's orders. There was to be no abusive influence of that kind on Boromu Island.

Two Indonesian soldiers were coming down the beach, the usual security patrol. When Hoang saw them, he tensed. He said something quickly to Tran and then stood up.

"If you want to help, Doctor," Tran interpreted, "Hoang say get them off island."

Wait a minute," Brindle snapped. "Who is it? . . . Hoang?"

But the young man was gone up the beach.

Chapter Eleven

Brindle was beginning to feel again, but it was not something he was pleased about. Since hearing of Kim Thi, he had been wracked by the shifting emotions of anger and jealousy. He was outraged that someone on the staff had apparently abused Kim Thi and jealous that the woman he was beginning to love had been taken by someone else. The latter was not an emotion he was proud of, but that was the way he felt.

"It's too much," he muttered to himself and clenched his fist.

From somewhere far within him, he began to feel that queasy, tingling sensation of regret, sorrow, and remorse for all that had passed and all that would come. He felt it coming on in a rush, and he could not hold it back, except by concentrating with the utmost attention on the familiar objects around him—the table, the chair, the bed, the water pitcher on the sink. With blank eyes he gazed at the book on tropical medicine laying open to the section on parasites. The words did not register, though, and he felt the tingling reaching up to his shoulders and then his neck and lower jaw, and when it reached his face, he felt hot salt in his eyes. He tightened his jaw then and stood up. He had been through this a hundred times and experience told him there was nothing to do but fight it. Going over to the shelf, he picked up an old vodka bottle and raised it to his mouth. Nothing. The smell of the alcohol relaxed him somewhat, however. He associated the smell with numbness, lack of pain, absence of memory, a sanctuary from the life out there for which he had never been built.

It seemed that the world and John Brindle had always played by different rules. And try as he might, he had never been able to learn or understand those rules.

Except. . .

Brindle stomped out of his room and hurried across the courtyard.

"What's the matter, John?" Aldridge asked as Brindle passed him.

Brindle stopped and gazed at the administrator questioningly. Had he been wrong about Aldridge? he wondered. Was there some darker reason for the older man being here?

"One of the refugee woman was abused last night," Brindle said, watching the administrator's face closely.

There was no question about the sudden hurt and empathy in Aldridge's eyes. Brindle was immediately sorry he had doubted him.

"Which one?" Aldridge asked.

"The one with the infected arm. Kim Thi Van Quang."

"Oh, yes. Well, we'll have to inform Captain Salinem. Does she know who did it?"

"I think so, but she was reluctant to tell me."

"I can imagine."

"Her brother did say one thing," Brindle offered. "It wasn't a refugee."

"What do you mean?"

Brindle felt the bitterness surging up again. "He said it was someone on our staff."

"Impossible!"

"That's what I said."

"Are you going to see her now?"

"Yes."

"Then find out who it was. If they are going to make accusations like that, she had better be able to tell us."

"I'll try," Brindle said. At the same moment, he saw Tran standing on the clinic terrace. The young man was watching them curiously.

"Tran!" Brindle called.

The young man did not move.

Brindle walked over to him irritatedly.

"No more rain today, Doctor," Tran said as Brindle mounted the steps. "Maybe tonight."

Brindle looked through the clinic doorway. One of the Indonesian aides sat there at the registration table.

"I want to talk to you, Tran," Brindle said. Taking his assistant by the arm, he led him down the terrace and around the side of the clinic to the storage shed.

"Ants all gone?" Tran asked.

"I assume so," Brindle said, "but who knows?"

"Hope Miss Michele bring plenty antibiotic."

Brindle looked at him. "Listen, Tran," he said. "Do you know anything about this sexual abuse?"

Tran shook his head. "Poor girl," he said. "I worry about her. She nice girl. Very pretty."

"Did you know she had been abused before we talked to Hoang on the beach?"

"No, Doctor."

"But you thought she might be?"

"I all time worry about pretty Vietnamese girls."

"Why?"

Tran frowned and looked away.

"Listen, Tran," Brindle urged. "If you know something about this, you've got to tell me."

Tran gazed at the ground thoughtfully.

"Come on, Tran," Brindle said.

"Not my place, Doctor."

"I thought we were friends."

Tran looked at him. "We friends, Doctor. All same, not my place talk."

"But they're your women," Brindle said. "Vietnamese girls. Don't you want to protect them?"

"All time worry," Tran repeated.

"All time worried, sure," Brindle said. "But not enough to do anything about it."

Tran frowned. "Ask Miss Van Quang, Doctor. Get name. Then all okay. Not my place talk now."

"I can't believe this," Brindle said.

"Maybe I wrong, Doctor," Tran explained. "If wrong, then no problem. But if right, then make big *palaver*."

"So it's someone important?"

Tran glanced at his watch. "Excuse, Doctor. Make rounds now. Must go."

"Okay," Brindle said, realizing that Tran was probably right. It was not his place to pass along gossip. Brindle needed to speak with Kim Thi herself. If the abuse had actually taken place as Brindle suspected, then he would have to know so that he could deal with it. And he would deal with it himself. He was tired of letting others take the responsibility for actions which he could have handled. Perhaps the first sign of regenerating self-respect was that he no longer saw himself outside of the swirl of events. Or perhaps with renewed respect came the power to bend events in his direction. He did not know, but he felt that this was something he needed to do. Perhaps it was to make up for that other incident, the one he never let himself think about. If an event in the present could ever have an influence on something that happened in the past, then he would begin to chip away slowly at that past event until its whole character had been altered. Perhaps with each chip his emotional response would change also, so that eventually he would be able to look back on it without the despair and remorse he always felt now. Brindle did not know if that was even possible, but he felt determined to try.

The sun had dropped behind the hills and jungle palms as Brindle set foot once again on the path to Kim Thi's hut. Through the trees he could see the beach, where gulls floated in the evening light like feathers blown in a slowly circling breeze. The sea was gray and streaked with glints of fading yellow. He could imagine a fishing boat pushed out from the beach so that a man in the prow could address the crowd. The man was saying, "*He who has ears to hear, let him hear.*" Now was the time of loneliness, Brindle thought, when the tide began to come in and the vast emptiness of the ocean seemed to press in on the land. In the camp women were lighting fires, and the scent of cooking rice wafted into the air. It hardly seemed possible to him that so much had transpired in the past twenty-four hours. It was just last night that he had been playing chess with Aldridge when the refugees had brought in the body of Nguyen—or whoever it was. And at the same time, Kim Thi had been abused. Was it possible that so much grief had happened on what had seemed to be such a calm evening? Brindle wondered.

He walked through the camp toward Kim Thi's shelter.

She was not there. Madame Van Quang was sitting alone by the cook fire. Even before Brindle could speak, the old woman turned and gazed at him with that wrinkled face and those dark bead eyes which held the sorrow of Asia and yet gave off nothing, and he knew that it had happened again. She did not utter a word and yet he understood, for he had seen that expression before. It was the look of fear and anticipated dread that a parent felt when the fate of their child had been taken from their hands. He had seen it many times in hospital waiting rooms, and had felt it once himself.

A sudden contraction in his stomach made him feel sick.

"Kim Thi?" he whispered pathetically.

Brindle began to feel his lack of effectiveness, his inconsequentiality, his meaninglessness in the whole scheme of life that was the essence of Boromu Island. And feeling this, he began to run.

The damp tropical air moved swiftly around him as his boots struck up the path. Surprised faces gazed at him or stopped and stared as he hurried among the huts. He did not know where he was running, he only felt the need to move, and in moving to go somewhere, and in going somewhere to help. Then he was on the beach, although he had never determined to run there, and the heavy, salt air tasted like sickness in his mouth. Dropping onto the sand, he breathed heavily.

He had to help Kim Thi, he thought to himself. But how? Then a hard edge of something like anger began to crystalize inside him. It came from somewhere far down, so that even he was unaware of its origin, and as it took hold, he looked up from his place on the sand and began to think clearly.

I've been so stupid, he cursed to himself.

Jumping to his feet, he began to run again—this time toward the Indonesian barracks.

The barracks of the Indonesian soldiers were two long buildings on the southern edge of camp. On the inland side of the barracks, near the helicopter clearing, was Captain Salinem's office and quarters. Brindle could see the light on in Salinem's office as he ran up from the beach. He should have gone to the administrative office first and gotten Aldridge to come with him, but he was not thinking in terms of chain of command now. He was only thinking of Kim Thi and where she might be at that moment and what was perhaps happening to her even as he hurried across the sand. Outside the barracks, three soldiers were passing around a bottle of rice wine and two others were playing cards. In the back of his head, Brindle realized that he might have to deal with these soldiers. He had never felt much of a kinship with the Indonesians, but now it occurred to him that they might even be adversaries. Reaching the office, he hesitated for a moment. What had Tran said? *"Maybe I wrong, Doctor. If wrong, then no problem. But if right, then make big palaver."*

Brindle realized that he was on untenable ground. If he barged into Salinem's office and was wrong, had miscalculated in any way, then there would be a terrific amount of embarrassment and apologizing. But if he was right, then there would be no subsiding of the anger which swelled in him now like a lost part of his soul, and there would certainly be a scene. And danger? Brindle did not care.

A guard standing duty outside the office eyed Brindle suspiciously as the doctor approached. Brindle realized at that moment that he had never before visited Salinem's office. Was that possible? In such a small camp? he wondered. And what did it say about him? The Indonesians made up the third reality that was Boromu Refugee Camp. First came the official reality, Aldridge and Michele and himself and the other WRO staff, then came the refugees, that transient mass of human debris that washed up on the shore from time to time, and finally, the unkempt, unappreciated Indonesians whose government made the camp possible. Each element had its separate identity and life dictated by the confines of the island and perimeter of the jungle.

From the look in the guard's eyes, Brindle could tell he was wondering what to do. Everyone knew Dr. Brindle, but this was an unusual situation. Was the soldier aware of what was happening in Salinem's quarters? Brindle wondered. Had he been ordered not to let anyone enter?

The answer came soon enough. When Brindle stepped up to the terrace, the guard snapped to attention and held out a rifle to bar his way.

"I need to see Captain Salinem," Brindle said sternly.

The guard shook his head and muttered something in Indonesian.

"Right now," Brindle commanded.

The guard shook his head again.

Brindle pushed away the rifle and stepped toward the door. The guard resisted at first but then gave in as Brindle shouldered past him.

The interior of Salinem's office contained a wooden desk and three chairs. On the far wall hung a large map of Indonesia and a smaller one of Boromu Island. A framed portrait of Soeharto and the Indonesian flag hung on a wall to his right.

A door to his left apparently led to the captain's living quarters. Brindle pounded loudly on the door.

"Captain!" he called. "Captain Salinem!"

He glanced back at the guard and saw him watching suspiciously from the doorway.

"Captain Salinem!" Brindle called again.

He was just reaching for the knob when the door flung open.

An obviously irritated and surprised captain stood there before him. He was wearing a black silk robe. The greasy strands of hair which he always combed so carefully across the top of his head were pushed forward now and Brindle thought, it only takes that much for some men to lose their dignity—just a slight ruffling of the hair.

"What on earth is the matter, Doctor?" Salinem asked.

"I'm looking for someone," Brindle answered, looking over the officer's shoulder to the room beyond. It was a small room with a table and chairs. A carved Indonesian elephant stood in the center of the table.

"Have you been drinking again, Doctor?" Salinem asked. "I am well aware of your problem."

"I'm not the one who has a problem this time," Brindle snapped.

"What are you implying?"

"That you have a Vietnamese girl in there," Brindle said. "Kim Thi Van Quang. And I want her out now."

"You are out of your element, Doctor," Salinem said sarcastically. "Why don't you go back to your clinic?"

"I'm warning you, Captain. Unless you want a scandal on your hands . . ."

"All you Americans are such pompous fools," Salinem said. "What makes you think you have any place here? Do you believe you can barge into my quarters like this and start making demands? You could not be more wrong. Now, why don't you leave quietly before I get angry and do something I will regret—or perhaps that you will regret."

"I'm not leaving," Brindle said stubbornly. "Kim Thi is my patient and under my medical care. If you're going to have one of your men shoot me, then do it. Otherwise, let her go."

Salinem gazed at Brindle now with undisguised hatred.

"You would make me do that, wouldn't you?" he asked.

"Yes," Brindle replied.

The captain gazed at the doctor for a moment longer and then the hot anger suddenly subsided from his eyes. It was not that the Indonesian officer had ceased to be angry, but rather that the wall of Asian aloofness which always separated them had reappeared. Salinem had slipped behind the phony, supercilious mask of politeness he always wore when dealing with Americans.

"Of course, Doctor," he said deprecatingly. "If I had only known she was your woman . . ."

"She's not my woman," Brindle said. "I'm her doctor."

"You may call it what you like," Salinem said. "If you will wait outside . . ."

"I'll wait here."

"Very well."

Kim Thi appeared a moment later, buttoning her blouse with trembling fingers as she moved along the darkened hallway of Salinem's quarters to the outer office. She glanced quickly at Brindle and then turned away, as if she could not bear the look in his eyes. It was a look he tried to hide from her, but the pain was there and he could not pretend that it did not exist. Putting an arm around her, he led her out of the office and down the steps. Pressed against him now with his arm around her shoulder, she felt much smaller than he had anticipated and, therefore, more vulnerable. With this sense of vulnerability, he felt a sudden respect for her courage, for a young woman who had pressed out into the South China Sea with only her mother, her brother, and her childishly simple command of English.

They passed the guard who still held his rifle in an attitude of dangerous confusion and then moved past the barracks. On the left a path led through the trees, and Brindle decided to take this way since it was the shortest route to the camp.

"It's going to be okay," he said in an attempt at consolation, but the words sounded ridiculously hollow in the tropical night air. They walked down the path without talking.

"John . . ." Kim Thi finally said, her voice a quivering whisper.

"Yes?"

But she did not continue. Whatever thought had crossed her mind had been sealed off from him, as if even as she spoke, her mind was weighing the consequences of her words.

"It's okay," Brindle said. "You'll be alright now."

She hesitated on the path and looked up at him. It was not the look a patient gave a doctor, and Brindle felt that as he gazed into her soft eyes, he had finally crossed over that barrier into the realm of feelings between a man and a woman.

"I afraid this make big trouble," she said, taking his hand.

"No, no," Brindle coaxed. "He won't bother you again. I promise."

"He no make trouble for you?"

"No," Brindle replied.

"No send back Vietnam?"

Brindle shook his head. "He can't do that. He doesn't have the authority."

But as he spoke, Brindle heard the sound of footsteps approaching rapidly from the direction of the barracks.

He turned to see two figures running toward them. The image of the runner shot on the beach came to his mind.

"Go," he said to Kim Thi, pushing her up the path. "Run!"

Kim Thi slipped away into the shadows with a swiftness that surprised even Brindle. When she had gone, he turned and waited. Within a moment two Indonesian soldiers came up the path and began to circle around him.

"This is not right," Brindle said.

One of the men leaped at him. Brindle lost his footing in the loose sand, and they tumbled to the ground. He managed to push the man away, but as he struggled to regain his balance, the second man kicked out hard with a boot and caught Brindle on the right side of his head. It was not an explosion of pain that Brindle felt when the boot made contact with his temple, but rather a feeling of shock that this was happening to him, and the sudden sensation that his physical movements were no longer under his control. Collapsing onto his side, he made a feeble attempt to cover his head as the boot struck again and again at his ribs and stomach.

Chapter Twelve

Something touched him, and he awakened to see Tran gazing at him with a look of concern and relief. Behind Tran, Brindle could see the examination light and cabinets of the operating room.

"He wake up," Tran said to someone else in the room. "Doctor open eyes."

Brindle turned his head slightly, a movement which caused his temples to ring with a nerve-shattering pain, and then he lay still again. Gazing at the light, the events of the evening began to slowly float back into his consciousness. He could taste the sand in his mouth from where he had fallen.

"Good," said the second voice, which he recognized as Aldridge's. "I was beginning to worry."

"I think all okay now," Tran said. He patted Brindle on the arm. "You in big fight, Doctor," he explained. "But you okay now."

"My head aches," Brindle groaned.

Tran examined Brindle's temple.

"Bad contusion here, Doctor," he said. "Someone hit you?"

Brindle shook his head.

"Kick?"

He nodded slightly, trying to prevent the pain from returning.

"Maybe you got concussion," Tran offered.

No doubt, Brindle thought. But he was not concerned about himself.

"Kim Thi?" he asked.

"She come get us," Tran explained. "Say you in trouble. Then she go."

Aldridge stepped closer to the bed, and Brindle saw him in the light from the examination bulb. The administrator's face was flushed and he looked worried.

"Can you talk?" he asked.

"A little," Brindle muttered.

Aldridge shook his head pathetically. "What happened, John?"

Beginning slowly, Brindle told them about his visit to Captain Salinem's office and the confrontation over Kim Thi Van Quang.

"So she was there?" Aldridge asked.

Brindle nodded.

Aldridge rubbed his chin thoughtfully and glanced out the window. "I'll have to contact the military authorities in Jakarta. And of course, we'll need to talk with Captain Salinem."

"Just get him out of here," Brindle urged.

Tran spoke up. "You do right thing, Doctor. This problem not go away. Here for long time."

"You knew about this?" Aldridge asked.

Tran looked suddenly repentant and turned away.

"Did he know about this?" Aldridge asked Brindle.

"I think everyone did—except us."

"Why didn't they say something?"

Brindle closed his eyes and felt a slight spinning sensation. "You forget, Hal, where these people came from."

"They should have told me," Aldridge said. "I can't help if I'm not aware of the problem."

"When do you want to meet with Salinem?"

"Tomorrow. If you think you'll feel up to it."

"I will," Brindle said. "In the meantime, Hal, could you have someone keep an eye on Miss Van Quang?"

"I'll have her brought to the clinic," Aldridge offered. "She'll be safe here."

"We move you now, Doctor," Tran explained. "Nice bed in ward."

"I can walk," Brindle protested, but the pain in his ribs caused him to reconsider.

"No, no," Tran insisted. "Better we take you."

Two aides came in, and Brindle felt himself being lifted from the examination table and onto a cart. Tran pushed the cart through the surgery doors and around the corner to the ward. Again he was lifted and then felt the softness of the pillow beneath his head. He felt like sleeping, and a glance at his watch told him it was past two o'clock.

"All okay now, Doctor," Tran said reassuringly. "All okay."

"Yes," Brindle muttered. "Just great."

∽∾

The meeting with Captain Salinem was scheduled for the following afternoon. Brindle awakened that morning to the sensation of fingertips moving soothingly over the hairs of his arm like wisps of butterfly wings. He knew it was Kim Thi even before his eyes opened or he fully emerged into awakening. She had come to visit, and this realization caused a surge of tentative joy to swell within him; tentative because he never trusted joy—even in the best circumstances.

"Good morning," he said, trying to clear the sleep from his voice. It was a different perspective now, gazing at her from a hospital bed, but the dark hair and dust-pink cheeks were the same. Kim Thi smiled, and he thought how easily roles were reversed and how ironic—the patient visiting the doctor in the clinic. She did not cease moving her fingertips across his arm in the small, butterfly strokes, and he understood this to be her way of expressing affection.

"I sorry you hurt, John," she said with such sincerity that Brindle felt as if she were taking the pain from him.

"I'm okay," he said. Reaching over with his left hand, he pressed her hand tenderly into his arm.

"Make big trouble for you?" she asked, not withdrawing her hand as he had feared but leaving it there beneath his.

"No," he said. "You don't have to worry."

"Captain Salinem?"

"I imagine he won't be with us much longer."

"Really?" she asked. "He go?"

"I think so," Brindle replied. He saw admiration suddenly flare in her eyes. Is this what it took to gain her respect? he wondered. A show of administrative power? Even when he knew this was not true? It was Aldridge who would send the reports and demand the changes. As a doctor, Brindle had nothing to do with that kind of administrative work. Or was it that he had stood up for her the night before and taken a beating? He could not imagine what she was feeling or how the political environment of her former life had shaped her thinking. He only knew that her hand beneath his felt as if it had always been there—that all this time he had been incomplete, waiting for her feminine touch to make him whole again, to restore the John Brindle he had known before. . . .

"You'll stay here?" he asked hopefully.

"No," she said. "Must go back soon. Help mother."

"She could come here too," he offered, knowing this would never happen.

"Maybe," Kim Thi said thoughtfully. "But Hoang no want come here. Mother stay with Hoang."

"Yes," he said. "I just thought . . ."

"You good man, John," she said. "You care all time about Vietnamese."

"I care about you," he said.

Kim Thi slipped her hand from beneath his and ran her fingers along the side of his face.

"Must go now," she said. "You come see me?"

Brindle nodded.

Kim Thi walked toward the door and then turned. "I no say thank you."

"You don't need to."

"Yes," she said. "Must say. . . thank you, John."

"You're welcome." He smiled, but the smile faded as quickly as Kim Thi left the ward.

Brindle turned onto his side and felt the tightness of the tape against his cracked ribs. In the midst of happiness, can one realize that one is a fool? he wondered. Isn't there that brief moment or interlude between even the happiest times where the voice whispers, *such a fool, so oblivious to the truth, so out of touch.* Brindle thought this now as he lay in the ward and gazed along the row of beds. They had been made up earlier by one of the aides. The beds looked clean and starched, with a hardness of reality that made Brindle feel as if he were coming out of a dream or a place in which his mind had been clouded by fog. Hadn't there been just the slightest touch of pity in Kim Thi's voice as she had said thank you just now? he asked himself. Had he all along fabricated this idea of a developing relationship between the two of them? Or was his own sense of emotional self-protection causing him to search for the inevitable faults? He suddenly felt tired, with a weariness that went far beyond the strains of the night before. How can I get through this? he wondered, not referring to the events of the day.

⮌

Captain Salinem was already seated at a table in the mess hall when Brindle entered for the afternoon staff meeting. The officer glared impatiently as Brindle eased himself carefully into the chair. Aldridge sat at the head of the table.

"Are you feeling better, John?" Aldridge asked.

"I'm okay," Brindle said.

"So sorry to hear about your accident, Doctor," Salinem said.

"It wasn't an accident," Brindle snapped. "You sent your men after me." Perhaps hatred intensified the senses, or perhaps he had never actually studied the officer before, but now

Brindle became acutely aware of the way the strands of hair which Salinem had slicked across his forehead seemed to ooze grease. The corners of his mouth were dark and down-turned in a permanent, disdainful scowl. His jaw was clinched with bitterness. The overall impression was of a man who was comically and yet dangerously vicious. Brindle suddenly felt as if he had kicked over a rock and uncovered something disgusting.

"It was dark," Salinem explained to Aldridge. "One of my men was killed only three weeks ago. Two soldiers on patrol saw a figure waiting for them in the shadows. Naturally the men reacted in a violent manner—to protect themselves."

"That's a lie," Brindle said.

Salinem turned to Brindle and gazed at him patronizingly. "How unfortunate that this had to happen to you, Doctor. I hope it did not cause you too much pain."

"I spoke to them," Brindle said. "They knew who I was."

"Did they reply?" Salinem asked.

"No."

"Then they obviously did not hear. Do you speak Indonesian?"

"You know I don't."

"Then it was a misunderstanding." Salinem sighed. "It is too bad the WRO doesn't better prepare its staff for the work here. It would make things so much easier."

"Knock it off," Aldridge said.

"That is exactly what I am attempting to do, Mr. Aldridge."

"It isn't just that Dr. Brindle was beaten up by two of your men. It is also that you have abused your power here, Captain Salinem. You know it is completely against camp rules for staff members to coerce the refugees in any way—especially in moral situations."

"Of course," Salinem said. "I am quite aware of your rules."

"Then why did you break them with Miss Van Quang?"

"First of all, Mr. Aldridge," Salinem snapped coldly. "I am an officer in the Indonesian Army. I am not required to answer questions from you or any other foreign civilian. I am only responsible to my superiors. However," he said, dabbing a handkerchief to the corners of his mouth, "because I find these petty questions so tiring, I will answer them this time only and be finished with it."

"That's all we are asking, Captain," Aldridge said.

"Very well," Salinem said. "I in no way coerced this Vietnamese woman to visit my quarters. Do you really believe I am that desperate?"

"That is the allegation Miss Van Quang has made against you," Aldridge explained flatly.

"And you believe her?" Salinem asked. "Some woman who arrives here on a refugee boat? Do you know this woman? What is her history? How can you begin to question the validity of her word against mine?"

"Dr. Brindle found her at your quarters," Aldridge said. "He said you were reluctant to let her go."

Salinem stood up angrily. "We are all aware of Dr. Brindle's occasional nights of drinking. I have never mentioned this before, but do you really think he is suitable for the work here?"

Brindle felt his face flushing but said nothing.

"Dr. Brindle is an excellent physician," Aldridge said. "His competency is not the question here. Surely you understand that I must contact Jakarta and give them a full report of this incident."

"Such a ridiculous threat does not bother me," Salinem said.

Aldridge shook his head. "I'm not threatening you, Captain. I'm only explaining. The WRO depends on the personal integrity of all its staff—and that includes the Indonesian soldiers who guard the camp."

Salinem smiled. "It is you, Mr. Aldridge, who are the guest of Indonesia. You must surely realize that I could have this camp shut down."

"I think you overestimate yourself, sir," Aldridge said.

∿✕∿

After the meeting, Brindle stood on the steps of the administrative office and gazed at the rain. The storm had blown in while Salinem was arguing, as if the malevolent force from the Asian mainland had been the embodiment of his contempt. There was no pretense now for a show of common courtesy between them; the line had been drawn, and Brindle had stepped over that line with Kim Thi.

Who cares? Brindle thought. He was beginning to get very tired of Boromu Island with its refugees, soldiers, heat, insects, rain, mud, and himself. He could escape all the others, but how could he get away from the thing which he most loathed? Reaching absently under his coat, he rubbed the tape along his ribs. His head did not ache now, but his side hurt with each turn of the body, each movement or action. Gazing up at the twilight sky, he saw that the rain had settled in and would not stop until early morning. He had wanted to visit Kim Thi as soon as the meeting was over, but he did not want to trod through the rain with his side hurting. As he watched the rain, the door behind him opened and Aldridge stepped out to the terrace. The administrator seemed oblivious to the rain, just as he was to so many other things on Boromu, Brindle thought.

"I've received a message from Michele," he said, tapping a sheet of paper. "She has obtained the antibiotic."

And a blue dress, Brindle thought. "Thanks, Hal."

Aldridge looked at the rain falling in the courtyard. "Is there anything else I should know before I send my report to Jakarta?"

"No," Brindle said. "How long do you think it will take to get a reply?"

Aldridge folded the sheet of paper. "A few days, I suppose. I can't imagine them waiting much longer. It's a rather awkward situation."

Brindle nodded. "The sooner, the better."

Chapter Thirteen

He was busy with medical cases for the next few weeks, which was good perhaps, for it took his mind off Kim Thi and Captain Salinem. Casualties of the monsoons were beginning to line up outside the clinic, and he treated them with the usual antibiotics, which were running low. He was concerned about a Montagnard woman who had come to the clinic to give birth. On examination, he had noticed that the mucous membranes in her mouth were pale. A look at her palms showed that they also had lost color. Brindle knew that even people with dark skin lost pink in the palms of their hands if they were anemic. This woman showed physical signs of anemia, but what could be the cause? His first thought was leukemia, but a palpation of the spleen showed that it was not enlarged. That ruled out malaria as well.

"Probably an iron deficiency," Brindle muttered, as he checked the woman's pulse. "These hill people rarely get a proper diet."

"Give medicine?" Tran asked.

"Not yet," Brindle said. "I'll have to do a hematocrit and a blood count and smear. Then we'll know for sure."

As with all his procedures on Boromu, Brindle had only enough medical equipment to do the most basic tests. He had put in requests for more sophisticated equipment, but it had not yet arrived.

Fortunately, the hematocrit was a simple test. After drawing the blood, he put it in a tube marked with graduations from zero to one hundred and spun it in the centrifuge. This gave him a reading of the red cells, white cells and platelets, and plasma. In a normal pregnancy, a woman's red cell count would register at about 28 to 30. The test showed that the Montagnard woman's hematocrit was twenty—far below the norm. A complete blood count showed that she had a red cell count of 2.64 million and a white cell count of 6,200.

"Well, she's anemic all right," Brindle said as he leaned back from the microscope and wrote down the numbers on her chart.

"Cause problem with baby?" Tran asked.

"It shouldn't," Brindle said. "But the more time she has before the delivery, the better. I could have her almost up to low normal if I had two weeks. But I doubt if that's going to happen."

"Yes, Doctor," Tran agreed. "I think this baby come soon."

"Okay," Brindle said, stretching. "Start her on the ferrous sulfate tablets. One tablet three times a day."

"Yes, Doctor."

Brindle gazed at the red cells in the counting chamber of his microscope again. " If I just had the gluconate, I could give her an injection," he said, focusing the knob. "That would have a much more rapid response."

"No have this?" Tran asked.

"No. And we'll have to give her something to counter the constipation. With all this iron, she's going to need it."

"I give first tablet now," Tran said.

"Right," Brindle remarked, making another note on her chart. Removing the hemacytometer slide from the microscope, he held it up to the light. He had always cared about his patients, but now he felt emotionally involved because he loved one of them.

"Good luck, baby," he whispered as he pulled off his gloves. And he knew there was someone he wanted to see.

Brindle arrived at Kim Thi's hut just after breakfast, when he knew she would still be helping her mother. The rains had stopped in the night, and the morning air smelled freshly of salt and sand. He sat on his stone in an attitude of complete ease, as if he had not a care in the world—which at that moment he did not. He had found there was something about being in Kim Thi's presence which caused all other cares to fall away or dwindle into unimportance.

"Captain Salinem said it was an accident," Brindle explained as he watched her preparing a pot of rice. "Can you believe that?"

"He go now?" Kim Thi asked.

Brindle took a sip of his tea. It was too hot.

"In about a month. It will take that long for Jakarta to send out a replacement."

"One month," Kim Thi mused. "Many days."

"Not so long," Brindle said. "At least we'll be rid of him."

"Yes." Kim Thi smiled, but she did not appear reassured.

"And . . ." Brindle began to say that Michele Fallon was returning, but he stopped himself. There was no point in complicating matters. It seemed nearly impossible that Michele had been gone for only three weeks. Brindle took a sip of his tea and gazed at Kim Thi thoughtfully. *She and her family would be moving on to the Philippines in a month or two*, he told himself, *and where would that leave him?* There was no need to answer this question, for he had known all along where that would leave him—had known since his first meeting with Kim Thi. The emotion didn't last, he told himself bitterly. Only the memory would remain, and even that would be transformed over time into something unrelated to the original feeling. *People shaped the memories of their past to fit their needs in the present*, he told himself. So, he thought with condescension—if one could really speak to oneself with condescension at any given time, weren't we really speaking not to ourselves but to those past physical and emotional reactions we had experienced? Did it happen the way he remembered? he asked himself. Or had he changed and molded it into something else—a distortion of that rainy night, the truck, the terrified hands gripping his arm . . . ?

"More tea?" Kim Thi asked, holding out the battered pot of water.

"No, thank you," Brindle said.

"You think about something?" she asked, watching his eyes.

Brindle rubbed his side. "No," he said, feeling that he had slipped for a moment, but that he was all right again. "Only that I want to keep you safe."

"Safe?"

"Yes. Where no one can hurt you."

"United States," Kim Thi said. "All okay in United States."

"You think so?"

Kim Thi patted his hand. "USA big country. Much money. Freedom. No communists."

"I suppose not."

"We no here forever, John," she explained. "Sometime go Philippines. Bad thing happen, yes, but we no stay forever."

He knew this was true, but still, her presence in his life was slowly making a place which would leave another void when she departed. *But that was thinking in terms of the living John Brindle*, he told himself. As the existing John Brindle, there was no hope of ever filling the void, but only living for a brief moment in the slight flicker of pleasure that she could offer him.

"I have to go," he said. "The helicopter from Jakarta is coming in this morning."

She did not quite catch all of this.

"Helicopter," he repeated.

"Oh, choppa," she said. "Choppa come today?"

"Yes."

"Make big noise."

"Terrible," Brindle commented. "But it's the fastest way to get anywhere from here."

"You go?" she asked with some concern.

"No, no. I'm meeting a friend." At least he hoped this were true. Was Michele still a friend? He would find out soon enough.

"You come back tonight, John?" she asked.

"I don't know. I may have to deliver a baby this evening." Kim Thi did not understand.

"Baby," Brindle explained. "A woman is going to have a baby." He had left word for Tran to contact him at Kim Thi's hut if the Montagnard woman's delivery progressed faster than expected, but nothing had happened so far.

Kim Thi laughed and said something to her mother.

"What's so funny?" Brindle asked.

"My mother help many babies come out," Kim Thi said. "She work this job."

Her mother said something.

"She say you make good helper too."

Brindle smiled. "Tell her it's not the kind of helping I like."

When Kim Thi translated this, Mrs. Van Quang looked puzzled for a moment, but then she began to laugh and chatter away.

"She say all men same," Kim Thi translated. "Vietnamese, American. All same. Want same thing."

"I'm glad you can laugh about it," Brindle said.

ᢍᕽᢍ

The helicopter stirred up a cloud of sand and palm fronds as it touched down in the clearing. Brindle watched with Aldridge from the tree line as the door opened and Michele stepped out. She came toward them with her head down, and Brindle saw the dark blonde hair held by a young hand, the white blouse, tropical flowered skirt, tanned legs, and leather sandals. She cradled a package under her arm. Behind her the pilot was busy unloading the supplies.

"Welcome back," Aldridge said and gave her a hug.

"It went fast," Michele said, looking at Brindle. "Hello, John."

"You've cut your hair," he said.

"You know me," she laughed, "always on the cutting edge of fashion."

Indeed, Michele did look healthy and happy, and Brindle wondered sympathetically how long it would last. He did not believe it was possible to beat the stagnant corruption of Boromu Island, but perhaps Michele had found a way, for she certainly appeared to be refreshed.

"Here," she said, holding out the package to him. "I hope it's what you had in mind."

"I'm sure it is," Brindle replied somewhat awkwardly, for he had caught a glimpse of hurt in her eyes, a restrained emotion. Had he been insensitive in asking her to purchase the dress for Kim Thi? he wondered. Did she still care for him, or was that look simply from memory—the way one might gaze fondly at a photograph of a place which would never be revisited?

"Thank you," he said.

"What is it?" Aldridge asked.

"Just a little something I asked Michele to pick up for me in Manila."

"And you got all the supplies?"

"Yes," Michele replied. "And I walked them through customs just as you asked."

"Great," Aldridge said. "Then we should have everything we need."

"Let me help you," Brindle offered, taking her bag.

They walked down the path toward her bungalow through the rain-dampened foliage. Walking beside her as he had so often in the past, Brindle caught a scent of Michele's perfume and it brought back with a kind of enveloping remorse all the evenings of loneliness and depression. How could someone so lovely and young be associated with sadness? Brindle wondered. Of course it was only from his perspective. Could there have been a time when the sight of her brought him happiness?

"So, you're okay?" she asked, not looking at him but gazing steadily ahead on the path.

"In reference to what?" he said obstinately.

"I was hoping . . ." but she let that fall, the sentence fading in the hard tropical light. Whatever she had been hoping would remain unsaid, perhaps because the mention of it would bring back that look in her eyes. Brindle felt instinctively that he wanted to start anew with Michele, meaning that he would establish a new relationship between them with her arrival. He would not mention anything of the past, nor share the feelings he had experienced on those miserable drunken nights when she had been present. If she wanted to talk about religion, he would not try to stop her. There was no harm in discussing something that you have given up.

"The ribs are feeling better," he offered.

"That was a brave thing to do, John."

"I don't know," he said as they reached her bungalow. "Isn't courage nullified when you have nothing to lose?"

Immediately, he regretted having spoken. Hadn't he just promised himself to avoid the old attitude, the old bitterness? Would Michele perceive that he had changed when he continued to speak negatively?

"How are things going with Captain Salinem?" she asked.

"He hates me."

"Then you're lucky he's leaving next month."

Brindle set her bags on the terrace. He still had Kim Thi's dress under his arm, and it felt as awkward to him now as an obtrusive person.

"If I wake up dead some morning, you'll know who did it."

"That's not funny."

"It could be," he said. "Just think of his greasy hair."

Michele looked at Brindle searchingly, her blue eyes settled on his. For a moment there was tenderness in her gaze, but then it changed.

"Well," she sighed. "It was a long trip and I've got a lot of work to do."

"I'm sure you're tired," he said. "I'll see you at dinner."

"Oh, I almost forgot," she added. "I got you that case of tequila. I'll have one of the boys deliver it to your room."

"I'd rather you didn't," he said without hesitation. "Could you just hold onto it for me? I'll let you know if I want it."

"Things have changed," she commented.

Brindle walked back to the clearing to help Tran with the medical supplies. With Michele's arrival, a certain amount of reason and justification had returned to the camp. He would take her aside soon, perhaps after dinner, and tell her about Kim Thi. Once she understood how much he cared for this young Vietnamese woman and how much Kim Thi had affected his life, then surely Michele would be supportive. That would put an end to the awkwardness and bring every-thing into the open. He had not told Aldridge about the rela-tionship, but Brindle felt the need to speak now. It surged within him like something physical, and it was not something petty or dirty, but something joyous, pure, without conflicts or the usual restraints.

When he reached the clearing, he saw Tran backing up the camp truck.

"That's good enough," Brindle said, holding up a hand.

"Many supplies, Doctor," Tran called happily. "Do much good."

"If the ants don't get them first."

"All time kill ants," Tran said. "Be okay now."

Brindle picked up one of the boxes and slipped it onto the truck bed.

"I wish all our problems were that easy to get rid of," he commented.

"Spray, spray, no more ants," Tran said, laughing.

As Brindle picked up the next box, he saw Captain Salinem coming through the trees on the far side of the clear-ing. The officer did not speak to them as he passed but gave

Brindle a withering look of contempt and kept walking. Brindle was curious about where Salinem was going and stopped to watch. With a feeling of dread, he saw the Indonesian climb the steps to Michele's bungalow and knock. When she opened the door, they spoke for a moment and then he stepped inside.

"Michele," Brindle muttered, shaking his head.

He tried to catch her alone before dinner, but she seated herself quickly at the table and entered into a discussion of Japanese politics with Aldridge. The discussion seemed to drag on interminably, and as he watched them, not talking himself or even listening really, but only waiting his chance, Brindle had time to study Michele. It seemed to him that Michele had become charming yet distant during her three weeks in Manila. Perhaps they were only going through the formality of friendship now, he told himself. Perhaps you could not go back to a friendship after the feelings of romantic love had entered, even if the romance was felt by only one person. And of course, he told himself, that was a presumption on his part.

After coffee had been served, he thought he saw his chance. Aldridge had excused himself for a moment and Michele had taken her cup over to the window. Brindle moved up beside her.

"I've been wanting to speak with you," he began, the words feeling totally foreign in his mouth. Was that from embarrassment or bitterness? he wondered. And what did he have to be bitter about concerning Michele Fallon?

Brindle hesitated. "I wanted to talk to you about . . . Kim Thi."

"Is that the girl you bought the dress for?" Michele asked.

"Yes."

"I think we've talked about her before, haven't we? Wasn't she the one with the infected arm?"

"Right," Brindle said, frowning. Why was this so difficult? Did he subconsciously have a problem with the relationship? Was there somewhere hidden in his innermost self a feeling that a patient/doctor relationship was wrong? Was it because Kim Thi was a refugee? Because Michele was a fellow staff member? Or was it none of the above? Was it simply that he had trouble expressing his emotions to others—especially Michele?

Brindle did not know, but he was determined to continue.

"I wanted to explain . . ." he began, but at that moment one of the mess workers came up to him with a note.

"You should get yourself a pager," Michele suggested.

"I had one, but it was ruined by the dampness."

Brindle read the note.

"One of the refugee women has gone into labor. I've been expecting it all day," he said.

"Delivering a baby. How sweet."

"I have to go."

"Of course, Monsieur Docteur," she said. "I'm sure your horse is waiting."

"Can we talk later?"

"You know where I live."

And so does someone else, he thought, as he hurried across the courtyard to the clinic.

∿

The Montagnard baby decided to enter the world at a quarter past two in the morning. It did not yet know about time or fatigue, but only that the moment for entry into the world had come. Brindle had been dozing in a chair by the delivery room door when he felt the gentle shake of a hand.

"Contractions come more quickly now, Doctor," Tran said as Brindle roused. "Maybe you take look."

Brindle entered the delivery room and saw that the woman's eyes were closed. She was in the midst of a contraction and was breathing in short gasps. He checked her and found that she was dilated to six centimeters.

"Ready?" the aide asked as she stood beside him with a tray.

"Not yet," Brindle said, yawning. "This is her first child. It may take a bit longer."

The aide did not understand this but gazed at the mother with concern. There was no need for explanation.

Twenty minutes passed.

"Tran?" Brindle said.

"Yes, Doctor?"

"Check her pulse."

Tran put his thumb and forefinger to the woman's wrist and gazed at his watch. "Pulse okay."

"And her blood pressure?" Brindle felt a gnawing sense that there was something wrong with this delivery, yet he could not identify the problem—if there were any.

"Pressure okay too, Doctor," Tran responded, but then he hesitated. "No, wait. Begin drop a little."

"Dropping?"

"Yes, Doctor. Go down."

Brindle mentally scanned a list of reasons why the woman's blood pressure might drop. Then a chill came to him, and he gazed down at his gloved hands.

"No!"

The woman had begun to bleed vaginally.

"Something wrong?" Tran asked.

"I think she's got placenta praevia," Brindle said.

"Bad thing, Doctor?"

"Very bad. If I only had an ultrasound!"

Brindle wiped his forehead with the back of his arm.

"Doctor. . ?"

"Let me think," Brindle snapped.

With an ultrasound he could have checked to see the condition of the placenta. If it were only a slight hemorrhage, he would prefer to wait for a short time and deliver the baby vaginally. But if the bleeding was severe, she could bleed out in a couple of minutes. The woman's anemia intensified the situation.

He had to find out what was happening inside the womb, but how could he do that without an ultrasound?

C'mon, John, he muttered to himself.

An idea came to him.

"Okay," he said. "I think I've got it. We can inject radio opaque dye into her bladder through a catheter and give her an x-ray. Iodine is a heavy molecule, resistant to x-rays. We'll have to use a water soluble dye. So what do we have that contains iodine?"

Tran and the aide gazed at him helplessly.

Brindle examined the woman again. The bleeding was steady but light.

"Metrizamide liquid!" he said suddenly. "I think we've got some. Tran, get her set up on the x-ray machine. I'll get the dye and the catheter."

"Yes, Doctor."

Within three minutes Brindle had prepared the dye and had inserted the catheter. He waited impatiently as Tran took the x-ray. He was just holding the negative up to the examination light when the aide came into the x-ray room. She said something hurriedly in Vietnamese.

"She say bleeding worse, Doctor," Tran explained.

Brindle dropped the x-ray and ran into the delivery room. The vaginal bleeding had intensified dramatically. "We have no choice now," he said. "If we don't do a C-section, we'll lose both the mother and baby."

"Prep for surgery?" Tran asked.

"Make it fast," Brindle ordered. "There's no time."

"Chloroform?"

"That would kill her quick," Brindle said. "And a general anesthetic is too dangerous with anemia. We've got to give her open-drop ether."

"I get, Doctor."

While Tran administered the ether, Brindle searched for clamps. If the woman was bleeding out, he would need them to stop the arterial side. He would need three.

"She all asleep," Tran offered.

"Okay," Brindle said. "Here we go."

He made a classic incision, running his scalpel right down the middle through the belly wall and uterus. It took him about two minutes. But was it fast enough?

"I've got the baby," he said after a moment, lifting the child into the aide's waiting hands. She took the baby and quickly cut the umbilical cord. Tran was waiting to clear the mucous membranes.

"She's bleeding out!" Brindle said.

"What can do, Doctor?" Tran asked.

"If I can get it clamped," he said. He placed two of the clamps, but the third kept slipping off.

The woman was going into shock.

"Pulse dropping," Tran said. "Blood pressure dropping."

"I need six hands and a defibrilator!" Brindle shouted.

"Pulse gone, Doctor."

She had gone into cardiac arrest.

Brindle began CPR and continued for five minutes.

"It's no use," he said finally, glancing at the clock. "She's gone."

"Not your fault, Doctor," Tran offered. "This hill woman very sick. No chance."

Brindle examined the baby. The Apgar scores were normal, and she appeared to be healthy.

"She looks good," he said as the aide wrapped the baby girl in a blanket. "Where's the father?"

"No father," Tran explained. "Father step on mine in Phuong Hoang Pass."

Brindle sighed. "Looks like she's on the long road to adoption." He pulled off his scrubs wearily. "I was going to talk to someone tonight. Now it's too late."

"You talk in morning," Tran suggested. "All same."

"Yes," Brindle said, flicking off the operating lights. "All same."

Chapter Fourteen

The Indonesian patrol pushed up the jungle path at daybreak and moved toward the higher ground of Boromu's central plateau. After the monsoons, the vegetation smelled heavily of decay, and their boots, wet from the dampened leaves and plants which slapped at them as they walked, sank in the soft mud of the path. They were five miles from camp, and it had taken them half the night to reach this point—a mile or so north of the ambush site where the three refugees had been shot the month before. The men in this patrol were not the same as those who had fired on the refugees, though of course they had heard of the incident. In fact, none of them seemed to know exactly who had done the shooting on that previous patrol. It seemed as if the soldiers involved had been sworn to secrecy. The patrol now moved in single file, not talking but slapping loudly at mosquitoes from time to time and stopping occasionally to remove leeches from each other's necks or other exposed areas of skin. They were half a mile from the road when the point man squatted and held up his hand to halt. The others joined him, and they talked in hushed voices.

"Smoke," said the point man.

"Where?" asked a soldier behind him.

"I don't know, but I can smell it."

"There," said another man.

The patrol split into two groups. The first group moved up the path about fifty meters and then cut to the right. The second group stepped off the path and headed cautiously toward the smoke. Pushing through the dense brush and trees until the vegetation began to thin out, they came to a small rocky clearing. On the edge of the clearing, which was no more than twenty meters across, was a small campfire and a shelter made of leaves and branches. The fire had been doused, but the embers were still warm. One of the soldiers squatted beside the fire and examined it carefully. Not one but many fires had been made in the area between the stones. The soldiers began to fan out and search for tracks in the brush.

While the patrol was searching the campsite, a dark figure, who only minutes before had been squatting complacently beside the fire, slipped on a patch of rotted leaves, tumbled down the slope, and then jumped up and began running again. From time to time he glanced over his shoulder or stopped altogether and listened intently to determine if he were being followed. *It was fortunate for him that those Indonesian dogs were so noisy on patrol*, he told himself, *or they might have caught him.* As it was, he had just had enough time to douse his campfire and take off through the trees. He doubted that they would be able to track him, but he was not taking any chances. He had already made several converts among the refugees who were to meet him that night—men who had changed their minds about betraying the great dream of Vietnam and its communist leaders. He would use them to cause trouble for the camp. The converts—he actually still thought of them as traitors—believed they would return to Vietnam with him, but that had never been an option. He had come to Boromu Island alone, and he would return the same way. The traitors would be dealt with at that time.

He moved on through the trees until he came to a small stream. He would wait here until the late afternoon, he decided, and then head for the camp. He would be there at nightfall, just in time for the meeting. His fingers itched to kill another guard, and he touched the knife on his belt instinctively. *It was just a matter of time now*, he told himself. Soon he would be off this island, and the camp would be left in flames. From his breast pocket he pulled out a small black book, its pages soggy from the constant dampness, and began to read a course on Marxism. From time to time he glanced up the slope in the direction of his old camp, but there were no sounds of approaching soldiers, only the chattering of birds in the trees and insects along the stream.

"It is as I thought," he muttered to himself in Vietnamese. Closing the little book carefully, he returned it to his pocket and buttoned the flap. He needed to begin thinking about the meeting this evening. There was much to be done and he had to be careful. A white butterfly floated across the stream and settled on a bush near him. He held out his finger, but the butterfly did not move. When he touched the edge of the wing, the insect fluttered into the air. The butterfly reminded him of what Ho Chi Minh had said about fighting the French in the early days of the revolution. Minh had called it a conflict between a grasshopper and an elephant. Now I am the grasshopper, the man thought, and I will make the elephant pay for his intervention. He watched as the butterfly disappeared into the tall reeds. Then he began making plans that would affect everyone at Boromu Refugee Camp.

～⁓

"You look very handsome now, Doctor," Tran said as he stood back and regarded Brindle. The Vietnamese assistant held a pair of scissors and a comb in his hands.

"Is there anything you don't know how to do?" Brindle asked as he felt the back of his neck.

Tran tapped the comb to the side of his face thoughtfully. "When communists come, I do many job, Doctor. But I never drive taxi. All time, never drive taxi."

"You sound like you regret it," Brindle commented, brushing the hair away from his shoulders.

"Taxi driver good job. Meet people, go all time, see many places."

"And get robbed or shot."

"Not so bad," Tran said. "No work in rice paddies. No leeches. No snakes."

"I see your point." Brindle stood up.

"You go see Miss Van Quang now?"

"Yes."

"Miss Fallon back . . ."

"I know," Brindle said.

Tran removed the sheet from around Brindle's shoulders. "She good lady."

"I know she's a good lady," Brindle said. "We've had this conversation before."

"Okay."

"How's that Montagnard baby doing?"

Tran took a broom from the railing and began to sweep the snippets of Brindle's hair off the terrace.

"She okay, Doctor. Aides take care of her."

"Well, then," Brindle said. "I'm off."

"Miss Fallon . . ."

Brindle ignored him and walked down the path to the camp.

He had wanted to look his best when he gave Kim Thi her present. It was, after all, a special occasion. He had never done this before. Yes, he had given many presents in his lifetime, but this was something new. Brindle regarded the giving of this package as the first in a series of special things he meant to do for Kim Thi. He realized it was probably a sophomoric gesture—this getting cleaned up and giving her a dress as if they were going to a prom or on a first date—but he did not care. How long had it been since his last drink? he wondered. Ten days. That gave him a chill—that he had known instantly how long it had been. Still, he thought, it had been ten days and that was something.

He had chosen to visit Kim Thi just before sunset because he wanted her to see the dress in the light. Often he waited until after dinner to visit and drink the proverbial cup of tea.

Through the palm trees now he could see the sun still high above the water.

He was mildly disappointed when he reached her hut and she was not there. She was probably on the beach, he thought, and headed in that direction.

Kim Thi was sitting at the water's edge with several other women. They had built a lean-to from palm branches to provide shade and were talking. Kim Thi sat with her arms around her knees. Beside her was a wicker basket with a pot of rice on top of it. The women turned and looked at Brindle as he appoached.

"Hello," Brindle said, flushing. He continued to be embarrassed by these situations—especially now that he had come for a special purpose. He felt as if he were a teenager meeting his date's family for the first time.

"Hello, John," Kim Thi replied, smiling. "We talk about America."

"That should be interesting."

"Hope go soon." She then translated into Vietnamese for the benefit of the other women. They all nodded in agreement.

Brindle knelt beside her. The tide was coming up, leaving a line of foam just beyond their feet.

"I have something for you," he said, tapping the package under his arm.

Kim Thi's eyes brightened. "For me?"

"Yes," Brindle said, looking at the other women who sat gazing at him with unveiled curiosity. "Can we go back to your hut?"

Kim Thi picked up her basket, and he walked beside her toward the camp. It was pleasant, he decided as they moved across the sand, for the two of them to be doing ordinary things—like just walking along as if they were any other couple. He had come to realize that people who had someone took so much for granted. He wanted to hold Kim Thi's hand but could still feel the beady gaze of the women behind him. Also, her hands were busy with the basket and pot of rice.

"May I carry something for you?" he asked.

Kim Thi smiled. "All okay."

She took a narrow path through the trees, her feet moving with practiced casualness over a clump of twisted roots, as if she had made this journey a hundred times, and perhaps she had. Brindle realized that if his world was small—defined by the boundaries of the jungle west of the clinic and the beach— then hers was even smaller.

"So," he said, after she had put down her things, "here it is."

Kim Thi took the package and unwrapped the paper. He had expected to see some sign of delight or pleasure on her face as the paper fell away and revealed the dress, but whatever emotions transpired within her did not show. In fact, as she turned the pale blue cloth over in her hands slowly, the fingers examining the material, he felt let down. He had expected something more. Perhaps she did not like the dress, he told himself, or perhaps she did not have a need for it. Anyway. . .

"I put on," she said, interrupting his thoughts. "You see."

Brindle sat beside the cook fire and waited while Kim Thi slipped into her hut and put on the dress. Through the trees, he watched the sun dip below the horizon and the sea change color from green to slate gray. Just out there, he told himself, was Borneo and then Malaysia, and then the Philippines. It didn't seem so far away now. "*He who has ears to hear, let him hear*," the voice replayed in his thoughts.

"Okay?" Kim Thi asked, standing before him.

Brindle had not thought about styles. Michele had chosen a dress that looked as if it must have been from China. It was sleeveless with a rounded neck. Very demure but on either side was a slit that ran nearly up to the hips. Kim Thi had overcome this problem of delicacy by wearing a long white skirt under the dress. The total effect was one of refined attractiveness.

"You look like a princess," Brindle said, smiling.

"Thank you," Kim Thi said. "Good for puppets?"

"Perfect."

"When we go?"

"Saturday."

"Then I put away," she said. "No get dirty."

On his way back to the clinic, Brindle thought about asking Michele why she had chosen that particular dress. It was not what he had anticipated. He had pictured Kim Thi wearing a cotton summer dress, but he had not mentioned this to Michele, only that the dress was to be a light shade of blue. That was his mistake, he realized; he should have been more specific. Anyway, it was incredible how Kim Thi had been able to transform the dress into something beautiful. So he would not mention anything to Michele about his disappointment. He still wished to talk with Michele about Kim Thi and did not want anything to discourage their conversation.

She was not at the mess hall when he arrived for dinner, however, which roused his suspicions and also caused him to feel a twinge of disappointment. He realized that he had been looking forward to speaking with Michele—not just speaking but finally confiding with her in a way in which she had always hoped.

"Where's Michele?" he asked Aldridge.

"I'm not sure," the administrator answered, breaking off a piece of bread and dipping it in his soup.

"And Salinem?"

"I doubt that we'll be seeing him again at dinner. He hates us, you know."

"All of us?" Brindle asked. "I thought it was just me."

"Well, you most of all, certainly, but I'm sure he has hostile feelings towards us all."

"Including Michele?"

Aldridge looked at Brindle inquisitively. "What do you mean, John?"

"I saw Captain Salinem visiting her bungalow yesterday."

"Really?" Aldridge asked, sounding surprised.

"I'm sure it's nothing," Brindle said, but at the same moment an ugly image of Captain Salinem's greasy hair pressed against her soft white cheek began to run through his mind. He immediately lost his appetite and pushed away the bowl of fish soup. Where could she be? he wondered. At the office? He had just decided to get up and go find her when a hand squeezed his shoulder.

"I'm sorry about the Montagnard woman, John," Michele said sympathetically, standing behind him. "I know how hard that must have been for you." She was carrying a stack of folders under one arm while balancing her dinner in her hands. Apparently she had been at the office. He felt relieved and disgusted with himself at the same time.

"Yes," he responded. His first thought had been to say something flippant or negative, but some new kind of self-restraint had caused him to answer truthfully. It *had* been difficult. As he had struggled helplessly in the operating room while the poor woman bled to death, he had thought of Kim Thi. Would all suffering refugees from now on remind him of her? he wondered.

"So now what?" Michele asked as she finished her plate of rice and vegetables and the mess worker came with the coffee. Brindle had not eaten but had sat quietly while Michele and Aldridge finished.

"You're not going to stay healthy if you don't eat, John," Michele said.

"I had some soup," he said, but the thought turned his stomach. He had never been able to eat when he was anxious.

"Would you like to go for a walk?"

"Fine."

"I have some work to do," Aldridge interjected. "Perhaps we can meet later for a game, John?"

"Can I get a rain check on that?" Brindle asked. "I was up most of the night with that delivery, and I'm beginning to come down fast."

"If you're too tired . . ." Michele added.

"No," Brindle said. "I could use some fresh air. I just don't know if I'm up to challenging this old buzzard. He's ruthless, you know."

"Okay." Aldridge laughed. "We'll put off the massacre until tomorrow."

Brindle and Michele walked down to the beach. Through the palm trees they could see fires glowing dimly in the camp and the shadows of people moving around them. Above their heads the stars were shining bright.

"A clear night sky," Michele remarked. "How wonderful."

"The West Monsoons are supposed to end in late February," Brindle commented. "The East Monsoons don't begin until June."

"Maybe my clothes will finally dry out," Michele said.

"And the bed sheets," Brindle added.

"And my shoes."

They walked along the beach in silence for a few minutes. Brindle listened to the steady roll of the surf, not knowing where or how to begin.

"So," Michele said finally. "We were going to talk about Miss Van Quang."

"Her name is Kim Thi."

"That's very pretty."

Moonlight glimmered off the wet sand. The beach ahead of them sparkled.

"I wanted to explain," he said.

Michele leaned against him as she took off her sandals and began to walk in the surf.

"It isn't necessary, John. I was happy to get the dress for you. I hope it fits."

"It's great," he said. "I just wanted you to know . . . to understand what has been happening to me lately."

Michele stepped over a piece of driftwood. "I'm listening."

Where to begin? Brindle thought. "I never meant for anything to happen," he said. "She was just another patient with a curious injury. Well, I don't know if that's true. I noticed her when she was getting off the launch at the dock."

"What did you notice?"

Brindle paused. How could he describe to Michele that undefinable quality which had attracted him to Kim Thi? Would she understand that he had instantly sensed the innocence, the need to be protected, the femininity? It would never come out right if he tried to describe it in those words. He was talking about feelings, not literary clichés. So he would not try, and perhaps that was for the best.

"I don't know," he lied. "There is just something special about her."

Michele folded her arms as if she were cold.

"And now you're in love with her," she stated.

Brindle hesitated for a moment. "Yes."

Michele stopped walking and looked out at the darkness of the sea.

"Is this supposed to be making me feel better?"

"I was this close from the edge," Brindle said earnestly, holding his thumb and forefinger so close that they were nearly touching. "That's why I wanted to tell you. I've felt myself falling into that black oblivion a hundred times."

"And meeting her pulled you back?"

"Yes."

"How?"

"Just by being there."

"I tried to be there for you. Wasn't that enough to pull you back?"

"It should have been, Michele, but for some reason it wasn't. I don't know why."

"The reason is obvious."

"Yes," he said. "It is."

The walk back to Michele's bungalow seemed to take hours. She did not speak but moved ahead of him silently on the path. Watching her white blouse moving in and out of the shadows, he thought of all the times she had taken his arm under just these circumstances. Now she no longer needed or wanted his support.

"Goodnight," he said when they had reached her door. "Thanks for listening."

She turned the knob. "I'll see you in the morning," she said softly, closing the door behind her. He was left standing alone in the fading moonlight. A storm was blowing in, and he could feel the change in wind direction and moisture in the air.

"I thought it was too good to be true," he muttered, heading for the clinic. He would make a final check on his patients and if nothing required his attention, he would go back to his room and get some sleep. The night duty aide glanced up at him from her magazine as he entered.

"Pen?" she asked.

"What? Oh, no," he answered. "Just checking on the patients." He walked along the row of beds in the ward. They were all sleeping or resting quietly, and he returned to the night duty station and then the terrace.

Later, he could not recall what he had been thinking as he walked along the side of the clinic to his bungalow, but he did remember the jump his heart had taken when he saw something move on his terrace. He had frozen in mid-stride then, barely breathing, as his eyes focused on whatever it was that had budged. It moved again. Someone or something was waiting beside his door.

Brindle was just turning back to the clinic when he heard a voice whisper his name.

"Docteur Brindle."

He had to think now. Would someone be calling his name if it were a trap?

The whisper sounded again.

"Docteur."

The pronunciation was Vietnamese.

"Yes?" he called.

There was no reply.

"Tran?"

Silence, though he could feel the presence of someone in the shadows just to the right of the steps. A floorboard groaned slightly.

"Who is it?"

The figure stood up and he could just make out a profile in the moonlight.

"Duong?"

The figure nodded without speaking.

"You scared me to death," Brindle exclaimed. "Come inside."

When the door was opened, the young refugee moved quickly into the room. He was obviously very frightened and began to speak slowly in Vietnamese, apparently trying to make the doctor understand. The words came out like wind chimes in a breeze, but Brindle could not follow them.

"I'm sorry," Brindle said, shaking his head. "I can't understand . . ."

"Nguyen," Duong said in a frantic whisper. "Nguyen."

Brindle's stomach turned cold.

"Vo Nguyen?" he asked.

Duong nodded and pointed in the direction of the camp.

"Oh, no." Brindle sighed and walked to the door. He glanced outside to the darkness where a steady rain was beginning to fall, warm, unrelenting, and oblivious to his needs or cares. It was as if someone had opened a box and let out something evil into the night wind. The evil had settled into the moisture of the air and gave Brindle a chill.

"Where?" he asked, closing the door in an effort to keep out the evil. But Duong only gazed at him blankly.

"Okay," he said, motioning the young man to a chair. "It's truth time. I'll get Tran."

"Nguyen," Duong repeated, fumbling nervously with his hands.

"I know," Brindle said. "I'll be right back."

Even as Brindle hurried through the darkness to get Tran, sheltering his face from the rain, he felt that something had changed within the very nature of the camp. It was as if he were an animal which had inadvertently wandered into a trap without knowing or sensing danger, and even now, without feeling pain or fear, was caught, doomed to a fate beyond his control. But then, he told himself with disgust, he had been in that trap for the past two years and had felt it pushing and pushing, the teeth getting nearer and nearer until he could practically smell it. Still, he had done nothing. Was that because somewhere along the line he had realized the futility of fighting? Had he really acquiesced to the point where he continued on numbly, simply waiting for the blow to strike? He felt some lack of capability when he thought of this. How could he have gotten himself into this situation without realizing at some point the danger involved?

No, he muttered to himself. *I never did*. And perhaps that was more painful to him than any conscious action, for it betrayed a weakness in everything he had thought and planned. Once he began to doubt his logical thinking, was there anything else left on which he could rely? *Yes*, he told himself, his medical training. He had learned medicine like any other craftsman and was able to help the refugees because of this in a very practical way. Sometimes he wished he had never gotten involved in human relationships but wanted instead only to go on treating patients and confining himself to his room—and, he thought resignedly, to his bottle when things got bad. Ahead he could see the light on in Tran's room.

"You right, Doctor," Tran said after questioning Duong. "He see Vo Nguyen tonight in camp. Not dead."

"I had hoped . . ." Brindle began.

"Other dead man mistake," Tran offered. "Not Vo Nguyen."

"I guess not," Brindle said, glancing at Duong. "What was he doing in camp?"

Tran spoke to Duong for a moment.

"He meet with men," Tran explained. "Refugees who want go back Vietnam."

"Is that all?" Brindle asked.

"No."

"What are they going to do?"

"Nguyen no say, but Duong think he make big trouble."

"We've got to catch him."

"Maybe possible, Doctor," Tran said. "Nguyen return to camp again tomorrow night."

"Great," Brindle said. "Does Duong know where they're going to meet?"

"No," Tran replied. "All time different place."

"Okay," Brindle said, thinking. "We've got to keep this very quiet. Tell him not to speak to anyone else about Nguyen."

"He no talk," Tran said confidently.

"I'm sure," Brindle said, watching Duong's hands moving nervously, the fingers seeking each other as if for reassurance.

Brindle glanced at his watch. It was nearly midnight. "Take him back to your room and keep him there. All day tomorrow too. I don't want anyone to know where he is. Okay?"

Tran nodded and spoke to Duong. The young refugee stood up, and together they stepped out into the rain. Brindle closed the door after them and sat thinking on the edge of his bed. It was time to inform Aldridge, he told himself. But not until morning. Aldridge had not yet completely recovered from his bout with malaria, and he needed his sleep. If Brindle went over there now and told him about Nguyen, the administrator would be up the rest of the night. Anyway, Brindle told himself, nothing could be done until the following day.

Chapter Fifteen

"I can't believe it," Aldridge said wearily. "I thought we had that business cleared up. You said we had a positive ID." He rinsed his razor under the tap in his room and gazed speculatively at his half-shaven face. The left side was still covered in foam. Brindle had arrived before breakfast, and the administrator was busy shaving.

"I thought so too," Brindle said with some feeling of truth.

"So we're back to ground zero."

"Not quite. We know he'll be in camp tonight."

"Yes," Aldridge said. "I'll inform Captain Salinem."

"I'd like to sit in on the meeting if I could," Brindle suggested.

Aldridge rinsed his face and reached for a towel. "I don't think so, John. We don't need any more complications."

"I didn't start this, Hal. You know that."

"Of course not. I just think it would be better . . ."

"Okay, okay," Brindle said. "Just remind him that they meet after dark and never in the same place. They won't be in the camp proper but out in the jungle somewhere. I imagine they'll be on the north or west side. Probably not the south. It's too close to the barracks."

"I'll tell him," Aldridge said.

There was a dryness in the morning air which Brindle felt immediately as he stepped out of Aldridge's room. He lingered for a moment and ran his hands through his hair. It had been another long night, but he did not feel so bad this morning. Perhaps that was from the absence of alcohol in his system. Or perhaps it was because of an idea which had occurred to him during the night. He had been lying in his bed, trying to sleep as usual, when he began to think about the Montagnard baby. Since her delivery and the death of her mother, he and the child had shared the same destiny of having lost a loved one. *If fate had brought them together, then why shouldn't they continue on that way?* Brindle asked himself. As the presiding physician, it was his responsibility to fill out the birth certificate. All he had to do was put down his own name as the birth father and the child would not only be legally his but also have American citizenship. If he were really going to raise her as his own, then what could be the harm? He knew the life that many orphans lead in Indonesia, the squalor and poverty, the lack of affection and touch. And this baby was not even Indonesian . . . she was a nonentity without nationality or status. She deserved better, and Brindle wanted to give her that chance. *Anyway,* he thought to himself, *it was something to think about.*

Brindle wished he had a new copy of the *San Francisco Chronicle* and a decent cup of coffee. He felt like taking the morning off and just relaxing. He was beginning to wish now that he had taken Michele up on her offer to visit Manila. He really needed to get away from the camp for awhile. But then he wouldn't have been able to spend as much time with Kim Thi. His days with her were dwindling down fast; he could feel it in his stomach. As soon as her name came up on that list for the Philippines she would already be gone mentally. It always happened that way—even with the staff.

Across the courtyard a squad of soldiers were carrying a large roll of tarp toward the helicopter clearing. Another group was carrying poles and rope. *The wayang drama,* Brindle told himself. He had almost forgotten. The performance was Saturday evening. He followed the workers along to the clearing and watched as they laid out the poles and unrolled the tarp.

"I guess I should have gotten a new dress myself," Michele said, walking up the path beside him. "It looks like it's going to be a big deal."

"Of course," Brindle replied, "a wayang drama is a big deal."

"Maybe you could give me a little briefing then—so I'll know what to expect."

"Well," Brindle said thoughtfully, "the typical wayang drama is about royal political intrigue—you know, with a beautiful princess and a prince and kings and an evil advisor. It always ends in a big battle."

"It sounds like something from Disney."

"Much more sinister and symbolic," Brindle said. "Everything in the drama represents something else."

"Like what?"

"I'll explain it to you tomorrow night. Are you going to breakfast?"

Michele smiled. "Actually, I was looking for you."

"I was talking with Hal."

"Yes," she said. "I saw you coming out of his quarters."

The soldiers had the tarp up now and were securing the ropes. Brindle imagined they could fit forty or fifty people under the tarp if it rained.

"I could use a cup of coffee," he said. "Do you mind walking toward the mess hall?"

"All right." Her voice was pleasant, as if a strain had been taken off her during the night. The tenseness and moments of withdrawn silence were gone. She seemed her old self again, and this pleased Brindle. Perhaps things were turning around after all. It had just needed some time.

"I'm sorry about last night, John," she apologized, gazing at him with reticence. "You were sincerely trying to tell me how you felt, and I reverted back to the old forsaken woman."

"You were okay, Michele, really."

"No," she said. "I wasn't."

They had reached the edge of the compound. On the right was the mess hall. Michele plucked a leaf from a passing bougainvillea and brushed it across her cheek. "Isn't it funny how we never seem to fall in love with the people we can talk to the most easily?"

"I never thought about that before," Brindle said, holding the screen door open for her. "Perhaps it's true."

"Maybe it's the lack of mystery."

"Not with me," Brindle scoffed. "I hate mystery."

"So do I," Michele agreed. "Give me plain, dull reality anytime. At least then I know what I'm really getting. And of course, I would have to marry someone with faith."

"I know what I'm getting," Brindle said with a smile.

"What's that?"

"A cup of coffee."

She looked at him, studying his eyes and mouth. "I like to see you smile, John. You do it so rarely."

"I haven't had much to smile about since last night."

He poured a cup of coffee and offered it to Michele.

"No, thank you," she said. "What happened last night?"

Brindle gazed around the mess hall. A worker was mopping the floor in front of the kitchen. "Let's sit over here."

They moved to a table on the far side. Brindle put a spoonful of sugar and a splash of cream into his coffee and began to stir. "It's like the worst thing I can imagine happening right now," he said in a low tone. "The worst thing. And of course it makes me look like a fool—not that that matters."

"Did you blow a diagnosis or something?"

Brindle took a sip of the coffee and suddenly felt an overwhelming remorse sweep over him—unjustified and unexpected—and along with it came images of Kim Thi in every place he had ever seen her in the camp. Perhaps he had never realized until just now how difficult it was going to be to continue existing and working in the camp once she had gone. Every incoming tide, every sway of the palms along the beach, the rain showers, the footpaths, the shanties with their cook fires drifting into the evening air, the sunsets, even the clinic and the smell of antiseptic would remind him of her. And he would have to go on living with that—her presence and the lack of her presence—long after she had departed. He knew it was true, because just now the smell of coffee rather than tea had caused his heart to ache. But why? he wondered. Wasn't he going to take her to the wayang drama tomorrow night? Yes, but that was not the problem. The problem was that each time he was with her now only intensified his feelings—so much so that he would pretend they would always be together, that he would always be able to love and take care of Kim Thi, that even the cackling old Mrs. Van Quang would one day be a part of his family, and that he would be able to help Hoang. But this was not true. It would never happen. With a sudden cold despair, he realized that the more he saw of her now, the more his heart would be torn out when she left. It was quickly becoming a question of protecting himself. But did he want to be protected? Was there anything really to protect?

"No," Brindle answered, as much to himself as to Michele's question. "You remember the body we identified with the mutilated face?"

Michele nodded. "The infiltrator . . ."

"It wasn't him."

"How do you know?"

"Because," Brindle said, "the real guy was spotted in camp last night. He's trying to stir up trouble again."

"Oh, no."

"That's what I was talking to Hal about."

"He must be so angry."

"To say the least. He's probably meeting with Captain Salinem right now. He didn't want me to go with him."

"They've got to get Nguyen this time," Michele said. "If he kills another soldier . . ."

"I know."

"Just when you think it's almost over . . ." she murmured, shaking her head.

"It *is* almost over," Brindle commented, but he was not referring to Vo Nguyen.

∾

After his morning rounds, Brindle went to look for Kim Thi. The ambiguity he always felt around her was beginning to chip away at the joy he felt at being in her company. He needed answers, and if not answers, then at least he needed to pose the questions so that he could not look back later and tell himself that he had never tried. Perhaps it was only a matter of asking. Perhaps he had expressed his interest in her too hesitantly. Whatever. He would find out soon enough.

"Docteur, Docteur," a group of children called to him as he walked along the path through the camp. A boy wearing a dirty straw hat came up and took him by the hand.

"Hi, buddy," Brindle said.

The boy squinted up at him in the sunlight, grinning broadly. When Brindle arrived at Kim Thi's hut, he found her on her knees bending over a pail filled with water. Mrs. Van Quang stood over Kim Thi, her hands covered with shampoo suds. Kim Thi was getting her hair washed.

"Can I be next?" he asked in amusement.

Kim Thi looked up at him and smiled. "You funny all time, John."

"That's the second time in one day," Brindle said. "I must be changing."

"What?"

"Nothing."

Mrs. Van Quang picked up a bucket of water and began to rinse Kim Thi's long dark hair.

"I don't suppose you want to go for a walk?" Brindle asked. "There is something I wanted to ask you."

"Must comb and dry hair first, John," Kim Thi said, closing her eyes as the water ran down the sides of her face. "Then go."

"Okay," Brindle said. "Do you mind if I stay and watch?"

"Watch woman comb hair?" Kim Thi asked. "Not fun."

"It depends. I could watch you doing anything and enjoy it."

Kim Thi picked up a towel and began to gently rub her hair. "You different."

"I hope so." ·

It took much longer than Brindle expected for Kim Thi to comb out her hair and then dry it, but at no time was he bored. When she had finished, Kim Thi changed from her sarong into a blouse and pants, and they headed down a path that followed through the trees toward Surabi Point.

"Too hot on beach now," Kim Thi explained as they walked beneath the trees. "Sun high. Just wash hair. Too hot."

"This is nice," Brindle said.

There was a thump behind him.

"Look," Brindle said. "A coconut."

He picked it up and looked at the tree above his head.

"It would be funny to have traveled all this way only to get whacked by a coconut," he said. "Maybe I should stand here a little longer. Do they fall in pairs?"

Kim Thi examined the coconut. "Good. Okay," she offered.

"Then I'll keep it." He reached for the Swiss Army knife in his shorts, but remembered he had given it to Kim Thi. "I was going to carve our initials," he explained, marking the green skin with his thumbnail.

"No, no," Kim Thi said, laughing. "Eat."

"Okay." Brindle tucked the coconut under his arm.

Through the trees he could see Surabi Point and the lines of waves foaming on the rocks far out to the right.

"You see that wind?" he asked Kim Thi. "Well, just yesterday, or the day before, that same wind was rising off the plains of the Never Never in Australia, and now it's here, blowing the waves onto Surabi Point."

He did not know how much of that Kim Thi understood, but she shaded her eyes and looked obediently at the rocks. They continued on the path through the trees.

"Kim Thi?" Brindle asked, blushing. "Do you mind if I hold your hand?"

"Hold hand?" she repeated. "Okay."

She held out her hand and Brindle took it. The feeling was different from what he had expected. Her skin was dry and cool, and he felt no affection at all from the fingers which intertwined with his. She was simply resting her hand in his because he had asked. This made the asking of his question all the more difficult, because now he had a predilection of the answer she might give him. He felt ridiculous discussing a serious relationship with a woman he had never even hugged.

"Kim Thi," he said again, searching for not only the courage but also the right words. "I was wondering . . ."

She stopped walking and gazed up at him.

"Yes, John?" she asked. She could not have understood the implications of his words, for he had not spoken enough yet to even give her the general direction of his thoughts. But perhaps because she was a woman, she understood the meaning of his actions without speaking. It seemed to him anyway that they had always communicated on a non-verbal level.

"You will be going on to the Philippines soon and . . ."

"Yes," she interjected, "Philippines. Then U.S.A."

Her unselfconscious delight showed no hint that she would miss him.

"I care about you," he continued. "I . . . love you, Kim Thi."

She squeezed his hand. "You good man, John. All time good to me."

"I don't have to work at this camp much longer," he explained. "I can resign, really, at any time."

"You no work here anymore?" she asked. "You go away?"

"Only to be with you," he said, hoping she understood. "When you get to the United States, I want to come see you."

"You come see me?" she asked. "You come my house? Anytime, okay."

"And when I come, Kim Thi, I'll have a question to ask you."

"Anytime, John. Okay."

"I want to know if you'll marry me."

"Marry?" she asked, and he could see her mentally searching for the definition of the word. "You want for wife?"

"Yes. I love you."

Kim Thi reached up and touched his cheek. She ran her fingertips over the sun-wrinkles beside his eyes.

"You good man, John. Make good man for woman. But . . ."

His heart dropped. He had been afraid of just that word, as if anything which came after it could only have one meaning.

"But . . ." she continued. "No good life here. Bad thing happen. New life in States. All new."

"I know that . . ."

She put her hand to his lips. "But you come my house. We see."

"All right," he said, smiling reluctantly. It was, after all, the only response for which he could have realistically hoped. Kim Thi was no sentimental fool or dreamer. Her life was based on harsh reality. "I'll come see you," he said softly.

∾

While Brindle and Kim Thi were walking back from Surabi Point in the fading light, a group of Indonesian soldiers slipped out of their barracks through the south entrance so as not to attract attention. Their plan was to move quietly around the camp to the northwest and then fan out into a string of positions at one hundred meter intervals. They were all in contact by walkie-talkies. Another group of soldiers waited in the jungle on the west side of the clinic. They would be ready if needed. It was the perfect night for an ambush. The weather report predicted that rainstorms would not hit the island until after midnight. By that time, it was expected that Vo Nguyen would be dead and that his co-conspirators would either be scattered or arrested.

Back at the clinic, Brindle paced the floor. So much depended on the soldiers getting Vo Nguyen, he realized, and there was nothing he could do about it. He had not even been informed of the plan. The only thing Aldridge had told him was that there might be casualties.

"Of course there might be casualties," Brindle said, irritated. "What was Salinem's reaction?"

"He didn't seemed to be surprised at all," Aldridge replied. "I don't think he ever really believed that body with the mutilated face was the real man. But it's just one more thing for him. I don't know if he cares."

"Why should he?" Brindle commented. "This is no longer his fight."

To pass the time, Brindle went into the operating room and checked his sterilized equipment. The most logical injury would be a gunshot wound, and he was prepared to deal with at least two at a time. Tran had placed an additional stretcher in the hallway. Brindle walked out to the ward and checked the charts of the patients who had been admitted earlier in the evening. A nine-year-old girl had been suffering from sporadic vomiting and diarrhea, and Brindle was having her checked for intestinal parasites. This malady was more common in the dry season because of poor sanitation and unhealthy drinking water, but there was still a strong possibility. He would know within a few hours.

As he stood beside her bed and studied the chart, he happened to glance up and see that she was awake. Moonlight from the ward window fell upon her face. Brindle was surprised to see that her eyes were wide open and that her features were set in deep concentration. He assumed she was going to be sick again and reached for the bedpan, but then he realized that she was listening to something outside. He walked over to the screened window and stood quietly. For a moment all he could hear was the rustle of palm branches, but then he heard another noise and turned back to the girl. She looked at him and nodded. She had heard it too. The sound was carried on the wind from somewhere in the jungle north of the camp. It seemed to be at least a kilometer away. Brindle tensed as he listened now for the sounds he heard were the popping bursts of automatic weapons.

Chapter Sixteen

It had started at ten o'clock that evening when a soldier at sentry post five had called in to report. A group of refugees were approaching his position, he had whispered into the walkie-talkie. When asked how many, he said there were three. A few minutes later, he reported that more men had arrived. He could not tell how many there were now because of the darkness. He was told to hold his position while the backup group from behind the clinic hurried into place. The number-five man reported again that the refugees were squatted down on a wide area of path and were discussing something. He was too far away, however, to hear what they were saying. From that point on, he was told to maintain radio silence until the backup group arrived.

Fifteen minutes later, the shooting started. A group of soldiers moved in from the east and cut off the infiltrators from the camp. The second group moved straight toward post five from the south. When both groups were in position, so that the number-five man was now linked up with the second group, the order was given to open fire.

The infiltrators, caught on two sides and taken by surprise, had jumped up and began to scatter frantically. One man screamed when he was hit and toppled over. Another was shot in the head as he tried to stand. The order had been given not to let anyone escape, so the firing continued. A young man who had been in the center of the group when the shooting started had scrambled on hands and knees for twenty meters through the undergrowth and then begun to run for his life.

He had kept low and had stumbled often, but each time he had gotten quickly back to his feet and had kept going. At one point he had heard the pop-pop of an automatic rifle nearby and had dropped to the ground and held his breath. Then he had crawled on until he could see the fires of the camp ahead. Reaching the edge of the clearing, he leaned against a rubber tree and tried to slow his breathing. A moment later he heard the snap of footsteps coming toward him from the jungle and pushed away from the tree and moved into the camp. Soon he was indistinguishable from any of the other refugees who moved around the shanties in the darkness, except that as he passed one hut, the gold necklace clutched tightly in his left hand glinted in the firelight.

"They'll be bringing in the casualties soon," Brindle said to Tran as they stood on the clinic terrace and gazed toward the jungle. The firing had stopped some time before, and Brindle could imagine that the soldiers were carrying the wounded on stretchers toward the clinic. As the minutes ticked away, though, a feeling of disbelief slowly settled over him. It was taking too long. Was it possible that no one had been hit—with all that gunfire? Or had there been no survivors? Brindle thought of Captain Salinem and his hatred of communists. He also thought of the Indonesian soldiers and their desire for revenge. He realized that the last few sporadic shots he had heard could have been more than just random firing at escaping refugees.

"Maybe no one hurt," Tran offered. "Or . . ."

"Yes," Brindle interjected. "I think so too."

"But that okay," Tran said. "Communists bad people. Make life in camp no good."

Brindle looked at him. He began to make a comment but then checked himself. He had never lived under communist rule or had his property or business confiscated. None of his family had been killed during the war, nor had he been through ten years of declining economic hardships. So he had no right to criticize or judge Tran. Nevertheless, if the Indonesian soldiers had actually gone around and finished off the wounded, then how could Brindle defend their moral superiority over his own?

Who are you to talk? he asked himself. *Of all people.*

"I'll be at the office," he told Tran, stalking off.

Aldridge was standing on the terrace of the administrative bureau with Michele and gazing in the direction of the shooting.

"Did you hear that?" Brindle asked them.

"Yes," Aldridge responded. "We've been monitoring their radio transmissions. A group of men was spotted on the northwest side of the camp. The soldiers moved in."

"I hope they got him," Michele said.

"There haven't been any casualties," Brindle remarked.

Aldridge rubbed the side of his face nervously.

"I was afraid of that."

"We can't just . . ."

The radio in Aldridge's office crackled, interrupting Brindle.

"Come inside," Aldridge said.

Brindle followed the administrator and Michele into the office and stood listening as the radio crackled again.

"Six dead," Aldridge said, translating.

"Any wounded?"

Aldridge listened for a moment, his head down to the radio speaker.

"No, I don't think so."

"Prisoners?" Michele asked.

"No."

"Then let's hope one of the dead is Nguyen," Brindle said.

Aldridge flicked the handset on the radio.

"Captain Salinem. This is Aldridge, over."

"Yes, Mr. Aldridge," the captain's voice sounded after a moment.

"I think it's important that we try to indentify Nguyen right away."

"I agree," Salinem said. "I will send a squad of men to escort you and your witness to post five."

"We'll be ready," Aldridge said. "Out."

He put down the handset.

"You'd better get Duong," he suggested to Brindle. "And bring a good flashlight. The moon's down. You won't be able to see your hand in front of your face out there now."

Brindle went to Tran's room. Duong was hesitant to go but realized that he had no choice. When they returned to the administrative office, the squad of soldiers were waiting. Michele was standing on the terrace.

"Are you going with us?" Brindle asked her.

"I'm afraid of snakes," she said with a shiver. "Anyway, someone needs to stay by the radio."

Aldridge looked grim. "Let's get going."

They moved north through the compound and along a path that skirted the edge of the camp. Brindle felt an unreal sensation about the experience: walking through an Indonesian jungle in the middle of the night to view the bodies of six men who had been killed in an ambush. It was as if it were happening to someone else—and he wished it were.

They walked on in single file for about twenty minutes. Brindle was perspiring and heard mosquitoes humming around his ears. He kept an eye on Duong, who walked ahead of him.

When they finally stopped, Brindle looked around. The jungle had closed in on them, and he could no longer see the stars.

"This is it," Aldridge said. "Just over there." He shined his flashlight, and the beam fell on something white among the foliage.

Brindle could still hear the hum of mosquitoes and the chit-chit of insects in the bushes. A few soldiers stood off to one side talking quietly. It seemed odd to him that six men had given up their lives here only an hour before. There was a pervasive silence, as if the ominous presence of the jungle made their human actions seem trivial. The bushes and plants on either side of the path had been trampled. Brindle swung his flashlight off the path, and it fell upon the face of a dead man. He was lying on his back. Another man was next to him, and another. The bodies had been lined up.

Aldridge spoke to the soldiers and then came back to where Brindle was waiting.

"Four of them had identity cards," he said. "So we know who they are—or at least who they said they were when they registered. Those two on the end are unidentified."

"So which one is Nguyen?" Brindle asked.

"That's what we're here to find out," Aldridge replied. He turned to Duong and said something in Vietnamese. The young refugee nodded and began to carefully examine the faces of the dead.

Brindle walked along the row, shining his light on each body. None of them looked familiar. Worse, none of them seemed to fit the description Duong had given them of Nguyen.

"What's that?" he asked.

Two of the soldiers were looking at a gold pocket watch.

When they realized that Brindle had seen it, one of the soldiers slipped the watch into his jacket.

"Let me see that," Brindle said.

The soldier gazed at him blankly.

"Hal," Brindle called "will you tell this guy I want to see what he has in his jacket?"

"What's the problem?" Aldridge asked.

"I think they took something off one of the bodies. It could be important."

Aldridge spoke sternly to the soldier in Indonesian. The soldier glanced from one of his friends to the other and then reached into his jacket. He pulled out the watch and handed it to Aldridge.

"I told him he could have it back if we don't need it," Aldridge explained.

Brindle looked at the watch under the beam of his flashlight. It had obviously been an expensive watch at one time, but now it was old and scratched.

Aldridge said something to the soldier who responded with a look of guilt on his face. "He says he found it here."

"Did he find anything else?"

Aldridge translated, and the soldiers spoke together for a moment.

"They say no," Aldridge said at last.

"Nothing?"

Aldridge shook his head. "I guess not."

Brindle was beginning to get angry. "Tell them that I could have them searched."

"I doubt if Captain Salinem would approve of that," Aldridge noted.

"Probably not," Brindle said, "but they don't know that."

"Okay," Aldridge said. He snapped an order at the soldiers. They looked at each other in confusion. Finally one of them reached into his pocket and pulled out a small, intricately decorated wooden box. He handed the box to Aldridge. A second man handed him a small gray bag that contained two pearls.

"How did you know. . . ?" Aldridge began to ask, but at that moment Captain Salinem arrived. A soldier with him lit a flare which burned bright white and lit up the scene.

"Now that we can see," Salinem said. "Let's get down to business, gentlemen. Have we identified Nguyen?"

Brindle turned to Duong, who shook his head nervously.

"You mean," Salinem said incredulously, "we have six dead men and not one of them is this accursed infiltrator?"

"Apparently not," Aldridge said and shrugged.

"This is too much," Salinem said. "Did he get away?"

"I don't think he was ever here," Brindle offered, gazing at the inlaid ivory on the wooden box.

Salinem would not speak directly to the doctor. "What does he mean?" he asked Aldridge.

Aldridge turned to Brindle in frustration.

"John?"

"Take a look at these guys," Brindle suggested with growing sorrow. "They weren't communist infiltrators. They weren't even drug smugglers." He tossed the box to Captain Salinem, who regarded it with suspicion. "This was a black market meeting. They were just trying to buy or sell a few trinkets."

Captain Salinem looked at the line of dead bodies. "Were we supposed to know that, Doctor?" he asked contemptuously. "You can see for yourself how dark it is out here. And who was it that told us there would be a meeting tonight, hmm? We are here because of you. Do not try to blame us now for another of your unfortunate mistakes."

"I'm not blaming you," Brindle said. "I'm just saying that these aren't the right men."

"May Allah save us from incompetent Americans!" Salinem snapped and turned up the path. Stepping out of the flare light, he disappeared into the jungle.

It was past midnight when Brindle got back to his quarters. He was tired with a weariness he hadn't felt since medical school. Pulling off his muddy boots, he set them by the door. Then he took off his clothes and searched himself for leeches. He did not find any, so he wrapped a sarong around his waist, grabbed a towel, and walked down the terrace to the shower room. His mind was racing with thoughts of misunderstanding and guilt. Six refugees were dead. What had happened? Duong had come to him the night before and said that Nguyen had been spotted in camp. Brindle had told Aldridge about it the next morning. What more could he have done? As the tepid water sprayed down over his face, Brindle began to think. He felt that he was missing something here. If Duong were telling the truth, then the ambush this evening had simply been a tragic mistake. That also meant that they had missed the real meeting and that Nguyen was still out there somewhere. If Duong was lying, then what would be his motive? Had someone gotten to him? Surely Captain Salinem would not have gone to such elaborate measures to kill a few refugees. He could have done that in any number of ways without involving the WRO staff. Perhaps that had been his intention—to embarrass Aldridge. Or perhaps Duong had been frightened into working for Nguyen. That was more likely. Still, Brindle thought as he dried off, he had to believe that Duong was telling the truth. He had seen the fear on Duong's face, the trembling at even the mention of Nguyen's name. *The best laid plans*, he told himself.

He was too hyped to get any sleep, so he pulled on his shorts and a t-shirt and walked out to the terrace. He had just sat down when he saw Michele coming across the compound.

"Hal told me about the mistake," she said. "I can't believe it. Those poor men."

"Tell me about it," he replied.

"What could have gone wrong?"

"I don't know," Brindle said, tasting the bitterness of the event in his mouth. Nothing was quite right tonight: not his thinking, not the actions of others. He felt as if his cynicism had somehow been tranferred to the physical environment.

"I hear that Captain Salinem was irate."

"Yes," Brindle said. "All those bullets are expensive, you know."

"John," she said. "How can you joke about it?"

"I have to. Otherwise . . ."

"It's too tragic."

"Something like that."

"Is that what you do as a doctor? Joke about it?"

"Sure. When a patient is brought in who is really messed up—we call that a 'train wreck.' Like 'We have a train wreck in O.R. 2.'"

"And tonight?"

"Was definitely a train wreck."

"So what happens now?"

Brindle suddenly felt his fatigue return. "I don't know."

"You're not making any sense," she said. "I hope you're not going to drink yourself into oblivion tonight."

"It's a good idea," he said wearily. "But I've kinda sworn off the stuff for now."

"Well, I'm proud of you for that," Michele said.

"There's nothing to be proud of."

Another mosquito hummed past his ear.

"Let's go inside. The mosquitoes are beginning to eat me up."

"I'd better turn in," Michele said. "Another group is coming in tomorrow morning."

"Is there anybody left in Vietnam?"

"Only that one guy who promised to turn out the lights." Brindle laughed.

"See you at the dock?" Michele asked.

"Wouldn't miss it."

"And we've got the wayang drama tomorrow evening. It's going to be a busy day."

"Not to mention the continued search for Nguyen."

"It's going to be horrible when the families come to identify those two bodies. I hope I don't have to be there."

"You will," Brindle said. "You'll have to do the paperwork."

"I suppose so. I hate that part of the job."

Brindle sighed. "I'll do it for you, if you want."

"Would you?" Michele's face brightened. "I will be busy with the new arrivals."

"Yes, I'll do it. Don't worry."

"Thanks, John," she said.

Brindle felt the sting of a mosquito on his arm and turned toward his door. It was the least he could do, he thought—the least he could do for anyone. He was too familiar with death now for it to bother him much, and the wails of grief would never be as loud as the ones he heard in the silence of his room at night.

He went to bed.

∾∾

Three kilometers away, Vo Nguyen was spreading out his ground sheet on a bed of palm branches. He had strung another ground sheet from a rope tied to a tree branch overhead to keep out the rain. He was hungry, thirsty, and angry. The refugees he was supposed to meet tonight had promised to bring him food and water. But they had not come, or, rather, he had been unable to reach them. It had been a few minutes past ten when he had approached the camp from the direction of Surabi Point. He had traveled in a wide arc through the jungle to prevent being tracked and to check for patrols. He had not found any patrols, which surprised him somewhat, but he was also pleased because that would make the rendezvous less dangerous.

As usual, he had planned to arrive at the site early so that he could observe it for at least thirty minutes before the others arrived. He had not realized as he moved silently through the jungle that he was actually very close to sentry post six. The darkness had forced him to stay on the jungle paths, *and* this was taking him directly toward the waiting soldiers. He was within twenty meters of the sentry post when a burst of automatic weapons broke out in the trees on his right. Nguyen crouched and waited, but the firing did not come any closer. When the firing stopped, there were a few sporadic shots and then silence again. Nguyen crept cautiously in the direction of the shots. Could his refugees have stumbled onto an Indonesian patrol? he wondered. But the firing was in the wrong direction. They had planned to meet at the fallen palm tree near the beach which was off to his left.

He saw a soldier step from behind a tree and move away from him. Nguyen's hand reached for his knife. It would be easy for him to move up quietly behind the soldier and jab a knife into his back. But that was not a part of the plan and could cause problems later. It could be dangerous too. Nguyen did not know how many other soldiers there were or why they were in the jungle. When the soldiers began to light flares, he crept backwards until he had reached the path again and then headed north. Whatever had happened in the jungle had ruined his chance for a meeting tonight, but Nguyen was a patient man. His men would simply fall to the backup plan and meet the next night at the same location.

"Indonesian dogs," he muttered. "Probably firing at themselves."

This amused him.

"Yes," he said. "Probably firing at themselves."

Pulling out the little book from his pocket, he tried to read another lesson on Marxism, but it was too dark. So he put the book away and closed his eyes.

He could wait until tomorrow, he told himself. General Giap had waited in the forests of the Red River valley for years. Nguyen could wait one more day.

Just one.

Chapter Seventeen

"Have they been told yet?" Brindle asked, wiping the sleep from his eyes.

Tran nodded. "Mr. Aldridge put up names early this morning, Doctor. He talk to people in camp. They know."

"What about the other two?"

Brindle had put the two unidentified bodies in the operating room, but he would not be able to keep them there for long—not in this heat.

Tran shook his head. "No one come. Maybe no family."

"That's possible," Brindle said. "We'll keep them in the O.R. until midday. Then we'll have to move them to the morgue."

Brindle glanced at his watch. "We'd better get down to the dock."

"Medical kit all okay," Tran said.

Brindle patted him on the back. "Remind me to write you a letter of recommendation."

"For what job, Doctor?" Tran asked.

"Any job," Brindle said. "Taxi driver, president, whatever."

Tran laughed. "Okay, Doctor."

It was windy on the beach, and there were low gray storm clouds on the horizon. *Not a good time to be out in the South China Sea in an open boat*, Brindle thought. There would be fewer boats going out from Vietnam now that the monsoons had come—at least for another month. The refugees who were coming in this morning on the launch must have had a rough time.

"We're going to need some stretchers," Brindle said to Tran.

"Why, Doctor? All same like before."

Brindle pointed to the launch. It was just bumping up against the dock. "Look how many of them are slumped over. They are going to need help."

Michele came down the dock toward him. She was upset. "They're in pretty bad shape, John. Apparently two died on the ship last night."

"How long were they on the water?"

"They're not all from the same boat. . . but the worst one was out eight weeks."

"We'll take care of them," he said.

The first man off the launch could not have weighed more than one hundred pounds, although he appeared to be a young adult. As he came toward the doctor, supported on two sides by camp workers, he held out his hands as if he were blind. Tran spoke to him.

"He say eyes okay when he get on boat, Doctor. But no can see now."

"Okay," Brindle said, mentally running through a list of ophthalmological problems people might have after drifting on the sea for weeks. His best guess was that the man was probably suffering from a temporary loss of sight due to injury to the superficial cells of the cornea. This would have been caused by overexposure to ultraviolet rays of the sun and reinforced by those reflected off the water. But that was just a guess. "Get him up to the clinic."

The other refugees were coming down the dock. Even from a distance, Brindle could spot the cases of malnutrition and dehydration.

"Get that one on a stretcher," he said to Tran. "I'll take this one."

A woman passed them. She appeared to be disoriented.

"Whoa," Brindle said gently, taking her by the shoulders. She looked at him, but he could tell that nothing was registering. She mumbled something.

"What is she saying?" Brindle asked.

"She say all time, cousin, cousin," Tran explained.

"Maybe her cousin was one of those who died last night," Brindle offered. He motioned to one of the workers, who took the woman by the arm and escorted her up the beach to the clinic.

It was late morning before Brindle had time to grab a cup of coffee. When he reached the mess, he collapsed into the hard metal chair. His body ached, and he felt a dullness in his head from lack of sleep. All the time that he had been working with the new patients, he had been thinking about Kim Thi. It was inevitable now that he would think of her, and he did not try to stop it. It was as if she were always with him, walking beside him and talking to him. He carried on mental conversations with her throughout the day: wondering what her response would be to this or that situation, wondering how she would react to such-and-such a comment. He could not wait to see her in the new dress and to escort her to the drama. He realized, stirring a spoonful of powdered cream into his coffee, that this would be their first public appearance together as a couple. Brindle would be making a statement with their arrival at this performance. He wondered, rather inconsequentially, how Captain Salinem would react. Naturally, Captain Salinem would believe that he had been correct about Brindle's actions that night at his office. Salinem would assume that Brindle had rescued the girl for personal reasons and not because it broke camp regulations. Brindle wondered if he would have reacted so angrily had the girl in Salinem's quarters not been Kim Thi. *Probably not*, he told himself. But it was still wrong, and Salinem knew it.

"Ah, John," Aldridge said, sticking his head in the door of the mess. "I've been looking for you. How did it go with the new arrivals this morning?"

"Didn't Michele brief you?"

"She hasn't had a chance. I've been meeting with Captain Salinem all morning."

Brindle nodded. "We had more than the usual amount of problems. One woman seems to be suffering from psychic trauma. She keeps calling out for her cousin."

"Probably someone she left in Nam," Aldridge suggested.

"I suppose so."

Aldridge rested his right foot on one of the chairs. "Look, John. You don't have time to play shrink for every refugee with a traumatic problem. They all have traumatic problems. They've all seen an incredible amount of trouble. More than we'll ever see."

"I know . . ." Brindle said.

"Let's just get them patched up and sent on to the P.I. That's our job."

"Sure," Brindle said.

Aldridge dismissed the subject with a wave of his hand. "That's not what I came to talk to you about anyway. We've got a real problem with Captain Salinem."

"Don't tell me," Brindle said sarcastically. "He wants to take everyone in camp down to the beach and shoot them at dawn."

"Not quite so drastic, but you're not far off," Aldridge said. "He wants to burn the jungle and smoke out Nguyen."

"You're kidding."

Aldridge shook his head in exasperation. "Absolutely not. He says he is finished playing games with this infiltrator. He has asked for reinforcements, and they should arrive on Tuesday. That's when he wants to start the fire."

"I've heard of that being done in small areas," Brindle remarked. "But the whole jungle? The government would never give him permission to do that."

"That's what I told him," Aldridge said.

❦

The final preparations for the wayang drama were being completed as Brindle left the mess. Benches had been constructed and placed in rows beneath the tarp. A stage with a screen and lantern had been set up at the far end.

Brindle did not return to the clinic but instead cut to the right past the office and down the path to the camp. It was a beautifully hot day. The clouds which had appeared so threatening on the horizon earlier in the morning had blown off to the north. He wanted to see Kim Thi. Usually a gut feeling told him when she would be available, and when he arrived, it was often the case. He did not have that feeling now, but he wanted to see her. He wanted to talk with her and to see her smile at the mention of the dress. He wanted to see the sun shining on her black hair, the slender curve of her waist, the swelling pink of her mouth. It did not really matter if they talked at all, he realized; he simply wanted to be near her. So he entered the camp.

Indeed, Kim Thi was at her shanty when he arrived, but her reaction was not what he had expected. She and her mother were sitting close together by the cook fire and talking in hushed voices, almost conspiratorially. Brindle had an urge to turn and leave quickly before they saw him. It was obvious that this was an inappropriate time for him to visit. Yet, if they saw him leaving, it would be embarrassing. He decided to clear his throat and make his presence known. When he did, Kim Thi glanced up and saw him standing there. A look of fear came into her eyes.

"Not good time now," she whispered fiercely, gazing at the nearby huts. "Not good time."

"What do you mean?" Brindle asked. Her reaction had caused all the old insecurities to flood up again. He immediately felt like a fool and questioned everything that had happened over the past months. Perhaps he had completely misunderstood their relationship.

Kim Thi looked at him and whispered again, "Not good time. You go. I come clinic."

"What's the matter?" he asked, knowing that his stupidity was intensifying her anxiety. She had wanted him to go, and he should have turned and left immediately. But his insecurities were causing him to linger. Maybe if he remained one moment longer, he would begin to. . .

"Go!" she snapped, turning away from him. "Please!"

Brindle backed up a few steps and then turned abruptly, unaware of his boots hitting the ground, or that he was moving at all. He felt hurt and then angry, these shifting emotions sweeping back and forth over him like clouds over water. He hurried back to the clinic, his face flushed and sweating, but as his foot fell on the first worn step, he realized that he would not be able to concentrate on anything medical at the moment. He needed to go back to his quarters and to think. *What had happened?* he asked himself. *What had he done?* Dropping onto his bed, he gazed up at the balled knot of mosquito netting. John suddenly felt unbearably hot. It was always so hot and humid and infected and insect-permeated on this island. He suddenly hated Boromu with a terrible, all-encompassing anger. He hated this place. He hated himself. He even was beginning to hate Kim Thi for making him feel this way. Oh . . . God! What he needed *was* God! But the Savior had *not* come to his aid when he had needed Him on that rain-slick highway. No one had been there when he had needed help. "So forget them all!" he snapped bitterly. "I don't need anybody! I don't have anybody!" He wadded up the mildew dampened, sour-smelling pillow and pressed it against his face. "I don't *deserve* anybody!"

At last he had come to the bottom of his despair and with that had sounded a small element of truth. It was true. He did not deserve anyone. He had had his chance and had blown it, or it had been blown for him, or something. But there was no instance now in which he deserved to be happy. How could he be, after he had rejected God?

Where was the bottle? he wondered, swinging his legs off the bed. Then he remembered that he had asked Michele to keep the new case for him. *What a stupid idea*, he told himself. What could he have been thinking—playing the squeaky clean young doctor, the new man, the living John Brindle! What could he have been thinking?

"John?" a voice came through the door. It was a soft, apologetic voice. "John?"

Brindle did not have to wonder who it was, for he had heard that voice in his dreams night after night.

"Kim Thi," he whispered, jumping up from the bed. Going to the mirror he saw the remorse on his face and quickly ran his hands under the tap.

"John?" the voice asked again, and he could hear the floorboards creak. She was leaving.

"Wait!" he called. "Kim Thi!"

He opened the door, and she was there, standing shyly off to one side.

"Come in, please," he said.

Moving through the door with a determination that surprised Brindle, she allowed him to see for a brief moment that inner core of strength which had carried her from Nha Trang onto the open sea and finally to this camp—as if this camp were the final goal of her journey, which it was not.

Brindle could only look at her. It was as if his dreams had manifested themselves into this one moment, so that as Kim Thi stood before him, gazing at him with perhaps as much sorrow in her dark eyes as he had just felt, it seemed like more of a dream than a reality.

"I sorry, John," she said with such sincerity that he could not help but believe her. "I no want you feel bad."

He realized then that he had not yet spoken, though his mind was flashing with unplayed scenes.

"What's the matter?" he asked flatly.

"Okay, sit down?" she asked.

"I'm sorry. Here, take the chair. I'll sit on the bed."

Kim Thi looked around the room curiously.

"This your place," she stated.

"Yes," he said, wondering if she could see the emptiness, the depression, the need to find himself in someone else. Did it cover the walls and furniture of his room like paint, or was it more the texture of smoke? He wondered how much of this was evident, or if she only saw a small, bare room with a metal bed and a washstand. *Was loneliness visible*, he asked himself, thinking of Michele that night and her letter to a friend, *or did it require imagination to sense the desperation of others?*

"Much trouble," she said. "Hoang much trouble."

"What do you mean?" he asked, not even waiting for or being able to really concentrate on an answer, but rather watching the way her mouth moved as she talked, the pink of her fingertips—the fingertips which had brushed so affectionately against his arm in the clinic—moving nervously now over her black pants. "What about Hoang?"

"Hoang big trouble," she said, as if a slight change in wording would transmit all the information he required to understand the situation.

Brindle stood up from the bed in frustration. What a fool he had been! Her insistence that he leave the shanty had not been directed at him for emotional reasons—and only a spoiled, self-centered American would perhaps think that it had been—but because she had been worried about her brother. It had been so out of character for the Kim Thi that Brindle thought he knew to have acted that way. Of course there must have been another reason. As he paced the room, he considered sending for Tran. But at the same time, he did not want anyone else to share this moment with Kim Thi. He selfishly wanted to resolve the problem by himself.

"Okay," he said calmly. "What trouble? Tell me from the beginning."

Kim Thi touched the long scar on her forearm. "Necklace," she said. "Necklace."

Chapter Eighteen

It had been a long afternoon, and Brindle paced the clinic terrace impatiently. The sun had just settled like pink fire into the palms, but it seemed to Brindle that it had been lingering there—almost as if to taunt him—for an hour. He did not know exactly when Hoang would arrive at the clinic or from which direction. He had told Kim Thi that her brother would be safe here and that Brindle could offer him shelter. She had explained that Hoang was now hiding somewhere in the jungle. But where he was hiding and how far away, Brindle did not know.

"Do you think he will come?" Aldridge asked from one of the canvas chairs.

"I hope so," Brindle replied. "He can't hide in the jungle indefinitely. He has to come in sometime if we're going to get him out of here."

Aldridge nodded and glanced at his watch. "I hope he doesn't wait too long. The drama starts at nine."

"I told him to come at sunset. He still has a few minutes."

"Yes, yes. Well, it's just too bad that he got mixed up in that black market stuff. How do they think it's going to help them get off the island? I still don't understand that."

Brindle stopped pacing and leaned against the railing. "Kim Thi told me Hoang was working on an angle to get them to the Philippines. It had something to do with getting money for the necklace. I told her it didn't work that way. When their number came up, they were moved on. That's all there was to it. No payoffs, no bribes. Just wait for their number."

"And Michele handles the list," Aldridge added. "She is above reproach."

"Of course," Brindle said.

The sun was halfway down the trunks of the trees now. Leaning against the railing, Brindle considered what Kim Thi had told him. Hoang was in trouble because everyone in camp believed he had told the authorities about the black market meeting. Wasn't his sister the doctor's girl? the refugees had asked. What kind of arrangement had Hoang made with the Americans? Perhaps a quick trip to the Philippines? Then there were the relatives of the men who had been killed in the ambush. According to Kim Thi, they had sworn to get Hoang.

Things had certainly gotten messed up, Brindle thought, *and poor Hoang was in the middle of it.*

The sun had dropped behind the water now, and the figures Brindle saw moving across the courtyard were indistinct in the twilight. Out of the corner of his eye, he caught movement on the terrace and turned to see Hoang coming up beside Aldridge's chair.

"Hoang?" Aldridge asked, turning and looking at the young man.

"Yes," Brindle replied.

Hoang looked frightened and angry.

Kim Thi's brother hated him now, Brindle realized. Hoang had wrapped him up with the ambush and everything negative that had happened on the island since their arrival, and he hated him. And yet Hoang had to rely on him for protection. That must have made his anger all the worse.

Brindle motioned for Hoang to follow him into the clinic.

"He's here," he said quietly to Tran as they entered.

"Okay," Tran said. "We put him in examining room."

"Please tell Hoang what we have in mind," Brindle said.

"He know," Tran replied. "He stay here all time till go Philippines."

Hoang gave Brindle another angry look and then stepped into the examining room. When it was quiet in the clinic, he would be moved to another room. Perhaps they could make up one of the small storage areas with a mat on the floor for him, Brindle thought. He would try to avoid Hoang as much as possible. But for now, he had other things on his mind. It was only two hours before the drama.

After his shower, Brindle combed his wet hair and gazed at himself in the mirror. How odd, he thought, that the facial contours seemed to change, alter from one moment to another depending on whether he had seen Kim Thi. Was love really that physically transforming, or was it simply the way he viewed his face? Without a doubt, spending time with Kim Thi had done something to him. It had revived the living John Brindle, and now it seemed to be transforming even the outer man into something he had not seen for two years—himself as he was before. He ran a hand over his face. It was no good dwelling on things like this, he told himself. He was still the same man he had been six months ago, and that man would always be there in quiet moments of self-doubt. Brindle felt as if he carried the depressing image of his former self around like a prominent scar.

Buttoning his shirt, he stepped back.

"Flowers," he muttered to himself, "I should take her some flowers."

Brindle had seen some orchids growing in the jungle. He would offer to pay the camp workers if he would get them for him. Glancing at his watch, he saw that it was nearly eight o'clock. He would have to take care of that quickly.

As he was heading for the door, he realized with some surprise that the old urge was upon him again. Far down within himself, he had been thinking of alcohol. He wanted a drink. He wanted to calm his nerves before meeting Kim Thi. An image of the tequila bottle came into his thoughts like a photograph, like a taste in his mouth that he had been missing. *But why?* he asked himself. Why was tonight any different from any other time he had visited Kim Thi? Because, he told himself with cruel awareness, tonight was his first real experience with Kim Thi. He wanted to impress her—as if that was even possible, for he had no idea what value she placed on his actions.

"We're not getting into that," he muttered to himself derisively. Anyway, he had left the tequila with Michele, and it would take too much time for him to get a bottle from her room. Then he also would have to explain to her why he wanted the tequila, and that was more humiliation than he could tolerate at the moment.

"Flowers," he muttered to himself again, purposefully trying to distract his mind. "Orchids."

The evening air was soft, and he could see the stars of the Southern Cross through the palms as he walked along the path to Kim Thi's hut. He still had the taste for alcohol, or rather the need for a taste in his mouth, and this bothered him. He had never thought of himself as an alcoholic; he only drank to kill the pain and depression—not because he loved it. Of course, he had grown to appreciate the lack of feeling, but the root of the problem had never been because he liked to drink. In college he had been a moderate drinker; in medical school he drank only socially. Thinking clinically now, with that abstract distance of a doctor, he thought it was interesting how the desire had slipped up on him without any conscious effort. Another scar from the past.

"Relax," he told himself, though he knew there was reason to worry. The situation with Hoang had spoiled everything—not just the evening performance but any chance he had of a growing relationship with Kim Thi. How could her affection for him grow if Hoang felt the opposite? Perhaps hatred did not breed hatred, but certainly it caused some doubts to come into the mind. Kim Thi would begin to wonder, to question, to become more secretive, less trusting. And how could he build a relationship on feelings like that? Even tonight, Brindle thought, Kim Thi's thoughts would not be on the drama. She could not be expected to enjoy a performance of shadow puppets when her brother was in danger. It seemed ridiculous.

Hoang was not in any immediate danger, Brindle reassured himself, but there was always the potential threat. That is why he had posted a guard at the clinic.

Kim Thi was waiting when Brindle arrived at her hut. She was wearing the new dress, but the impression of loveliness was marred by the anxiety in her eyes. Even in the lantern light, he could sense her worry.

"These are for you," he explained, handing her the orchids.

She held them up to her face. "For me?"

"Yes."

She touched his hand. "Thank you, John. I make dry. Keep all time."

He glanced at his watch. "We'd better go. It's almost nine."

Kim Thi looked at the lantern.

"Maybe no can go," she said. "Hoang much trouble."

"It's all right," Brindle assured her. "We have him at the clinic. He is safe."

Kim Thi shook her head slowly in disbelief. "Maybe no can go," she repeated.

"We have to," Brindle said, smiling. "I've already got the tickets."

"Tickets?"

"Never mind," he said, dropping the attempt at humor. "Hoang is going to be okay. You don't need to worry. I've posted a guard at the clinic."

Kim Thi looked at him questioningly.

"Same guard who kick you?" she asked.

"No."

"But you no see face in dark. Maybe same guard."

Brindle rubbed his side in frustration. What a shame, he thought. He had been waiting for this evening for so many weeks.

Kim Thi had noticed the disappointment on his face.

"So, no problem?" she asked.

"None," Brindle said. "Hoang will be fine."

"And we go Philippines?"

"On the next ship."

She smoothed out her dress thoughtfully, and Brindle noticed the way the blue cloth fit over her slender hips.

"Maybe okay," she said, gazing at him shyly.

"Great," Brindle said, holding out his arm. "Shall we go?"

"I see Hoang after?"

"Someone may be watching. You'll have to wait for a few days."

Kim Thi nodded. She knew about lack of privacy, about being watched.

The musicians, known as *gamelans*, were already playing when Brindle and Kim Thi arrived in the clearing. The music, so plaintive and mysterious, drifted through the palm trees. The tent was decorated with colored lanterns, and the rows of benches were packed with soldiers and other camp workers.

"Captain Salinem will be here," Brindle warned Kim Thi as they approached the tent. "I hope that doesn't bother you."

Kim Thi frowned. "No," she said defiantly, and her courage caused Brindle to love her even more.

Michele waved. "Kim Thi, you look beautiful," she said.

Kim Thi smiled shyly.

"Where's Hal?" Brindle asked.

"He got a call from Jakarta just as we were leaving the office. He should be here in a few minutes."

"And Salinem?"

Michele looked around the tent. "He was here a minute ago. He must be taking care of something."

"Where is he sitting?"

"There," Michele pointed to the bench in front of her. "I thought it would be rude to sit any farther away."

"Okay," Brindle said.

Captain Salinem came into the tent at that moment. Ignoring Brindle and Kim Thi, he hurried up to Michele. "No, no, Miss Fallon," he said, with a slight desperation in his voice.

"You must sit here." He ushered her to a space on the front bench. "This is for the guest of honor."

Michele gave Brindle an apologetic look and moved up a row. She and Salinem were now sitting in front of them and off to the left.

"I hope we haven't missed anything," Aldridge said, coming up to the bench with an Indonesian dressed in gray slacks and a white shirt. The man was obviously a government worker, for he carried himself with an air of self-importance. Brindle would not have been surprised if the man had been wearing sunglasses. Government officials always seemed to be wearing sunglasses.

"I had to take a call from Jakarta," Aldridge said.

"Anything special?"

"About the new replacement." The administrator nodded imperceptibly toward the man with him. "Just paperwork."

Brindle looked at the man.

"This is Mr. Haryati from the Interior Ministry," Aldridge explained. "He is making a short tour of our camp."

"I wondered who got off the helicopter this morning," Brindle remarked, shaking the man's hand. It felt small and damp. "Welcome to Boromu."

"I am not used to this much humidity," Haryati said, dabbing a handkerchief to his face. "Is it always so hot here?"

"This is a cool spell," Brindle offered. "Come back after the monsoons."

"My sympathy goes out to you gentlemen. I do not think I would last very long on this island."

"Neither do we," Brindle said. He could feel bitterness coming up from within him like something he needed to expunge, like a sickness. He hoped that he could stop it before he embarrassed either himself or Aldridge. He also had Kim Thi to think of now.

"Dr. Brindle handles all of our medical cases," Aldridge explained to the official. "It's very rare that we have to medivac a patient to Jakarta."

"I have heard about you, Dr. Brindle," Haryati said, studying him appraisingly.

Brindle wondered what the man from the Interior Ministry had heard, but he did not respond. He was trying not to let anything more spoil the evening. It had already been shattered by Hoang's predicament, and he was attempting to hold onto the one thin element of happiness that was left to him—the presence of Kim Thi seated next to him on the bench.

"And this is Miss Van Quang," Aldridge continued, politely refraining from mentioning that she was a refugee.

The official nodded courteously.

Brindle scooted over on the bench, and the two men sat beside him.

"Mr. Haryati knows all about wayang drama and has offered to explain it to us," Aldridge offered.

"Do you speak Vietnamese?" Brindle asked.

"No," Haryati said. "I am afraid not."

"Well, then," Brindle said. "Kim Thi should sit next to Hal. That way he can translate."

"My pleasure," Aldridge said.

Brindle moved over so that Kim Thi sat between him and Aldridge. Haryati sat on Aldridge's right.

A soldier in the back was dimming the lanterns.

"It's beginning," Aldridge said.

Michele turned and glanced back at them for a moment. When she caught Brindle's eye, she smiled weakly, looked at Kim Thi, and then turned to the front. The lantern light glowed like orange fire on her blonde hair.

A small man dressed in black moved around behind the screen.

"That is the *dalang*—the puppeteer," Haryati explained. "In Indonesia we believe that we are all just puppets and are moved by the ultimate dalang—God."

"That's very poetic," Brindle commented. He could see Salinem leaning close to Michele, explaining something to her. *The captain has all the moves*, Brindle thought.

"Any important political official is liable to be labeled a puppet manipulated by an unseen dalang," Haryati continued. "We always want to know who the real dalang is."

And who is yours? Brindle thought absently. He saw Michele lean quickly away from Salinem. *Be careful, Michele.*

A shadow of the first puppet appeared on the screen.

"That is Prince Gathutkara," Haryati explained. "There will be many formal introductions now. The characters must all become acquainted."

"Who is that?" Brindle asked. Another puppet had appeared with an ornate headdress.

Haryati watched the screen. "That is Dewi Surtikanti, the beautiful second daughter of the king."

The shadows of the two puppets moved across the screen. Their heads were in profile, but their shoulders and bodies were viewed from straight on. Music accompanied the movements of the puppets. With the darkness and flicker of the yellow lanterns, it was like being in a dream.

"The typical wayang drama is about royal political intrigue," Haryati said in a hushed voice. "There is always a big battle at the end."

"Like *Richard the Third*," Aldridge suggested. "Shakespeare."

"I suppose so," Haryati agreed. "But wayang drama does not represent real life. It has its own reality."

"In what way?" Brindle asked.

"The shadow," Haryati replied, pointing to the dark shape of Prince Gathutkara on the screen. "Because it is visible, it shares a characteristic with the material world. But because it is non-material, it shares a characteristic with the invisible world."

"I never thought about that," Aldridge said. "That's very interesting."

Brindle watched Salinem move closer to Michele on the bench. His thigh was now pressed against hers. Brindle was beginning to feel bitterness again and took Kim Thi's hand. She did not resist or respond, and when he turned to her, her eyes were on the screen.

A third puppet, a priest named Begawan, was introduced.

As the story began to unfold, Prince Gathutkara learned that his father had disappeared. He told his story to the Prime Minister, who called in Begawan. After much formal discussion, the priest offered to locate the missing father. Moving diagonally away from the lamp, Prince Gathutkara's shadow became progressively elongated and distorted. At the same time, Dewi Surtikanti moved toward the lamp and her shadow grew.

"Do you see the significance of that movement?" Haryati whispered as the action continued. "The lamp represents the sun which gives and maintains life."

Brindle nodded. "Who is that character?" A puppet with a sharp nose and long spidery arms had appeared.

"The evil advisor," Haryati said. "There is always evil in wayang drama, just as there is good. It is very predictable."

"The good wins, doesn't it?" Aldridge asked.

"Naturally," Mr. Haryati said, smiling knowingly. "But not without tragic losses."

Brindle felt Kim Thi's fingers close around his now. *Had she finally decided to respond*, he wondered, *or had she been distracted by thoughts of her brother or the drama?* He enveloped her hand in his, the fingers intertwining, and it felt right and natural. Just as Michele had said that she would always remember the new year's celebration and the young man with the dragon mask, Brindle knew that he would always remember this moment, seated with Kim Thi in the dimly lit tent as the wayang puppets moved across the screen.

> *"My father has been taken from me!" Prince Gathutkara said to Begawan as he moved toward the lamp.*

"Now, now," said the priest. "I will help you to find your father. I have promised the Prime Minister. You must believe."

"That is not possible," snapped the Prince. "Not since my father was taken from me. How can I find him?"

"We must confront the evil one," Begawan advised. "He is surely behind this treachery."

Dewi Surtikanti appeared from the right of the screen.

"I have been looking for you, Prince Gathutkara. I have news of your missing father."

"Where is he?"

"I think you know," said Dewi Surtikanti. "Search your heart."

"Yes," Begawan agreed. "Perhaps your heart can tell us."

"No," said Prince Gathutkara sadly. "It has turned to stone."

"Then how can you live?" asked Dewi Surtikanti.

"On hate," answered the Prince.

"If that is so," said Begawan, "then you have already visited the evil one."

"I know him," said the Prince.

"He is at the palace," offered Dewi Surtikanti, "but we must be very careful."

"You must not go," Begawan warned. "It is too dangerous for a woman."

"I will go by myself," Prince Gathutkara said.

"No," said the priest. "I will go with you."

Together, they exited to the left of the screen.

A hand touched Brindle's shoulder. He turned to see Tran crouched behind him. The assistant's face looked concerned.

"What is it?" Brindle asked.

"Hoang. . . ?" she asked in a whisper, grabbing his arm.

"No, no," Brindle reassured her. "Tran just has a question."

Brindle followed Tran out of the back of the tent and into the starlight. "What's the matter?" Brindle asked, looking back at the drama.

"Hoang leave clinic, Doctor."

"Where did he go?" asked Brindle. "Is he coming back?"

Tran shrugged. "He say he no want die in clinic. He say better go back camp. So I come get you. Very worried, Doctor."

Brindle patted Tran on the shoulder. "It's okay, Tran. We'll find him. It's too dangerous out there for him now."

"He go on path to camp," Tran offered.

"Okay," Brindle said, thinking. "I'd better get Kim Thi. We may need her help."

"Is there a problem, John?" Aldridge asked when Brindle returned to the tent.

"You know that situation at the clinic," Brindle said evasively and glanced at Mr. Haryati. "The patient has left."

"Do you need my help?"

"No, I don't think so," Brindle said, "but we need to find him."

They left the clearing and hurried across the courtyard to the path. From the moment Tran's hand had touched his shoulder, Brindle had felt a hollowness in his stomach, as if something irrevocable had happened. He tried to tell himself that it was only nerves and possibly even a case of hypoglycemia from not drinking, but something told him otherwise. Why had Hoang felt that he would be killed in the clinic? He was safe enough. Only a few trusted people knew he was there, and a guard had been posted. So why had he run?

A wide storm front had blown in from the southeast and covered the moon, so it was very dark walking along the path. Brindle wished he had brought his flashlight, but there was no time to run back to his room and get it now. They needed to find Hoang as soon as possible.

"Hoang . . ." Kim Thi whispered nervously. "Hoang . . ."

clinic? He was safe enough. Only a few trusted people knew he was there, and a guard had been posted. So why had he run?

A wide storm front had blown in from the southeast and covered the moon, so it was very dark walking along the path. Brindle wished he had brought his flashlight, but there was no time to run back to his room and get it now. They needed to find Hoang as soon as possible.

"Hoang . . ." Kim Thi whispered nervously. "Hoang . . ."

They had reached a dark section of the path where the palms grew so thickly overhead that even on full-moon nights it was difficult to see, and then Brindle tripped. In his haste, he had not been watching the ground, and his foot had caught on something, causing him to fall. Letting go of Kim Thi's hand, he had tumbled forward and landed on his hands and knees.

"Ah!" he groaned, remembering the last time he had fallen like this and the two guards who had kicked him. But there were no guards here, only the hum of insects, the cry of a night bird, and the rustling of palms. As he reached across the dark sand to regain his balance, though, his fingers pushed against something soft and Brindle began to shiver. It was the sleeve of a shirt, farther up was a shoulder, and then damp hair. But it was not water which had caused the moistness in the hair, and when Brindle removed his hand, his fingers felt sticky. He knew, even as he scrambled in his pocket for a match flashlight, that the flame would illuminate the features of Kim Thi's brother. *Oh, no* he thought to himself weakly, *this can't be happening.*

At that moment, Kim Thi began to wail in a voice filled with primal grief. Listening to her and feeling the hollow chill of absolute inadequacy, Brindle could only close his eyes and turn away. He did not understand her Vietnamese, but he was familiar enough with Kim Thi's actions. He had cradled his daughter in just that same way after the accident in California, her damp hair and limp arms pressed against his chest. It was not hope which had caused him to react that way, but a sudden, hundred years. Kim Thi would come to realize this also, he knew.

"Hoang!" Kim Thi cried. "Hoang!"

People from the camp were running toward them. Brindle reached out to Kim Thi in sympathy, but she did not feel his touch. He realized with deep remorse that she never would again. She had moved far away from him in her sorrow, and the severity of her pain had caused any ties in their relationship to dissolve like inconsequential foolishness, like the dust of things which he had kept hidden.

And perhaps that is what it was, Brindle thought sadly.

Chapter Nineteen

Brindle could not have known as he woke on Sunday morning with the taste of loneliness and defeat in his mouth, like the aftermath of a binge, that events on Boromu Island had gone far beyond his control. He still believed that he had a responsibility to those whom he cared for—both friends and patients and, of course, Kim Thi—and that his actions could in some way affect their lives. It was a belief born out of need, for he desperately needed to feel as if he could help those around him. It was a futile gesture, but he was not willing to accept any other possibility at the moment. For then what would be the purpose of going on? He could have so easily stopped going on before, he told himself, and perhaps he would consider the idea again, but he felt the urge to finish what had been started at the refugee camp. It was the one thing which kept his feet swinging from the cot each morning and gave him the energy to take the steps toward the clinic. Even the cup of hot coffee which Tran had brought him did not dispel the feeling of catastrophe which filled his quarters like harsh sunlight filtering through his slatted windows.

Brindle rubbed a weary hand across his face. "What am I going to do?" he muttered, not so much in despair but as in utter fatigue.

His desire was to get away. The thought of going outside and dealing with the events of last night turned his stomach. He did not want to examine the body of Hoang or even to see Kim Thi. The thought crossed his mind that he would like to talk with Michele, to just sit calmly and watch her dark blonde

217

hair as she stirred her coffee, her shy warm smile, her friend-ship. He wondered where she was now. Glancing at his watch, he saw that it was nearly eight o'clock—very late for him to be getting out of bed. *But who cared*, he thought.

"I'm sorry," Aldridge said as Brindle entered the camp office. "I should have helped."

"It wouldn't have made any difference, Hal," Brindle explained, handing in his medical report. "Hoang knew what he was doing."

"Things are just getting too complicated. We're supposed to be here to help these people."

Brindle stood at the window. He watched two little boys carrying a burlap sack of rice down the path to the camp. The sack was stenciled with WRO in white letters.

"Perhaps the camp should be closed," Aldridge sighed.

"We may not have to make that decision if the winds change, Hal. Is Captain Salinem still planning to burn out Nguyen?"

"I assume so. I haven't heard anything else."

"On Tuesday?"

"Right."

"Then we still have two more days."

Off to his left, Brindle could see the edge of the clearing and the tent for the wayang drama. Could it have been only last night that he had sat there with Kim Thi, happy to be holding her hand, touching her, enjoying the gentle pressure of her hand in his? If love could occur so instantaneously, so that a tiny fraction of time could hold the full development of emotions, then couldn't the loss of that love also slow down time—allowing for the full impact of the loss to be dealt with and grieved over and understood within the early hours of one sleepless night?

"It's not the refugees, really, Hal," Brindle said. "It's what brought them here. You think you've left something behind when you escape, but you've really just brought it with you."

"Do you have any idea who killed him?" Aldridge asked.

Brindle shook his head. "Anyone with a machete."

"What about his sister?"

"I plan to visit her today. She took it hard."

"Of course. Is she in any kind of danger?"

"I don't think so. But I don't know anymore."

Brindle had planned to visit Kim Thi in the afternoon, but something held him back. For the first time, he found that he was not eager to see her. Perhaps he wanted to put off the realization that everything had changed, that she was no longer interested in him, and that he no longer had any influence over her emotions. Or perhaps it was simply pride. He had done everything he could for her, short of skipping her ahead on the departure list. It wasn't his fault that Hoang had been a fool and had gone to a black market meeting. Brindle had warned Kim Thi that they didn't need to bribe anyone to get out of the camp. Why hadn't they listened? It was their own stupidity which had gotten Hoang killed, not his own. But now he was paying for it by losing Kim Thi.

Mrs. Van Quang was standing outside her hut like a sentinel as Brindle approached. When she saw him, she squeezed up her mouth and eyes into an expression of sour disdain, and he knew there was no point in trying to deal with her. Even if she did not believe that he had been responsible for Hoang's death, she would surely not want Kim Thi to be seen in his company. Nor could he explain in any kind of language which she understood why he had not been responsible. Yet he had come into the camp to speak to Kim Thi, and he decided to give it at least one try before he gave up. At the first mention of her daughter's name, Mrs. Van Quang burst into a haranguing chatter which caused Brindle to step back in embarrassment. He did not know if Kim Thi was inside the hut—though he assumed she was—and this caused him more pain, believing that she was just there beyond those dried palm leaves and corrugated sheets, and that she did not want to see him. If that were the case, then their relationship had deteriorated far beyond any romantic feelings; it meant that they were no longer even friends. Brindle tried to remember back to his own feelings after the accident. Had he wanted to see anyone? he asked himself. The answer came immediately. Yes. If there had been anyone that he loved, then he would have wanted to be with them. Perhaps that was the key—if there had been anyone. There had been no one else, with the exception of his sister. He had walked the streets, gone to see a hopelessly ridiculous film, and stood at the edge of the bay and gazed out to the ocean (this seemed to help somehow). And all the while, he had watched himself going through the motions and had said to himself in an almost hallucinatory way, *I've just lost my wife and daughter. I'm standing here, but I'm in a completely different reality from the rest of you. It's almost funny, being so alone. I don't want to laugh, though. I'm not sure how it would sound. Looking at the bay was nice. I should go back there. Maybe that would keep me from feeling as if I've been blown to bits. No one seems to notice. They think this is a smile on my face. I've just lost my wife and daughter. And where is God? Where is God? Where is God?*

That's when he had prescribed Valium for himself and spent the next several days sleeping at his sister's house.

"I've been looking for you," he heard someone say. He turned to see Michele coming toward him between the huts. "I thought you might like to take a walk."

She smiled encouragingly, and Brindle wondered if she had talked with Aldridge or if she had just assumed he would be in need of a friend.

"Sure," he said, gazing back at Mrs. Van Quang, who had stopped chattering angrily. She continued to look at him with an icy glare, her jaws clamped, and her head shaking back and forth.

"Wow. She's ticked with you."

"I guess she blames me for Hoang's death."

"Let's go this way."

They walked along a narrow path to the beach. It was the same path Kim Thi always used and the same path upon which he had followed her that day when he had asked her to the drama. The same stretch of sand which had caused him happiness then now caused him to feel sadness and loss. It would be this way at the camp, he realized, as long as he retained any affection for Kim Thi—which meant that it would always be this way. But now Michele was walking beside him, and this was something he had wanted.

"I hope you understand," she said tenderly. "It wasn't your fault, John. We each have our job here, and yours is to take care of the sick and injured. You can't be expected to protect refugees who are in trouble. That's impossible."

"I don't blame myself," he said. "Hoang was stupid to have gone to the black market meeting, and he was a fool to have left the clinic. He was responsible for his own death. . . but I feel terrible about it."

"We all do."

"Anyway," he admitted, "I'm glad to see you."

"I think that's a first, John," Michele said, slipping off her sandals. "Not only are you glad about something, but you're glad to see *me*."

"Sure. Don't you think we're friends?"

They stepped out to the open beach. There was a pleasant breeze blowing in from the south. Michele pushed the hair away from her face. "I don't know what we are."

"Well," Brindle said, "I've always thought of us as friends, and I'm glad you're here. I wanted to talk with you."

"Okay. Let's talk."

Brindle stepped into the surf and felt the cold swirl of water around his ankles. Was this the moment of confession? he wondered. Should he tell Michele about the private thoughts which had tormented him for the past two years, about the knowledge which had formed him, about the motive behind his every action? Was that why he had wanted to see her? Until now, he had not really thought about it. He had merely felt the urge to be in her presence, to feel relaxed, safe. Was that it, that he had wanted to feel—even for a moment—

that surrounding safety which a family provided? Could Michele offer that to him? Was it even fair to expect it from her?

No, he told himself. This was not why he had wanted to see her. He needed an uncomplicated friendship with someone who understood him. He had never realized before how much of a strain the difference in cultures put on a relationship. In the presence of Kim Thi, he was always thinking, observing, and trying to understand. Now he was tired. He did not want the strain of differences; he wanted to feel completely at ease, unguarded. Perhaps this was what he had needed all along. He began to think he had been a fool not to let Michele into his life months ago.

"I'm listening," she offered, walking through the surf beside him.

"It's funny," Brindle said. "I've just been thinking about Kim Thi and all the time and effort I put into that relationship when . . ."

"What?"

"When you're the one I can talk to, the one who has always tried to help me."

"I could have told you that," she said with exasperation.

Brindle immediately regretted having shared this intimacy. It was not his intention to taunt her. "I'm sorry."

"There's no need to be, John. It was probably for the best."

They walked along for a few minutes without talking. Brindle watched a gull skimming over the water. He decided not to confide in Michele. There was no point in opening the door to his private torment and discussing the cruel whisper which played at the back of his mind. He had never told anyone about it and did not believe this was the time to begin.

"John, don't you think it's time to let God back into your life?"

"That's the last thing I want to talk about now, Michele," he said wearily.

"I know, but you've been living in torment for the past two years. Don't you want out? Wouldn't it be nice to have God lift you out of it?"

"He's not going to do that."

"He will, if you ask Him."

"No, He won't," Brindle said. "Things have happened that you don't understand."

"We've all done things, John. That's what repentance and forgiveness are all about."

Brindle shook his head, but he could feel it coming.

"Anyway," Michele offered, "how could it be any worse?"

Brindle clamped his jaw, but it was almost there now and his mouth was beginning to work without his control.

"It wasn't an accident," he said distantly.

"What do you mean?"

"That night on the road. . . it wasn't an accident."

Michele stopped walking and stood in the surf.

"What are you saying, John?"

"Sarah and I had been arguing. I don't know what happened."

"It can't be," Michele said in almost a whisper.

Brindle gazed at the ocean. "So now you know," he said, his voice trembling.

Michele looked him in the eyes. "You did it on purpose?"

"Yes," Brindle admitted.

"You set out that evening to have an accident?"

"Of course not."

"Did you want to hurt your daughter?"

"Never."

"So what happened?"

"We had been to a party. Sarah and I were arguing on the way home. It was raining. I saw the headlights of the truck coming . . ."

"And you turned into them?"

"I don't remember . . . but I must have."

"And you've been carrying this guilt around for two years?"

Brindle waved his hand. "Let's just forget it. I don't want to talk about it anymore."

Michele took him by the arm. "Listen, John," she said, "maybe we don't really know each other that well, but I've seen you at work here. I know how hard you try. I don't believe you would ever harm anyone on purpose—least of all your family."

"My wife and daughter are dead, Michele," he replied.

"But don't you see," she pleaded, "you feel guilty about it because you were driving. Naturally you feel responsible, but that doesn't mean you did it on purpose."

"Does it really matter?" he asked.

"Yes," she said adamantly. "And you've got to ask God for help. You can't do this on your own, John, you just can't."

"I'll think about it," he said.

❦

He did think about it that night, as the hours ticked slowly by till dawn. Sitting on the edge of his bed in the darkness, wishing the time away, he imagined he could hear again the voice which asked, almost as if it were his own demanding of him, "Whom do you seek?"

"You know who I'm looking for," he whispered angrily.

He couldn't make it on his own; he realized that now. By himself, he had managed to slip farther and farther into the pit. But calling on God and repenting of his hardness of heart was another thing. That required him to relinquish the bitterness he had felt for two years, and he was not sure that was possible. Perhaps Michele was right when she said that you could not be neutral. Since the accident, he had believed that he was standing aside, watching the spiritual battle take place without him. Now he understood that he had crossed the line, and had been effectively taken out of the game. If he could not escape the sorrow, then he was not a free man. And if he was not free, then who was his personal dalang? Who was manipulating his strings? Which part did he play in the wayang drama?

Brindle thought about praying and even clasped his hands together fervently, but he could not do it. He could not make himself repent of the bitterness.

"No," he muttered to himself, "Not yet."

✏

The following morning he made his rounds with Tran at his side. The psychic trauma case had improved, though the emotional strain had left the woman in a state of exhaustion. Another symptom of deep depression, Brindle thought, and made a note on her chart.

"Has she eaten anything?" he asked, checking her pulse.

"She no care about food, Doctor," Tran explained. "All time sleep."

"Have the aides keep an eye on her."

The malnourished patients were looking better.

"The man in bed three seems to be getting stronger," he commented to Tran. "Has he walked yet?"

"Small steps around bed, Doctor."

"Good. We'll keep him another day."

Tran studied Brindle thoughtfully. "You okay, Doctor?" he asked with compassion. "Everything okay? Sleep okay last night?"

"I couldn't sleep," Brindle stated, "but yes, I'm okay."

"Good, good," Tran smiling. "You look different."

"Do I?" Brindle asked. He picked up the Montagnard baby and held her in his arms. She felt light, as if there were nothing at all within the folds of the blanket but only the dark hair and the tiny, brown searching hands. She was three weeks old now—still too young to travel. A memory came back to him of pacing in a restaurant with Carrie in his arms while Sarah finished her dinner.

"What name you give this baby?" Tran asked.

Brindle rocked the child casually in his arms. "I don't know. You name her—something beautiful in Vietnamese."

"Okay," Tran said. "I name her Trieu after my daughter. Trieu Au was important woman in Vietnamese history. Fight for independence against Chinese."

"You have a daughter?" Brindle asked, surprised.

"Two daughter," Tran replied. "Trieu nine when I go in boat."

"I never knew that."

Tran jabbed his hands into the pockets of his medical coat. "I see again some day," he said. "In America, I send for family."

"If there's anything I can do . . ."

Tran smiled encouragingly. "You write letter? Maybe letter from Doctor Brindle help family come U.S.A."

"Sure, Tran. As soon as you get settled in the states, I'll write a letter to the immigration office."

The baby began to cry, and Brindle handed her to an aide who was waiting with a bottle.

"I'll see you later, Trieu," he said, running his hand affectionately over the baby's silky black hair.

❧

After his rounds he went to Michele's office, but she was not there. Then he saw her coming across the compound from the clinic. She must have been looking for him. As she came closer, Brindle saw that she was frowning. Her lower lip was curled upwards and her brow was furrowed. There must be a problem, he thought to himself. She only looked that way when there was a problem.

Michele saw him and waved.

"I was looking for you this time," he said as she stepped into the shade.

"Yes?" she asked, her frown brightening to a smile.

"I need to ask you something. It's kind of a legal, moral question."

"Are you asking me as a friend or as Hal's assistant?"

"Both, I guess."

"Do you want to go into my office?"

"It's too hot. How about if we walk over to the clearing?"

Michele glanced at her watch. "Okay. I have a few minutes."

What Brindle wanted to ask her was something which had not even clearly formulated in his thoughts, but which caused him to feel a calm joy every time the idea came into his head. It was a thought which had begun so far back in the recesses of his mind that he had not even fully recognized it himself for several weeks. But looking back on it now, he realized that it had originated even as he was listening to the Montagnard baby's heartbeat after the delivery. She had only moments before passed her mother in life—one coming into the world as the other moved away from it—and he had thought, she needs me now. She has no one and I have no one. We are a pair.

But did he really want to share this with Michele?

"So what do you want to know?" she asked, looking at him.

Brindle chewed his lower lip and gazed across the clearing. "It can wait," he said, finally. "I need to think about it some more."

"Okay," Michele said. "Whatever."

"So what's bothering you?" he asked. "You didn't look so happy when you were crossing the courtyard."

"Oh, that." Michele sighed. "Something odd happened in my office this morning . . . Well, I guess it's odd. Maybe it was nothing."

"What happened?"

"My desk," she said. "It was really neat."

"I see what you mean," Brindle scoffed.

"I mean, it was all straightened up—everything in its place, papers stacked—all that."

"And it usually isn't?"

"Sometimes, but not yesterday."

"So the cleaning lady straightened it up for you."

"We have a girl who comes in to sweep the floors and chase out the lizards, but she doesn't work on Sundays."

"Then you think someone was messing with your papers?"

Michele shrugged. "I had a stack of files on the edge of my desk—the refugees who are going out on the next boat. I have a feeling that someone knocked them off and then put them back—but did a much neater job than I would have done."

So, if someone was messing with your files, the question is—why?"

"Maybe to see who was shipping out."

"Do you look at the files again once you've selected the departing group?"

Michele shook her head. "No, not usually. Once I've made the selection, I give them to my assistant to type out the names."

Brindle began to think that Kim Thi had known what she was talking about after all.

"If someone wanted to switch the files—say, perhaps take one out and put in another—could they do that after you've made the selection?" he asked.

"I suppose so, but I put a red tag on them."

"How difficult would it be to peel off the sticker?"

Michele hesitated in the shade of a palm tree. "I see what you mean."

"I'm not saying that's what happened," Brindle said, "but I've heard rumors. Kim Thi said that was why Hoang was at the black market meeting—to get enough money to buy their way to the Philippines."

"That's ridiculous!"

"I told her the same thing, but maybe she was right. Everything else has gotten so screwed up around here, why shouldn't there be a problem with the boarding list?"

"I'm beginning to get angry," Michele said.

"What are you going to do?"

"I'll have to do the departing files all over again," she sighed. "That's going to take a full day. Then I'll make a list myself and keep it with me."

"We could be wrong," Brindle advised. "Wait until your assistant types up the new list and then check it against yours. If there are changes, then you'll know something is up."

"I'll let you know," she said.

Brindle smiled. "Maybe we could talk again after dinner."

"If I finish the files . . ."

When she had gone, Brindle glanced at his watch. It was time to return to the clinic. Crossing the compound, he saw a familiar figure sitting on the steps.

"Hello, Kim Thi," he said meekly.

Chapter Twenty

Vo Nguyen crouched behind a palm tree and slowly moved his head until he could see down into the camp. From this position, he could see the rusted tin roof of the clinic and beyond the camp office to the supply hut. It was the supply hut he was interested in observing. With so much rain from the monsoons, the vegetation around the camp was too damp to burn easily. Even the floorboards of the clinic and office were saturated with water to the point where they would not burn but would only smolder. Nguyen was no longer interested in trying to make a point or to frighten the Indonesians; he wanted destruction; he wanted to see the camp in flames. It would be a fitting revenge for the thousands of deserters who had betrayed the great communist dream of Ho Chi Mihn. Nguyen would smile as he watched them burn. The best way to start the fire would be to douse the buildings and huts with kerosene, and he knew that containers of the flammable liquid were locked in the back of the supply hut. He would have to break into the supply hut and steal the kerosene. It would be dangerous, but he would wait for a few days. Calculating in his mind, he decided that it would take at least four men to do the job effectively. Six would be even better, but he had not yet contacted five men whom he could trust. Three men had met with him the night before and they had seemed to be reliable, but Nguyen knew there was a big difference between discussing sabotage and actually carrying it out. And these three men were refugees—cowards who had run away from the revolution once before. *Why not again?* the infiltrator asked himself.

Slipping onto his belly, Nguyen crawled forward through the undergrowth and to the left, until he could see the front door of the supply hut. As he did so, he noticed that the American doctor had come from the camp office and was talking to one of the refugee women. *I should have killed him when I had a chance in the fog*, Nguyen thought calmly, gazing at the doctor. For one brief moment after stabbing the guard, Nguyen had considered killing the doctor too. The American had just been standing there on the edge of the dock by himself. It would have been easy. But then Nguyen had heard voices in the haze and had slipped away. He wondered how many refugees would be dead now if the doctor had not been there to save them? He did not know, but Nguyen imagined there would be many. Glancing at the supply hut again, he decided that he would try the front door first. If the door was too secure, then he would break the lock on the side window. The chaos would begin at midnight. As he crawled away through the damp grass, Nguyen imagined he could already feel the heat and crackle of the flames.

"I sorry," Kim Thi said to Brindle, not meeting his eyes but gazing off to his right at a place on the ground. "Mama no understand. Hoang dead. So sad."

Brindle watched her nervously curl a strand of dark hair behind her ear and thought to himself, *It's all there*. With the death of her brother on Saturday night and the rejection by Mrs. Van Quang on Sunday, Brindle had managed to put a few miserable nights of torment behind him. He had worked hard at the clinic all morning and was beginning to feel a slight wedge of distance between himself and Kim Thi. But apparently, it was not enough. The moment he saw her, it was all there again, the feelings, the pain of loss, the desire. *Human emotions hide behind such elusive camouflage*, he thought to himself. And the fool in him, the perpetual youth with its naive dreams, held out a slight hope that perhaps their relationship could continue after all. Perhaps he had been overly harsh with Kim Thi. Perhaps she did still care for him. He felt the words conjuring up inside himself now and knew that within a moment they would be spoken—but he did not feel good about it. He felt as if his actions were inevitable and that he was no longer reacting from his heart but from that place in his soul where desire was created. Brindle knew that desire was not love, and he suddenly felt remorse at the loss of something which had never had the chance to flourish. He felt compelled to try, however, because his longing for Kim Thi had not diminished to the point where he was able to let it go.

"I've missed you," he said tentatively, believing there was truth in the words but not knowing where the truth lay. He had missed her, there was no denying that. However, he was beginning to see things again without the inconsistency of emotional upheaval—which meant his life was returning to a certain stability.

"We friends, okay?" she asked, meeting his searching gaze for the first time. He did not see tenderness in her dark eyes now but only a cool apprehension of the situation. She was much tougher emotionally than he had given her credit. Perhaps it had even been her idea to slit the skin and place the necklace inside her arm. He could believe that of her now. Kim Thi was purposefully distancing herself, establishing that they were now friends—which had the implication that perhaps for a time they had not been—and that any hint of romantic feelings was long past. Brindle felt himself withdrawing, pulling back into that small area between his shoulder blades defensively. And he was surprised as he did this, that distrust so quickly slipped into the place where affection had been.

"Yes," he said, feeling depression settle over him. "We're friends."

The depression stayed with Brindle as he made his rounds that afternoon, and lingered like the scent of alcohol on his clothing when he attended the staff meeting that evening. He had assumed the feeling would vanish when Kim Thi was no longer within his sight, but this had not happened.

"Do you really think that I would burn the jungle?" Salinem was asking when Brindle seated himself at the table.

"That's what you said," Aldridge replied.

"I was angry. Have you not said things in anger that you later realized were imprudent?"

"It has been done," Aldridge said.

"So what *are* you going to do, Captain?" Michele asked.

"Reinforcements should arrive on Wednesday. We will then cover every inch of Boromu until we find the infiltrator."

"I'm glad to hear that," Brindle said, but Salinem ignored him.

"The next transport group leaves for the Philippines in two weeks," Aldridge continued. "It would sure help, Captain, if you could find Nguyen by then."

"I assure you, Mr. Aldridge, that his body will be hanging from the palm tree outside the camp by then."

"What a pleasant thought," Brindle muttered.

Salinem looked at him harshly. "You and your western sensibilities, Doctor. It is no wonder that your country is degenerating into anarchy."

"But we do it with style, Captain," Brindle said. "We have CNN. The Romans never had minute-by-minute coverage during their rise and fall. Neither did the Third Reich."

"That is true," Salinem said with disdain. "And when the end comes, you will all be at home, watching it on instant replay."

"Gentlemen," Aldridge snapped. "We have more than enough trouble to keep us busy here. Let's try to keep focused."

Michele had only asked the one question during the meeting, and, watching her, Brindle realized that she looked nervous. Throughout his interchange with Salinem, she had fidgeted with her hands—rubbing one thumbnail against the other. Thinking back on her question, Brindle wondered if there were more to it than the obvious reply. "What *are* you going to do?"

she had asked. Brindle wondered now if she was even referring to Nguyen.

She was waiting for him on the terrace when he came out of the office. It was a pleasant evening, and he could see the stars through the trees. A storm with heavy winds had swept through the camp earlier, but now the atmosphere was calm.

"You were right, John," she said quietly. "The list has been changed."

"How many names?"

"Twenty."

"Wow . . ."

"Exactly twenty percent," Michele said. "Can you believe that?"

Brindle shook his head. "It's a shame."

A tear rolled down Michele's cheek. "Hal has worked so hard to keep this camp honest."

"It is honest," Brindle said. "But it isn't Shangri-la. There will always be problems."

"You sound so calm," she said. "I wish I could be that way."

"No, you don't," Brindle said. "You have to give up too much to be this way."

"I'm beginning to hate this place!"

Hate was a strong emotion, Brindle thought. Perhaps he should be angry himself, but he found it almost humorous that someone had messed with the transportation list. Why not? Where there was human endeavor, there was corruption. It was inevitable.

"Use some excuse and call them in one at a time," he suggested. "We'll question each one and find out who's behind this. If they won't tell us, then they won't leave the camp. It's as simple as that."

"We're going to have some very angry refugees."

"They knew the rules."

"I'd better tell Hal. He's going to be so upset."

"What about Salinem?"

"No," she said. "I don't think so."

Brindle had seen many of the refugees as they disembarked at the dock. He had treated others at the clinic and had a fair memory of their faces. The first refugee to come into Michele's office was an older man who had been a patient at the clinic, though Brindle could not remember his case history. The man looked fit now and gave the doctor a smile of timid recognition as he sat in a chair before the desk. His WRO card was clutched in his hand. Michele had told the refugees the meeting was necessary to review their paperwork before departure.

Aldridge followed the man into the office and closed the door. When the refugee saw the three staff members gazing at him questioningly, his expectant smile slowly changed to worry and then suspicion. His eyes narrowed, and he clutched his knees nervously.

"Mr. Tu," Michele began politely, "we've had some problems with our transportation list, and we thought perhaps you could help us."

Michele's assistant, a young woman everyone called Lily, translated.

Mr. Tu asked something in Vietnamese.

Brindle suddenly recalled that Mr. Tu had been brought from the launch with symptoms of dehydration and had spent five days in the clinic. *When was that?* Brindle wondered. Possibly in December. He looked better now, though his cheeks were still sunken. But that could be from tooth loss.

"He want know, what is transportation list?" Lily interpreted.

Michele slowly explained to the refugee the procedures for departing from the camp. When she was certain that he understood, she continued.

"Now, Mr. Tu. This is a list I made up for the next group to leave this camp for the Philippines. You will see that there are one hundred names on the list." Michele hesitated while Mr. Tu bobbed his head in agreement. "But your name is not there."

When Lily translated this, Mr. Tu stopped bobbing his head and began to sweat.

"Yet you seem to think that you are going."

Mr. Tu looked at Brindle and then at Aldridge.

"Who told you that you were going?" Michele asked.

Mr. Tu scratched the back of his head nervously.

"Do you know what a bribe is, Mr. Tu?"

Lily had trouble translating this question.

"It's unfortunate, but you've apparently paid out some money or other valuable item to get your name on this list. Whoever took your money tricked you, because I have the real list right here, and your name is not on it."

When Lily translated this, Mr. Tu turned pale and looked as if he was going to faint.

"John?" Aldridge cautioned.

"I've got him," Brindle said. He had taken Mr. Tu by the shoulders. "It's hot in here. Maybe you could open the door."

Lily opened the door, and Brindle imagined that this helped, though he could feel no difference in the air flow. Perhaps it was the anxiety in the office which had raised the temperature.

"We need to know who you paid," Michele said kindly.

Mr. Tu gazed at her blankly and swallowed hard.

"I guess we're going to have to get tough," Aldridge said. He nodded to Lily, who began to explain to Mr. Tu the consequences of not cooperating. As she talked, the man shook his head slowly and gazed at the floor.

"Tell him to pack his bags," Aldridge said finally. "He's on his way back to Vietnam."

Mr. Tu began to talk rapidly, desperately, to Lily.

"He say he give two hundred dollars to Sergeant Purwanto. Purwanto say all okay for him leaving on this boat."

"I'm sorry you've lost your money," Michele said sincerely. "You will get off Boromu Island, I promise you, but you'll have to wait your turn."

"Should we send for Sergeant Purwanto?" Brindle asked.

"Not yet, John," Aldridge answered. "Let's question a few more first. We need more than one source on something like this."

"Okay," Michele said to Lily. "Bring in the next one."

How childlike adults are when they get caught, Brindle thought as he watched refugee after refugee come into the office. There was the withdrawn silence, the impudent thrust jaw, the refusal to believe until the blow fell—the threat of returning to Vietnam. Brindle felt that he could have made a checklist for the ten interviews he witnessed, filling in the appropriate box for each response as Michele asked the questions. He was surprised how many refugees refused to cooperate, even under the threat of deportation. But after a fourth man had specifically named Sergeant Purwanto as the recipient of the payoff, Aldridge was satisfied.

"That's good enough for me," Aldridge said finally. "I was convinced after the second man. Tell the others to go back to the camp."

"You realize," Brindle interjected, "that Captain Salinem may be behind this. A sergeant couldn't pull off something like this without the captain hearing about it."

"I know," Aldridge said. "However, the way I see it, our job is not to punish but to stop the corruption."

This was a new concept for Brindle. He had always thought in terms of punishment for faults committed. His life was built around the fact that if he didn't discipline himself, then God would, or Life would, or some other exterior factor would intervene. *How easy life would be if we could just move along without any consequences*, he thought. That would resolve so many problems. But Aldridge was right. The WRO staff was not in a place to judge. Hal simply wanted the bribery to stop.

"We'll have to go through channels," Michele offered. "That means we go to Captain Salinem first. In fact, we don't have the authority to discipline one of his men."

"And if he's behind this, then he's got us good," Brindle said. "We complain. . . he says he's dealing with it. . . and nothing happens."

"Oh, something will happen," Aldridge said. "The Captain doesn't want to lose face. He will have to discipline Purwanto."

Brindle went back to his room and stretched out on his bunk. He could hear the rustle of night wind in the palms and equated the sound with the loneliness which blew across the sand and up the slope from the camp toward his room. He could hear the faint murmur of Vietnamese voices, and although he could not understand them, they all seemed to be saying, "Just friends . . . just friends . . . just friends," in melodic repetition. He did not know how he was going to get over this one. In the past he could always change his life, and that had usually taken care of the problem. He was a firm believer in the theory of "out of sight, out of mind"—it seemed to work in his heart, and sometimes this troubled him. But there was nowhere for him to go now. He had driven himself to this foreign corner of the world—this remote island, and yet pain had found him here, had sought him out, had manipulated his needs and desires so that he had stupidly and foolishly made himself vulnerable. Now he was paying. It was not so much that he felt trapped as it was that he felt that there was nowhere else to go. *Life*, he thought to himself, *was not a matter of time but of options in relation to what you needed.*

Chapter Twenty-One

"Soldiers come," Tran said to Brindle as he entered the ward. "In launch from ship. You come see, Doctor."

"Just a moment," Brindle said. His stethoscope was pressed against the rib cage of a child who had symptoms of pneumonia. She was trying to breath slowly and deeply, but each time her small chest lifted, she went into a spasm of coughing.

"Tran, will you ask her to relax?" Brindle said. He moved his stethoscope across the small spine to the right lung.

The rattles were there.

"I wish we had a few of those respirators," he said, beginning to think about how he could rig up something. "But let's get her on antibiotics."

He pulled down the child's tattered shirt. She smiled up at him sweetly and began to cough.

"Soldiers come," Tran repeated.

"At the dock?"

"Yes, Doctor."

"I suppose I can spare a few minutes."

Boxes of equipment were piled on the beach. As Brindle and Tran reached the dock, the launch had just disembarked another group of soldiers and was heading out toward the ship again. The soldiers sat in groups smoking and talking while they waited. Brindle noticed that these men did not look like the Boromu guards. They wore dark green berets, appeared to be in better shape, and carried AK-47s slung over their shoulders on webbed slings. Each man also carried a webbed belt with four ammunition containers and a canteen. Their uniforms were dappled green and tan.

"Who are these guys?" Brindle asked.

"Paratroopers," Tran said.

"Looks like they mean business."

"I think all over for Nguyen now," Tran said, looking at the paratroopers. "He dead pretty soon."

"I hope you're right."

"Doctor? . . . Doctor?" Someone was calling him from the pathway. It was Lily.

"Miss Fallon say come for meeting, Doctor."

"Is Captain Salinem there?"

"Yes, Sir."

"Okay," Brindle said.

This was a moment he had been dreading. He did not fear confrontation, but he had been through enough with Captain Salinem. The open hostility expressed by each of them at meetings was beginning to wear him down. One of the difficulties with the remoteness and isolation of Boromu was that if there were a personnel problem, you could not get away from it. The person remained at your side like a constant irritation, like a sore which could not heal because of repeated aggravation.

As usual, the meeting had already begun when Brindle arrived. Upon entering Michele's office, he saw Captain Salinem pacing back and forth irritably, his walking stick in hand. He had expected as much. Even if Salinem were guilty of instigating the bribery, he would not confess his actions to them. Aldridge leaned against the wall next to a large chart with the monthly arrivals and departures of refugees from the island.

"This is intolerable!" Captain Salinem snapped. "You have definite proof?"

Michele nodded. "I'm afraid so, Captain. I have proof of the changed lists here, and four refugees have identified Sergeant Purwanto as the man they paid."

"I will see that he is punished," Salinem promised.

"The question," Brindle interrupted, "is who should be punished."

Salinem turned to him. "What do you mean?"

"Purwanto wouldn't have been involved in this by himself. You know that."

"Are you implying, Doctor . . ."

Brindle stood up. "What else have you done, Captain, that we haven't found out about yet? What about those refugees who were killed trying to escape? Were they really trying to escape, Captain?"

The slap came without warning, and Brindle felt a burning pain across his left ear and cheek. His left eye began to swell instantly.

"Captain!" Michele cried out.

Falling against the desk, Brindle had a blurred vision of Aldridge grabbing the stick from Salinem's raised hand, as if the Captain were preparing to strike him again.

"Go drink yourself to death, Doctor!" Salinem snarled. "You are a dead man anyway!"

"Captain!" Aldridge shouted. "Captain!"

Salinem gave them all a look of undisguised hatred and stomped out of the office.

Brindle felt Michele's hand around his shoulder. "John?" she asked. "Are you all right?"

"I don't know," Brindle said. He pulled his hand away from his cheek and saw blood on his fingertips. It was the second time in five days that his hand had come away bloodied. The last time had been with Hoang's blood. *Was there any difference?* Brindle wondered.

"I can't believe he hit you," Aldridge exclaimed. "But you shouldn't have confronted him, John."

"Someone had to do it," Brindle muttered, feeling with his fingers the tear on his cheekbone. He tried to open his jaw and felt pain.

"Come on," Michele said. "I'll get you to the clinic."

The paratroopers moved into the camp at mid-morning. While one group secured the perimeter, the remainder proceeded to do an intensive search. Each refugee was required to show their identification papers. Any male who resembled Nguyen's description was detained and checked by Duong. The floors of huts were examined for hiding places. A refugee who resisted was given a gun butt to the head. By sunset the camp had been thoroughly searched and locked down. A curfew went into effect beginning at eight o'clock. The refugees were told to stay in their huts. It was understood that the Indonesian paratroopers would not think twice about opening fire.

At dawn the paratroopers left the perimeter of the camp and moved into the jungle. Watching them fan out and move off, Brindle had the impression that he was observing beaters trying to frighten a tiger.

"They'll get him," Aldridge said. "And that will be the end of it."

"Do you think so?"

"Yes. And I heard from Jakarta last night. Captain Salinem will be out of here on Monday."

"A week early."

"Then everything will be back to normal." Aldridge sighed. "I don't know how much more of this I could have taken."

"Any more headaches?" Brindle asked.

"A few. Not so many with the new medicine you gave me."

"Take care of yourself, Hal."

"What about you?" Aldridge asked. "The helicopter will be here tomorrow morning."

"I'm all right," Brindle said, touching the scab on his cheek. "Anyway, what's the worst that could happen to me?"

"Don't talk like that, John. You spend a few weeks in Manila. When you come back, everything will be fine."

"Did you ever feel like something was going to happen, Hal?" Brindle asked. "Or rather . . . not happen?" He asked this

because for some days now, he could not imagine a life for himself beyond Boromu Island. Whenever he thought of the
future, it always came back around to this camp. He had
decided that it would be fitting if he stayed at the refugee
camp, for who was more a refugee than he?

Aldridge suddenly looked pensive. "Once," he said,
thoughtfully. "A long time ago."

"What happened?"

The administrator squinted out into the sunlight of the
compound. "I was waiting for someone," he said. "I waited all
day at the airport. . . and the next. I sat there for two days. I
was so sick of airport coffee, you can't imagine."

"A woman?"

Aldridge nodded.

"And finally you realized she wasn't coming?"

"Oh, no," Aldridge said, shaking his head slowly. "I knew
she wasn't coming before I ever drove out to the airport. I
knew maybe a week in advance. I heard it on the news."

"About her?"

Aldridge gave a short laugh. "No, about the fall of Saigon."

Ah, Brindle thought, realizing that so many questions had
been answered. "But you went anyway."

"I had to," Aldridge said. "I had to see for myself. And sec-
ondly, I've been wrong more times than I've been right, John."

It really did seem as if things were changing, as if something had been set in motion, or had always been in motion,
which he had not detected. We always think we are so aware
of what is happening around us, he thought to himself, and yet
later, when we have time to reflect, we ask ourselves what we
could possibly have been thinking. But it was more than that.
It was as if he had been playing by the wrong rules in an
unknown game for years, and now the game was ending. He
knew what he had done, though. He knew the actions he had
made and the people he had hurt. There was no denying that
much. He would have to seek them out and apologize. What
had Jesus said? That a man could not add one hour to his life,

yet God had provided for even the birds of the air—or something like that. It had been a long time since Brindle had read that verse. He would try to find it when he got back to his room.

Making his rounds at the clinic, he was surprised to find that the little girl with pneumonia had not improved. If anything, he realized as he held his stethoscope up to her back, the rattles were worse. He made a note to increase her antibiotic.

"You see Trieu now?" Tran insisted, coming from the nursery. "She very hot."

"What do you mean, hot?" he asked. "A temperature?"

Tran nodded. "You see, Doctor."

The baby was fussing miserably as Brindle reached into her crib and touched her cheek. A mild panic flashed through him. She was very hot—with a temperature, he guessed, of at least 103 degrees.

"How long has she been like this?" he asked, while undoing the baby's diaper so that he could gently insert a thermometer.

Tran spoke to the Indonesian aide. "She all okay this morning," he replied.

"Has anyone tried to pick her up?"

Tran spoke to the aide. "Yes, she pick up baby."

"What happened?"

"Baby cry loud. Hurt ears."

"That's what I was afraid of," Brindle said.

As he removed the thermometer, the baby vomited.

The aide reached for a towel.

Brindle looked at the thermometer. It registered a temperature of 104 degrees.

"I think she has E-coli meningitis," he said. "It's bacterial."

"So hot," Tran repeated.

"We need to get her on an antibiotic promptly. One hundred milligrams per day."

"I prepare injection?" Tran suggested.

"No," Brindle said. "We'll have to give it to her intra-venously."

Brindle went to the pharmacy and got a vial of the new antibiotic that Michele had brought back from the Philippines. Then he searched the baby's scalp.

"Get me a butterfly needle, will you, Tran?" he asked.

"Yes, Doctor."

He set up the IV on a scalp vein and then straightened up and gazed at the baby.

"There, there," he whispered to the infant.

She was sleeping now, but it wasn't a good sleep—she was knocked out by the fever.

"How long wait?" Tran asked.

"If she isn't any worse by tomorrow morning, then we'll know," Brindle explained. "The fever should be broken in twenty-four to thirty-six hours."

He glanced at the empty antibiotic vial in the pan beside the crib. It was a good thing Michele had brought the new box with her from Manila. It was enough to tide him over until the WRO shipment arrived from Switzerland. There was Chinese writing on the side of the box, and Brindle wondered vaguely where Michele had made her purchase. Then he turned his thoughts back to the baby.

"Hang in there, Trieu," he whispered again.

In the afternoon Brindle felt as if there was something he needed to do. Glancing at his watch, he realized this was the hour of day that he had usually visited Kim Thi. He thought about his place on the rock beside the cook fire, the battered cup of tea, the gentle conversation, and the way her dark hair fell around her face and shoulders. *Was that all over now?* he wondered. He wanted to see her. The desire was upon him—he was so much a victim of his desires—and he felt as if no logical thinking could prevent his feet from heading in that direction.

He knew that it was perhaps unwise for him to visit her, yet he also knew that if he did not make the effort, he would never see her again.

Ironically, he felt somewhat relieved when she was not at her shanty. There was only one place she could be at this time of day, so he walked along the footpath to the beach. Kim Thi was there, seated at the water's edge beside her mother and her girlfriends, talking and gazing out at the waves. *Were her friends consoling her?* he wondered. *Talking about Hoang?* Brindle lingered in the shadows of the palm trees. He felt hesitant about speaking to her now. *What was there to say, anyway?* he asked himself. Could they go on talking of pleasantries after all that had happened? Obviously not. So why bother? He was just making it more difficult for them both. Returning through the camp, he felt as if he were permanently leaving a part of himself back there on the beach, a part of himself that would eventually be lifted by the evening tide, carried out to the great expanse of South China Sea, and disposed of as easily as if it were dropped into a hole. Looking back at the water now, he imagined the rising and falling waves were like soldiers punching holes in canvas with bayonets. He was tired of conflict. From now on, he told himself with determination, he was going to mind his own business and try to get some semblance of his life, however fragmented, back in order.

He had promised to visit Michele after dinner, but he was worried about the baby and stopped by the clinic to check on her progress. He was beginning to feel now, with each time that he saw her, held her, felt the small brown hands groping for his fingers, a bond growing between them. They were both, after all, orphans in a way. She had lost her father, and he had rejected his spiritual Father. They were bound by that sense of loss, and by the sense that as her life had come into this world and her mother's had passed on, Brindle had been there waiting for her. But this feeling of hope was quickly diminishing. The baby's temperature remained at a stubborn 104 degrees.

"You're sure she is getting the antibiotic?" he asked Tran.

"Oh, yes, Doctor," Tran responded. "Just like you say. One hundred milligrams."

"Okay," Brindle said thoughtfully.

"Something wrong, Doctor?" Tran asked with concern.

"I was just hoping," Brindle muttered, letting the thought fade. He had seen temperatures as high as 106 degrees with meningitis, but those patients were usually terminal. He began to wonder if he should do a spinal tap and check the status of her fluid. If it was not clear, then her prognosis was bad.

⮑✕⮑

"How's the baby?" Michele asked, as she held out a cup of tea. She had put on the jazz tape again, and Brindle was beginning to feel that he understood the music. It had begun with a simple melody and now went on in a cascading flow of variations. Perhaps this new understanding had come from the drink he had taken before dinner. He had decided that he would no longer keep up the ridiculous pretense of abstinence. So what if he drank from time to time, he told himself. He could handle it, and anyway, that probably would be his last drink. If he were really thinking about. . .

"Her temperature hasn't broken," Brindle replied, interrupting his thought. "I'm worried about her."

"You said it might take twenty-four hours."

"I know," he shrugged. "It's nothing out of the ordinary. I had just hoped . . ."

"But if her temperature doesn't go down, then it could be serious, right?"

"Very."

"So what else can you do?"

Brindle took a sip of his tea. There was no half-written letter on Michele's table this evening. Perhaps she had found friendship in Manila. Or perhaps, like Brindle, she was beginning to distance herself from the past—though he doubted this was necessary. It seemed to him that life lay before Michele like an open promise. Everything about her pointed to the future and not the past.

"Nothing for the moment," he said in answer to her question. "We have to give the antibiotic time to work."

Michele looked at him. "You could say a prayer, John. If you really care about this baby, then you could say a prayer for her."

Brindle set down his cup. "No, I can't," he said harshly. "We'll just give the antibiotic time to do its job."

"You can't reject God forever," Michele said. "It's not possible."

"Who told you that?" Brindle asked. "I believe it is definitely possible."

But he was beginning to have doubts, and as he walked back toward the clinic, a thought came to him. He recalled the Chinese writing on the side of the antibiotic vial. In the third world you never really knew what you were getting when it came to medicine. It was very possible that the antibiotic was old or had been diluted. This was especially true of tetracycline. If that were the case, then he had nothing to give the baby to break the fever. The ants had seen to that. The meningitis would continue on its course and eventually kill her. A twinge of fear entered his stomach. Could it be, he thought, that he was about to lose another child, to let another infant slip through his fingers? A feeling of desperation came over him. Will it never end?. He felt the wall which separated him emotionally from the rest of the world, and from God, going up a bit higher.

In the ward he saw a woman seated beside the young pneumonia patient. The child was coughing in gurgling rasps. The mother gazed at him fearfully.

"She's no better either," Brindle muttered to himself. "It has to be the antibiotic."

Tran was in the nursery.

"How's the baby?" Brindle asked immediately.

Tran shook his head. "No good, Doctor. Still hot. You think maybe she die?"

"No," Brindle snapped, but there was no assurance behind his words. "Prepare a spinal tap."

"Spinal. . . tap?" Tran asked, puzzled.

"Sorry," Brindle said. "You've never done that procedure. Look, I'll show you."

After securing the infant, he carefully slid a stylet between the vertebrae and into the spinal column, slipped in the spinal needle, and retracted the plunger. The fluid which entered the syringe was clear.

"Whew," Brindle sighed. "That's good."

"What good, Doctor?" Tran asked.

"It's clear," Brindle said. "But that just buys us a little time. We have to get her onto a new antibiotic."

"I get from storeroom?" Tran suggested.

Brindle shook his head. "It's no good." He glanced at his watch. It was after eleven. "Will you send someone for Miss Fallon?"

"Maybe she sleep," Tran suggested.

"That doesn't matter," Brindle said. "We need to get some new antibiotic fast."

When Michele arrived it was obvious that she had just pulled on a pair of shorts and a t-shirt. Her hair was not combed.

"The antibiotic you got in Manila is worthless," Brindle explained as she came up beside him and looked at the baby.

"I'm sorry," Michele offered. "I had no idea."

"It's not your fault," Brindle said. "I would probably have done the same thing. But we need some new stuff right away or we're going to lose at least one patient—maybe two."

"Okay," Michele said. "I'll get on the shortwave to Jakarta. Maybe we can bypass the usual red tape and get a helicopter out here in the morning. That's if I can find someone awake and if they have the antibiotic."

"Let me know."

"In the meantime you could do something," Michele said as she hurried out of the room.

"What's that?" Brindle called after her.

"Say that prayer."

It was after one o'clock in the morning when Brindle returned to his room and his bed. He was exhausted and dropped down wearily onto the mattress. Kicking off his shoes, he rolled onto his back. He had spent the last two hours trying to rig up a respirator for the child with pneumonia. He had managed to come up with something that seemed to work, but she still needed an antibiotic. And the baby? The thought occurred to him that he might have seen Trieu alive for the last time. This sent a shiver of desperation through him, like a silent wave beneath the skin. He did not want to lose this child. He wanted to raise her as his own, to be a father again. Perhaps he had known that from the very beginning. Perhaps he had not really let it surface to his consciousness because he knew that God would put a stop to it. But of course God knew, as He knew everything, and therefore it was He who had given the child this illness. He had done this to spite Brindle, but it was not fair. No one else deserved to die for his sins, Brindle told himself. He had already lost his wife and daughter—and in many ways himself. He felt his hands wiping his eyes, and then coming together in a fervent grasp. What was he doing? he wondered. Was he surrendering? Had he finally suffered enough, survived in that black, emotional abyss enough so that he could no longer go on existing this way? Was it time to surrender? *Yes*, he told himself wearily. *It was time*. He had touched bottom when he had first set foot on Boromu Island, and now he was nothing but a heap of ashes waiting to be molded. *Well, perhaps Michele was right*, he told himself. Perhaps the void left in his soul by the extradition of God had been filled by something else—by a different dalang, and if that were true, then Brindle was no more free than he had ever been. It was time to rid himself of the bitterness and anger and ask God for help—not for himself, but for the sake of the child. In some way this seemed to mollify his surrender. Brindle was thinking more clearly now. He would open himself up to God again for the sake of someone else. Perhaps that was what he had needed all along—to re-establish his communion with God through intercession for another soul. Anyway, he told himself, *now was the time to try.*

But how?

Merely clasping his hands together did not seem humble enough for this act of contrition, so he rolled off the bed and onto his knees.

"God," he whispered, and the name sounded awkward in his mouth. It had been so long. "Holy Father," he tried again. "I repent my sins of bitterness and lack of faith and ask for Your forgiveness. I rejected You as the cornerstone of my life because I was angry and hurt. You may do with me as You wish, Lord, but I ask You to please help this Montagnard baby. Lay Your hands on her, Lord. Strengthen her. Heal her of this infection. Glorify Yourself through her, Lord."

As Brindle knelt in prayer, he suddenly felt as if a cool wind had entered the room and touched him gently on the right shoulder. The tingling spread down his chest and over his body. His shoulders relaxed, and he suddenly felt as if a great weight had come off him. He sighed deeply.

"Amen," he said, opening his eyes in the darkness of his room.

Now he would see. Brindle was not testing God. He was simply not sure that his prayer would get through—that it would not be hindered by what he had become in the past two years. He was trying to come so far up from the bottom that it hardly seemed possible God could hear his voice. But there was always the chance of a miracle. "For myself, or the baby," he muttered as he dropped back onto the bed and closed his eyes.

Chapter Twenty-Two

The pounding thud-thud-thud of an approaching helicopter awakened him at daybreak. Opening his eyes, Brindle gazed groggily around the room. Above his head was the balled-up mosquito net and corrugated ceiling. He blinked slowly. Yes, he realized, it was a helicopter. A helicopter. Hurrying to the door, he stepped outside and gazed toward the clearing. The helicopter was just touching down. It had the markings of the Indonesian Air Force. *How could that be?* he wondered. *At this time of the morning?* He rubbed a hand across his face. He was still exhausted and his head ached, but something was different. He felt as if he had opened a door and stepped onto an island similar to Boromu but where the colors were more vibrant, intense. Gazing across the courtyard to the administrative offices and then up to the gray swollen monsoon clouds, Brindle felt as if he had never really seen this camp before. *And what else haven't I really seen?* he wondered.

Michele was already at the landing site when Brindle reached the clearing. The pilot was unloading the boxes of antibiotic.

"You're amazing," Brindle said to her. "How did you manage this?"

"Actually," Michele said, smiling. "I'd put it up there on the same level as a miracle. Everything just fell into place. The authorities were really helpful. Can you believe that?"

"No," Brindle said, pausing.

"What's the matter?" Michele asked, looking at him. "What happened?"

255

"Let's get this stuff up to the clinic," Brindle said hurriedly. "Every minute counts."

Michele followed quickly behind him. "What did you do, John?"

"Never mind," he said.

"You said a prayer, didn't you? I should have known. It all fell into place so easily."

"It's nothing I want to talk about now."

"But you did, didn't you? You went to God for help. And you see what happened? Don't you see that He still loves you?"

"He loves the baby," Brindle said. He did not wish to sound bitter or distant, but he was not yet ready to discuss the events of last night. It was still too personal.

The antibiotic was already mixed, which meant it only had a shelf life of a few days. But that did not matter at the moment. In fact, it saved Brindle precious time. He attached the new antibiotic to the IV and checked that it was flowing correctly. Then he inserted the thermometer. "Check this when it beeps," he said to Michele and went out to the ward. The child with pneumonia was sitting up, her back supported by her mother.

"Here," Brindle said and filled a syringe with the new antibiotic. "This should help."

Disinfecting her arm, he gave her an injection.

Tran came into the ward.

"Has she been using the respirator?" Brindle asked.

Tran questioned the mother.

"Yes, Doctor."

"Good," Brindle said. "This is going to take some time, but she should start to feel better soon. Will you tell that to the mother? And tell her to keep using the respirator."

"You think it work this time, Doctor?" Tran asked. "Medicine good?"

Brindle nodded. "I think so."

Tran began to explain the situation to the mother as Brindle went back to the nursery.

"She has a temperature of 104 degrees," Michele offered.

"Right," Brindle said, "but it should start to come down now."

Taking the baby's chart, he reached into his medical coat and pulled out a pen. He had made up his mind the moment he had felt that twinge of panic. Something told him it was a God-given opportunity for a second chance, that both he and the child had nothing left to lose, and everything to gain. "I'm going to make a little change."

Michele looked surprised. "What kind of a change?"

"A life," Brindle explained. Erasing the name of TRAC, he filled in a new family name.

"Here," he said, showing Michele the chart.

"Brindle?" Michele asked. "You're giving this baby your name?"

"I brought her into this world, didn't I?" Brindle asked. "That gives me a certain responsibility."

"It's slightly irregular," Michele counseled.

"Look," Brindle said seriously. "I feel like this is right. Not just for me but also for the child. Maybe God planned it this way to get me back on track. I don't know. Will you help?"

Michele gazed at the baby and her eyes began to tear up.

"You want to start all over again," she said. "Of course."

Brindle nodded. "It's not really like adoption anyway," he explained. "As attending physician, I'm just claiming that I'm her biological father. Who's going to contest it?"

"Hal?" Michele suggested.

"I'll talk to him," Brindle said, remembering the two days Aldridge had spent at the airport in San Francisco. "I think he'll understand."

"Yes, I think so too," Michele said.

Vo Nguyen had experienced a few moments of fear when he had seen the paratroopers coming through the jungle toward him but not enough to lose his wits. At several key places in the jungle he had already dug out small tunnels—holes, really—where he could hide if a search became too intensive. It would mean a bad time of wedging himself into the damp earth, but he had done it before. How long he would have to stay in the hole would depend on how quickly the search passed and how well the area was secured behind them. He had met with his men at their usual location near the tidal pool and was cutting south around the camp when he saw the soldiers. At first he thought it was simply a patrol, but then he saw movement off to his right. The soldiers were moving forward systematically through the undergrowth. They were after him, Nguyen thought. Retracing his steps quickly but stealthily—for these men were probably also trackers—he hurried toward the thick vegetation near the beach. Soldiers were coming up from the north side of the camp now too, and he had just enough time to slip into his tunnel and cover it over with palm leaves before he could hear the crunch of footsteps.

He waited all day in his hole, and when he finally crawled out at dusk, he was hungry, thirsty, and viciously angry. His original plan had been to skirt safely around the camp until he was behind the clinic, but he decided now to be bold and cut straight through to the supply shed. The only moment of danger would be when he reached the camp perimeter and crossed that fifty meters of sandy clearing to the outer huts. He would have to reach it before the eight o'clock curfew. Carefully replacing the palm branches over his hiding place, he moved toward the camp.

Forty-five minutes later he slipped into the hut of one of his comrades. The man looked visibly shaken when he entered and saw Nguyen sitting there.

"Shhh," Nguyen whispered threateningly.

"The soldiers are coming back tonight," the man warned in Vietnamese.

"Those pigs," Nguyen said gruffly. "They could not find a water buffalo in the dark. I am hungry. What do you have to eat?"

The man went out to his cook fire and returned with a bowl of rice and a cup of water. He watched the doorway nervously as Nguyen ate.

"Where are the others?" Nguyen asked.

"There is only the one now," the man replied, giving the name of a second refugee. "He will meet us at the shed as you ordered."

"We may have to change our plans," Nguyen said thoughtfully. The plan had been to start the fire at midnight, and Nguyen was a stickler for details. It was the adherence to organization which had kept him alive for so long. But he also knew when the time came to break the rules.

"When exactly will the soldiers return?"

The man shook his head. Nguyen got the definite impression that this traitor did not want him to be here and was having second thoughts. Nguyen felt the knife on his belt. If need be, he would kill this man and do the job with the second traitor—or alone. It did not matter, really. He was quite capable of burning down the camp by himself.

"Then we go at eleven," he said. "Go tell the other."

This was a calculated risk. It was possible the man would leave and not come back. Nguyen doubted that he would tell the authorities, however, because then he also would be implicated. But there was a definite chance that the man would not return.

A few minutes passed, and then Nguyen heard footsteps outside the hut. The man ducked inside again. *So,* Nguyen thought as he watched the man wipe his face, *he is more afraid of me than of the camp soldiers. Well, he should be.*

"He understands?"

"Yes. He will meet us at the supply hut at eleven o'clock."

"Then I will get some rest," Nguyen said, stretching out on a mat. He was not concerned about the man's loyalty now, but out of habit, he rested with his hand on his knife. "Wake me in two hours."

While he slept, the wind shifted to the south and then died down to nothing more than an occasional rustle. The camp settled into a hushed stillness which was broken periodically by the cry of a baby or the chatter of voices.

At ten-thirty Nguyen awoke and glanced at his watch. The man was still sitting against the wall of the hut and gazing outside. He looked exhausted.

"It's time," Nguyen said. "Have you seen the soldiers?"

The man stuck his head out of the hut. "No."

"Then we go . . . for the glory of communist Vietnam."

He stepped from the hut without hesitation—it was always necessary to be aggressive in the face of civilians and particularly traitors—and the man fell into step behind him.

∾

"It's going to take some time for me to get used to thinking of you as a parent," Michele said as they walked back toward her room from the clinic. Brindle had insisted on staying at Trieu's bedside and had missed dinner, so Michele had brought him a bowl of soup and some bread. The baby's fever had broken at ten o'clock, and her temperature was beginning to drop, so they were both feeling relieved.

"Funny," Brindle said. "That's the way I always think of myself—in terms of being a parent."

"What did Tran say?"

Brindle laughed. "He said family all time good for man. Give him reason to work hard."

"That sounds like Tran," Michele said. She looked at him. "I know it's late, John, but if you aren't too tired, I'd love to hear about last night."

"I didn't do it consciously," Brindle replied. "It was as if . . ."

There was the sound of footsteps coming toward them across the courtyard. Brindle turned to see a young Indonesian woman moving through the shadows. She was one of the new clinic assistants.

"Yes?" Michele asked as the aide came up to the terrace.

"She's from the clinic," Brindle said. He wanted to ask if there was a problem, but he knew her English was not good enough for any kind of explanation.

The young woman looked at him anxiously. "You come clinic, Doctor," she said awkwardly, as if she had just memorized the phrase. "You come." Then she turned and slipped away.

"I'll have to go," Brindle said. "I'm sorry."

Michele put her arms around him. Her hips felt wider under his touch than he had expected. *So much of what we are is an illusion*, he thought to himself, as her mouth pressed against his for a moment. Her lips were soft and felt giving and tender as she pulled away.

"May I come with you?" she asked. "I don't want to stay here by myself. It's too lonely."

"I'd like that," Brindle said. "We'd better hurry."

∾

The lights were on at the clinic when they arrived, but there was an uncanny stillness about the place which worried Brindle. Michele took his hand as they stepped into the ward.

"Where is everyone?" she asked.

The patients were resting quietly in their beds, but Brindle did not see any of his staff. The night-duty station was empty.

"They must be around," he offered. "Maybe there's a meeting."

"Where's the girl who sent for you?"

They checked the operating and examining rooms. The clinic seemed to be deserted.

"I don't like this, John," Michele said. "Why would she come for you . . . ?"

"See if you can find Tran," Brindle interrupted. "He's probably in his room. I'll wait here until someone comes."

"But John. . ."

"It's probably just a messed up schedule," Brindle said. "See if you can find Tran."

Michele squeezed his hand. "I'll be right back."

He paused in the clinic doorway and watched her white blouse moving through the darkness toward the staff billeting. He was aware of the heavy silence of the night and the cicadas in the palm trees. Entering the ward again, he walked quietly down the rows of beds. The child with pneumonia began to cough, and Brindle held her shoulders for support. When the spasm had ceased, he eased her back onto the pillow. Finding a chair at the end of the ward, he sat near the wall and listened to the steady breathing of the sleeping patients. It gave him the same peaceful feeling he had experienced in Carrie's room when she was a toddler.

Maybe it wasn't so bad, he thought. He had been given a chance. Perhaps that was all anyone could expect—to be given one chance. Still, it seemed like so much trial and error went into that first and only opportunity. Wouldn't life be so very different if destiny allowed us to do it all again? he wondered. Would we make the same mistakes? Probably not, but we would make others. Or perhaps we would go on making the same bad choices time after time.

There was a creak on the floorboards in the hallway. Someone was coming. Brindle did not stand up but waited on the chair in the moonlit shadows.

"John?" he heard Michele calling softly.

"Over here," he said.

The child coughed again. There seemed to be less congestion in her lungs now.

Michele knelt beside him and took his hands. "I couldn't find Tran," she whispered. "I think you should get out of here."

"I hope he's okay," Brindle said.

In the moonlight, Brindle could see that Michele looked frightened. "Are they coming after you?" she asked. "Is that it? Is this what happened to Hoang?"

"I guess so," Brindle said. "Or at least . . . he thought it would."

"You don't have to do it this way. You can stay in my room or with Hal until morning. Then you'll be out of here."

Brindle shook his head. "Someone needs to stay with the patients. But I'll make a deal. If you'll leave now—so I don't have to worry about you—then I'll catch the chopper to Jakarta on Friday."

"You're worried about me?"

"Who else on Boromu has such a great jazz collection?"

Michele pressed her cheek against his, and he felt the dampness of tears. "I'll try to find Hal."

Good, Brindle thought. While she was trying to find Hal, this thing would be finished. They would not have lured him back to the clinic from Michele's room if they were going to wait all night.

Michele moved quietly down the ward to the hallway. Then she turned. "John?"

"Yes?"

There was a moment of silence. The child coughed.

"You can trust me."

"I know," he said. "I'll see you in the morning."

But he was worried about Tran. He could not imagine where his assistant could be at this hour. It was probably for the best, though. If Tran did show up, Brindle would only have to send him away. He did not want Tran to get hurt if there was trouble. Brindle walked to the window and peered between the bamboo blinds. He could smell something in the night air, as if someone was burning trash. At this late hour? he wondered. Then he saw an orange glow beyond the trees in the direction of the camp and heard a shot.

Something was happening.

Brindle ran down the path and saw the supply shed burning. Flames licked up through its wooden frame and curled around the corrugated metal roof. *It's lost*, he told himself, standing at a distance and feeling the heat on his face. He watched the embers floating up into the darkness. All the food supplies for the refugees were stored in that shed. It would take at least a week to receive a new shipment. But where was the guard? Then Brindle saw a figure lying in the sand at the bottom of the steps. He hurried over and pulled the body away from the blaze. The guard had been killed with a stab wound to the back in the same manner as the first guard. *So Nguyen was still alive and right here*, Brindle thought. Then the doctor heard more shouting in the direction of Aldridge's office. When he reached the compound, he saw Michele running from her office with a stack of files in her arms. The side of the building was on fire.

"It's Nguyen!" Brindle shouted. "Where's Hal?"

"Getting water!" Michele cried out. "Help me, John. All the camp records are in there!"

The flames had not reached Michele's office, but there was enough smoke to burn his lungs. Holding his breath, Brindle pulled open one of the filing cabinet drawers and scooped up all the files he could carry. Michele had already cleaned out two of the drawers. In three more trips he had removed all of the files, but anything left on Michele's desk was gone. He saw Aldridge hurrying across the compound with a group of refugees. They were carrying buckets of water.

"I'm going to the clinic!" Brindle shouted. "Have you seen Tran?"

"I saw him coming from the barracks before the fire started," Aldridge said, turning to the workers. "Get those water buckets going. No . . . over there."

Brindle hurried back to the clinic. It was not burning. He could see that plainly from across the compound.

Then he heard another shot; it came from the direction of the staff billeting. He saw a dark figure, dressed in black and carrying a container of kerosene, moving across the compound toward the clinic.

Not my clinic, Brindle thought. He began to run. By the time he had reached the steps, the figure had already sloshed the wall of the clinic with kerosene and was reaching for a match. He was moving incredibly fast, Brindle thought, taking the clinic steps two at a time. Just as Brindle reached him, the man whipped around and pulled out a knife. Brindle saw the glint of the blade in the man's right hand and a lit match in the other. Kicking out hard, he hit the man in the stomach and knocked him backwards. At the same time, he felt a pain as the man's knife jabbed into the calf of his leg. Crying out, Brindle dropped to the terrace as Nguyen toppled over into the spilled kerosene. The match fell from his hand and exploded into a fury of burning liquid. Nguyen was immediately engulfed in flames. He stood up and tried to beat out the flames on his clothes. Then he began to run. As Brindle fell back against the floorboards, Nguyen ran wildly into the compound. He ran about twenty meters and then collapsed.

"Oh, Jesus," Brindle cried. The pain in his leg was incredible. Rolling over, he began to pull himself away from the fire. Then he felt hands tugging at him and looked up to see Tran.

"I look all over for you, Doctor."

"We need water, fast," Brindle gasped. "And to evacuate the patients."

"I get water. Can you stand?"

"Yes, yes, now go!"

Tran ran down the steps.

Brindle leaned his back against the wall and pulled up his bloody pant leg. A quick examination in the firelight showed a deep gash in the gastrocnemius muscle running for two inches, just below the knee. At least Nguyen had not severed a major artery, Brindle thought. He might be able to walk if he could wrap the wound to prevent blood loss. Using one of the terrace chairs, he pulled himself up and tried to stand. He could manage if he didn't have to put too much pressure on his right leg.

Behind him now he could hear Tran and the others coming with water buckets.

"John?"

It was Michele.

"Help me get the patients out!" Brindle shouted.

Michele took the baby while Brindle helped the little girl with pneumonia. The trauma patient watched them distantly from her bed while the others struggled to their feet. Within five minutes they had evacuated the clinic. Tran and his refugee helpers put out the fire, while Michele stood with the baby in her arms.

"Will you take Trieu to your room?" Brindle asked. "I don't want any of the patients to go back inside the clinic until we're sure the fire is completely out."

"Of course," Michele said. "Can you treat your leg by yourself?"

"Tran will help me."

"Okay, then. We'll be waiting for you."

Brindle hobbled back inside the clinic to the treatment room. Tran was on the terrace with the workers, examining the damage to the clinic wall. They were lucky, Brindle thought, very lucky. Another minute and the whole place would have gone up like the supply hut—patients and all. He had not gone out yet to look at what was left of Nguyen. That could wait until later. Now he needed to take care of his leg. He could feel a warmth in his shoe which he knew was blood. It was not until he had stepped into the treatment room that he remembered why he had been in the clinic in the first place that night and not still in Michele's room. The Indonesian worker had come for him. Was it possible that had been only an hour ago? he wondered. He disinfected the knife wound on his leg and gave himself a shot of morphine. Then he heard someone in the hall.

"Tran?" he called. "I'm going to need some help with this suture."

But it was not Tran who stepped into the doorway of the treatment room and gazed at him coldly.

"Captain Salinem," Brindle said.

The captain did not move but stood staring at him. In his hand he held a 9 millimeter pistol.

So, Brindle thought with resignation, *God did sit in judgment and deal out punishments to those who comitted sin in this world. Then let it happen,* he told himself bitterly.

"Go ahead," he muttered.

"You are not afraid?" Salinem asked.

"If it's not justice, then it's mercy," Brindle replied.

"Even at the point of death, Doctor, you baffle me."

"Because I'm not afraid of dying?" Brindle asked. "You might not understand, even if I explained it to you. And anyway, you're wasting your time."

Salinem raised the pistol. "Why is that, Doctor?"

"Because," Brindle said, wincing as he slid his leg off the examining table. "I'm leaving on the chopper Friday morning. Why bother to kill me now, when I'll be out of your life anyway?"

"Do you think that will end it?" Salinem asked angrily. "You Americans have no sense of honor. You have insulted me, and I will not tolerate this."

"So you're going to shoot me and go to prison, and that will make you an honorable man?" Brindle asked.

"I will not go to prison," Salinem said smugly.

No, he probably wouldn't, Brindle thought. In the confusion no one would ever know who had fired the shot. And who would handle the investigation? Salinem himself.

"Listen, Captain. I've got blood running down my leg, and I'm really tired. So if you're going to . . ."

"Doctor?" Tran called. He was coming down the hall from the terrace. "All okay, Doctor?"

Salinem glanced down the hall and then turned back to Brindle. His finger tightened on the trigger of the pistol.

He's going to do it, Brindle thought to himself and closed his eyes. A wonderful sense of lightness came over him, as if everything was all right and would be okay even if Salinem's finger squeezed one more millimeter.

Then he heard the explosion of the shot and cringed in anticipation of the impact. A glass jar of cotton swabs shattered and fell to the floor behind him.

Brindle opened his eyes.

Salinem was gone.

"Doctor!" Tran came rushing into the treatment room. He glanced around fearfully. The smell of gunpowder mingled with the scent of ammonia and medicine.

"What happen, Doctor?" Tran asked, puzzled. "What happen?"

"A stray bullet," Brindle said, groaning. "Will you help me with this leg? It's killing me."

"You lucky man," Tran said, examining the shattered jar and the bullet hole in the wall above the shelf. "Only miss head by this much." He held up his thumb and first finger. "All time lucky."

"Yes," Brindle said. "All time."

Chapter Twenty-Three

During the night the monsoon swept over the island again like a nocturnal baptism, washing away the hot embers in the smoldering buildings and turning the gray ashes into paste. Brindle watched the storm coming from his position on the clinic steps and smiled faintly. *So nature was taking care of itself*, he thought wearily. *How much harm could man really do?* Sitting there, half asleep, he whispered a muted "thank you" into the darkness. "Thank you," he said again and pulled himself to his feet. He could sleep now, or at least try, if the throbbing in his leg did not keep him awake, though he felt that nothing could keep him awake any longer. The evening had seemed unreal. A part of him still hovered there before Salinem's pistol, waiting for the shot, expecting that at any moment he would be separated from his anguish. But then again, as if a part of himself was changing without his full consciousness, he sensed that he was moving forward at a tremendous speed, and that even the pistol shot had been a long time ago—in fact, another lifetime. Only the throbbing in his leg reminded him that the events had taken place only a few hours before.

As he had waited to see if the fire would rekindle in the clinic rafters, Brindle had thought about Trieu. Wanting the Vietnamese baby for his daughter was one thing, but there were other, practical considerations to be made from such a decision. Where would they live? How would he take care of her? No matter what happened, Brindle realized that he would not return to his old practice in Marin County. If he was ever to experience the feeling of being alive again—which he now believed would happen—it would be as a new man. Even as the moisture from the rain settled on his face and arms, he felt himself being raised from the ashes.

In the morning the laborious process of clearing away the charred wooden frames and sheets of buckled, corrugated metal began. Stepping from his room, Brindle noticed that the air was tinged with a bitter, greasy smell. Across the courtyard, Aldridge was already working with a crew on the storage shed. It would only take a few weeks to build the new structures, Brindle told himself. That was one of the benefits of impermanence. Had Nguyen really thought he could shut down the camp by destroying a few buildings? Or was there a larger scheme? They would never know now, because Duong had identified the blackened body in the courtyard as that of Nguyen. He did not seem such a large man, Brindle thought, to have caused so much trouble.

His first stop that morning was at Michele's room to check on the baby. When he knocked, Michele opened the door quietly and held a finger to her lips. Trieu was nestled into the covers on her bed.

"I gave her a bottle at six and then put her back down," Michele whispered as Brindle gazed at the child.

"The clinic is okay now," he said. "We can take her back anytime."

"Let her sleep," Michele whispered. "She had a rough night too. I'll take her back when she wakes up."

Brindle put his arm around Michele. He felt her blonde hair press against his cheek.

"Thank you," he said.

Her hands clasped around his neck and she smiled up at him.

"This is nice."

He kissed her.

"How's your leg?" she whispered.

"It hurts."

"But you're okay?"

He nodded. "Let's go outside."

Taking Michele's hand, he led her out to the terrace.

"I've been making some plans," he said.

"You're still taking the chopper on Friday, aren't you, John? I think it would . . ."

"Yes," he interrupted. "And I want to take the baby with me. I can send her on from Manila to San Francisco with Mrs. Esqueda—you know, the health officer? My sister could meet her there."

Michele thought about this for a moment.

"I'll send my sister a radio telegram this afternoon," he added, thinking of the letter he had let slip away. "She'll be surprised to hear from me."

"Okay," Michele said resolutely. "Then what? What about you?"

Brindle glanced across the courtyard to the burned administration office. "Then maybe I'll come back," he said.

Michele took his hands. "Really, John?" she asked, her eyes brightening. "I thought you couldn't wait to get away from this camp."

"I've changed," he explained, understanding for the first time that it was really true. He was no longer imagining changes within himself, perceiving subtle differences in attitudes, but he was experiencing the outward actions of change. Things were beginning to happen. He was making decisions which would continue on now and affect his life forever.

He could see that Michele wanted to know why, and her lips even parted to form the word, but she did not ask.

✑

"Well, that takes care of it," Aldridge said later, as he wrote his signature on the transportation orders. "You and the baby have authorization to fly to Manila on Friday."

"Thanks, Hal," Brindle said. "I really appreciate this."

"The placement of refugees—that's our job," Aldridge said and then added. "You don't want to tell us anything more about that stray shot?"

"There's nothing to say," Brindle replied.

The administrator looked at him. "Michele thought it was some kind of a set up. She's worried about you."

"I'll keep my door locked."

"At least," Aldridge said, smiling.

As he made his rounds Thursday evening, Brindle felt a sudden fondness toward these people with their easy smiles and gentleness; people who had escaped into the sea from Vietnam so that they could be here, gazing up at him from a clinic bed, on their way to a new life. He realized now that he would never understand them, but with that realization came an acceptance.

"Tran," he said.

"Yes, Doctor."

"Take care of the clinic for me. Okay?"

"We get new doctor while you gone," Tran said. "From Surabaya."

"I know," Brindle said. "Is there anything you want from Manila?"

"New sandals," Tran said thoughtfully, glancing at his feet.

"Sure," Brindle said.

A feeling of remorse came over him then, thinking of the last time he had gotten something from the Philippines for someone. It had been a blue dress for Kim Thi. Funny, Brindle thought. With everything that had happened, he had not thought about Kim Thi for the past several days. But she was still with him, like a vague presence or a dim thought which hovered on the edge of his waking moments. She had become like a wayang puppet which had moved too far from the light, so that her shadow on the screen had become distorted, leaving no clear, recognizable form. I should find her and say goodbye, he told himself. But he knew that he could not. Kim Thi had receded into that distant past which held memories of New Year's celebrations, sleepless nights, tequila bottles, and the existing John Brindle as he had been in all of his misery. The living John Brindle had no desire to go back there now.

Tran looked at him seriously for a moment. "If you no come back, Doctor . . ."

"Don't worry," Brindle said, patting his shoulder. "We'll see each other again."

"But if you no come back, you write letter—remember, letter?"

"Yes," Brindle said. "I remember."

ᦉ

On Friday morning, Brindle could hear the thudding whine of the helicopter as it approached from the southwest. Glancing at his watch, he saw that it was only fifteen minutes late. This time, he told himself, it was coming for him. How often in the past year had he longed to climb aboard that aircraft and leave the steaming rot of Boromu Island behind? But he did not feel that way now. In fact, he was hesitant to leave. *Why?* he wondered, as he stood with the others in the shade of the clearing. Trieu squirmed in his arms. She was wrapped in a blanket, and her tiny brown hands gripped the soft edge. *Why?*

"Well," Michele said, a tremor in her voice. "By tonight you'll be in Manila."

"It hardly seems possible," Brindle said.

"Maybe you should have someone look at that leg."

"I will."

Just then the helicopter came in over the trees and touched down in the clearing. They waited until the dust from the rotors had settled. When the door opened, a small man stepped out.

"That will be the new doctor," Aldridge said, walking toward the helicopter. "Do you need help with anything, John?"

"No," Brindle said. "I've got everything."

He and Michele were alone for a moment. He looked toward the camp. "Good luck getting this place back into shape."

"We'll manage," she said, running a hand nervously through her hair.

"And say goodbye to Captain Salinem."

"I haven't seen him since the fire," Michele said. "He'll be out of here on Monday anyway."

She looked at him, and Brindle saw the innocence, the struggle behind the hazel eyes.

"So," she asked, "You'll be back next month?"

"I'm not sure exactly when," Brindle said. "I'll let you know."

He kissed her and this time there were tears in her eyes.

The rotors of the helicopter started again. Brindle stepped into the clearing.

"You'll be in my prayers," Michele called.

Brindle climbed aboard the helicopter and buckled himself and the baby into a seat.

"You ready?" the pilot shouted.

"Yes," Brindle said, nodding.

The helicopter lifted off, dipped forward, and then accelerated rapidly into the air. As the island of Boromu fell behind them, Brindle gazed at the child in his arms. She was asleep now, and he hoped she would remain that way until they reached Jakarta. He had traveled with children before and knew that a restless baby could be a misery. Below them was the Java Sea, flowing in a vast blue expanse to the horizon. Brindle had finally come to understand that he actually loved life dearly; that what he had believed to be the internal death of himself, the living John Brindle, had been a cry within that black void of emotional numbness for help, a defense to protect what remained of himself as he had been before the accident, before the tragedy of error and loss for which he had been responsible, before his self-imposed banishment to Boromu Island. All his life he had cared for others, and all his life he had found it necessary to protect himself from that very quality. Perhaps he did not understand, even now, that the intensity of these feelings only came to those who cared enough to make themselves vulnerable.

The helicopter flew on towards Jakarta.

∾

Three weeks later, Michelle stood on the dock and watched the refugees loading onto a launch for the ride out to the transport ship. It seemed like months to her since Brindle had left. Captain Salinem's replacement had arrived, a small officer who wore his peaked hat pulled down on his forehead in an aggressive manner, but who in reality seemed to be bewildered by his responsibilities. Tran was helping the replacement doctor at the clinic. And the soldiers were still working on the new camp office and supply hut. Michele could hear the dull thump of hammers through the trees.

The morning sun was warm on the dock, and Michele pushed the hair away from her face. She wondered if Brindle was really coming back. It would have been so easy, she thought, for him to board the plane to Hawaii with Trieu and then fly on to the mainland. And who could blame him? What was there to hold him here anyway? she asked herself, not wanting to acknowledge the answer, for then she would begin to hope. Michele was not devoid of hope, she had her faith after all, but neither did she want to torment herself. She would just wait and see. If he came back, then that would be a definite sign.

Two Vietnamese women passed her and moved out to the launch. Michele realized with some surprise that it was Kim Thi and her mother. She had lost track of them for a while, but then their names had come up on the transport list for the Philippines. She had approved them quickly, knowing that Brindle would have wanted it this way. Watching them now with their bags, Michele thought that Kim Thi, in her black slacks, white blouse, and conical straw hat, looked like any of the other refugee women in camp. What was there about this one in particular which had attracted John?

Michele also wondered if Kim Thi ever thought of Brindle now. Perhaps she did in those fleeting moments just at twilight, when he used to visit her hut... or perhaps not. Michele wanted to believe that his affection had meant something to Kim Thi, had touched the young Vietnamese woman in some way. It probably did, but who knew?

To Michele, the refugees were like silent water moving around the camp, and she could never judge the depth nor perceive the current underneath. She had always assumed there was a current, just as there had been a face behind the dragon mask at the New Year's celebration, and a dalang behind the wayang puppets. Perhaps things which caused her soul to ache did not bother Kim Thi, but Michele wanted to believe the young woman had those feelings. She wanted to believe everyone did, for that matter.

"Here, let me help you," she said to a woman carrying a child and two bags. Michele took the bags from the woman and began to walk slowly with her toward the launch. If everything had gone as planned, she thought, Trieu would be arriving at the airport in San Francisco this afternoon. John's sister was waiting for the baby there. That would make Brindle's journey to Boromu Island complete in some unforseen way.

Michele helped the refugee woman into the launch and handed her the bags. She wondered if Brindle had gone with the baby. Perhaps he had, but she could not feel it. She wanted to know by some sort of female intuition the course he had chosen, but it did not come to her. So she would have to wait. Gazing thoughtfully at the ocean, she began to think of the child. Trieu Brindle, she mused. The name sounded funny, but perhaps it was the best of both worlds—of the Vietnamese and the American. Sorrow transcended boundaries, but adversity changed perspectives. Sometimes it took so much for just one life to be altered. No one would ever understand the price which had been paid. No one, she thought, except Jesus. He would surely understand.

After all, wasn't that what it was all about?